B NEW
BNEW

Bmc

W9-BWO-538
2487 00672 3702
055

DW

Large Print Ols
Olsen, Theodore V.
Rattlesnake

3558

WITHDRAWN

NEWARK PUBLIC LIBRARY
NEWARK, OHIO

GAYLORD M

RATTLESNAKE

*Also by T. V. Olsen
in Large Print:*

The Burning Sky
Canyon of the Gun
Deadly Pursuit
Eye of the Wolf
Haven of the Hunted
Lone Hand
The Lost Colony
McGivern
Run to the Mountain
Savage Sierra
The Stalking Moon
Treasures of the Sun

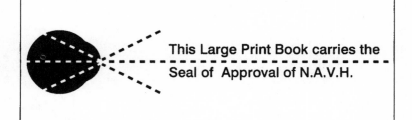

This Large Print Book carries the
Seal of Approval of N.A.V.H.

RATTLESNAKE

T. V. OLSEN

Thorndike Press • Waterville, Maine

Copyright © 1979 by Theodore V. Olsen

All rights reserved.

Published in 2002 by arrangement with Golden West
Literary Agency.

Thorndike Press Large Print Western Series.

The tree indicium is a trademark of Thorndike Press.

The text of this Large Print edition is unabridged.
Other aspects of the book may vary from the original edition.

Cover design by Thorndike Press Staff.

Set in 16 pt. Plantin by Elena Picard.

Printed in the United States on permanent paper.

Library of Congress Cataloging-in-Publication Data

Olsen, Theodore V.
    Rattlesnake / T. V. Olsen.
      p. cm.
    ISBN 0-7862-4156-X (lg. print : hc : alk. paper)
    1. Large type books.   I. Title.
  PS3565.L8 R38 2002
   813'.54—dc21   2002020720

NEWARK PUBLIC LIBRARY
NEWARK, OHIO 43055-5087

To Patrick Guilday
for sterling assistance

Large Print Ols
Olsen, Theodore V.
Rattlesnake

6723762

CHAPTER ONE

When the faint and faraway sputter of gunfire first reached him, Frank Tenney took notice of it with no particular interest.

Rifle shots. Several rifles going at once, from the sound. Not an uncommon one in a country where most people still made their way as much by horseback and buggy as by horseless carriage, where game laws were liberal and plenty of grown men still packed side arms. Hunters, most likely. Or a few skylarking locals getting in some target practice.

Rocking in his saddle with the ease of a lifelong horseman, Tenney continued northeast through the hills, and then his interest did pick up. For one thing, as nearly as he could tell, the shots were coming from roughly the point for which he was heading. For another, this pocket of country was part of his jurisdiction, for Frank Tenney was sheriff of Buck County. And the shooting, heavy and yet more sporadic than steady, had a flat, deadly note to it that told him it might be very much his business.

So he nudged his pinto to a quickened pace, but not too much faster. And he kept his eyes open. The semiarid land was more rolling than broken up, but the faintly marked road detoured around more than one ravine and rocky headland; the gentle hills were bearded with scrub timber that could hide anything.

Very little escaped Tenney's eye. Raised in this kind of country, he'd left it only for the time necessary to obtain a law degree in the East. And had vowed he'd never embrace any sort of life that would take him away from it again. At thirty his senses were honed as much by an outdoorsman's instincts as a lawman's. His stocky body was heavy and hard-knit; his powerful shoulders stretched the seams of a faded duck jacket. But there wasn't a slow muscle in his body; his eyes were cat quick in the shade of his curled hatbrim.

Without knowing just what to expect, he was ready for it as he came onto the brow of a tall hill and drew rein in a thick stand of pines. The slope below was covered with trees that thinned into scrub brush toward the bottom. On the open flat just beyond was a pine-log cabin and outsheds.

Tenney took his time sizing up as much as he could tell of the situation. Several rifles made a crackling din from isolated positions along the rambling slope. It took him a full minute of sighting through the trees to figure how many there were, and where. The fraying blooms of powder smoke told him there were four in all. But it was apparent at once that their sole target was the log house.

And at least two rifles in the house were giving a reply to their fire.

Tenney swung to the ground, threw his reins, and flipped off the snap-thong on the Luger pistol holstered at his side. Then he started downslope through the trees, walking quickly and carefully toward the closest shroud of powder smoke. This fellow was firing as fast as he could lever off shots. Coming in sight of him crouched behind a screen of tight-growing spruce, Tenney stopped and was about to yell at him when he saw the horse tied to a tree a few yards away. He recognized that silver-mounted saddle and, knowing his man then, didn't bother to shout.

He tramped down to the rifleman, halted behind him, and said grimly, "Boo."

The man whirled on his heels. The startled fear in his face erased to a tight grin. He said, "How you doing, brother-in-law," and swung around to fire at the house again.

Raising his voice a little, Tenney said, "Roger, I tell you what."

"What?"

"You shoot that thing off again and I'll dump you on your ass."

Roger Warrender gave a reckless laugh and fired. Tenney took a long step, planted his foot in the middle of Roger's back and shoved. Roger kited forward with a yelp, throwing his arms out wildly in a vain effort to catch himself. He skidded on his face in the pine-needle loam and then, cursing savagely, thrashed around on his side and stared up at Tenney as if he didn't believe it.

Tenney made no follow-up move, knowing it wouldn't be necessary. He stood above Roger with hands splayed lightly on his hips, just waiting. His squarish face, weathered to the hue of a coffee bean, was relaxed and stolid. His wide jaws had the stubborn set of a mastiff's, and his full mouth was tucked at the corners with a faint contempt. But his pale and flat-lidded stare was enough in itself to disconcert most men, for it showed nothing at all.

White-faced with rage, Roger scrambled to his knees, reaching for his rifle.

"Pick it up," Tenney told him, "and I'll belt your teeth out."

Roger stopped his movement. He eased slowly to his feet now, raking his long hair back from his eyes with a gloved hand. He was twenty-five, burly and blond and baby-faced. Most of the time, Roger was bumptious and friendly, a boyish, likable roughneck who refused to grow up. He looked as innocuous as a baby except when his temper was up; it flared and died like a match.

Scooping up his pearl-gray Stetson, he batted it against his whipcord riding breeches and clamped it on his head, eyeing Tenney carefully. "A real tough son of a bitch, aren't you, Frank?"

"Not yet," Tenney said. "You're just apt to make me that way." He bent over and picked up Roger's rifle. The barrel was scorching hot; he swore and shifted his grip to the stock.

The other guns were still banging away.

Tenney said flatly: "Who else is shooting?"

"Tony Soto," said Roger, trying to feign a bland indifference. "Billy de Groot. Trooper Yount."

"Tell 'em to quit."

"Listen, Frank —"

"Tell 'em."

11

Roger cupped his hands around his mouth and bawled, "Tony! Tony, you hear me?"

"Sure I hear you." Tony Soto's reply drifted from a patch of spruce farther downslope and off to the left. "What's up?"

"Get out of there and come up here. Billy and Trooper, too. Pass the word."

Soto yelled at a position still farther to the left. The shooting stopped. There were slow cracklings of brush as the three men worked their way up and along the pine-mantled incline, careful not to expose themselves to rifle fire from the house. But the people in the house had ceased fire too.

Soto was the first to come tramping into sight. Seeing Tenney, he let a grin split his lantern-jawed face. "Well, I be goddom," he said cheerfully. "How you always smell when there's trouble, Frank? Hey?"

"When I smell you just about anywhere," Tenney said, "it's trouble."

"Wow, sure, ain' that the trut'?" Soto, a wiry, dark-skinned youth in soiled range clothes, whooped a laugh and tramped up beside them. "Hey, Rodge, you tell this good relative of yours what is doing?"

"Not yet," Roger growled.

"Any time," said Tenney. "Start talking."

"When I tell the Senator — !"

"He'll likely kick you a foot lower and a sight harder."

"Don't be too damn sure!"

"Get talking or you won't have to wait that long."

Soto laughed.

Roger rubbed a hand over his round jaw, then let it drop. "That Injun down there —" he nodded toward the log house "— has high-graded some Big W beeves."

"You saw him, did you?" Tenney asked.

"Hell, I didn't see anything! Trooper saw —" Roger turned, yelling at another man, approaching upslope, "Trooper, tell this whistle-stop John Law about that track you found. Tell him!"

Trooper Yount was a sour-faced lath of a man in his fifties. A veteran of the old Cavalry, he had lost half his left arm in the Philippines campaigns, but he carried his Springfield rifle like an extra arm. He halted now, eyed Tenney with no particular surprise, and hacked out a stream of plug-cut juice before he answered. "I was on our top range yestiday workin' out from the line shack. I been keeping an eye out by Coahuila Crick, 'cause there's been sign there."

"What kind of sign?" Tenney said patiently.

"Rustlin' sign." Yount spat again. "Wasn't altogether sure till yestiday. Sign ain't sign till it points to somewhat. They was hoss track off 'n' on 'long the crick bottoms, but she was mixed with cow track and trampled up for fair. One rider, it looked like, but a man couldn't tell much. Anyways, I'm the only Big W rider works over that way, so it wa'n't none of our men."

"You sure of that?"

"Damn sure. But if this jasper was pushing off our cows, I couldn't be noways sure. Couldn't find no track that led off the bottoms. Till yestiday. I come on good sign showed one man had pushed off one cow, coming thisaway."

"Just like that, you knew who it was, eh?"

"Ain't nobody else settled on this corner of the basin. Hell, he's an Indin, ain't he? Steal any damn thing ain't nailed down. What else a man got to know?"

"Just maybe," Tenney said, "whether the track led straight here. That's if you bothered to follow it."

Trooper shrugged. "Lost it t'other side of the Santa Agrita. But the river's real shallow right there, and it stood to reason any cows got drove across there. It was coming dark 'bout then, so I quit looking. Besides, they was a hellsmear of a storm brewing and I wanted to get back under a roof."

Tenney glanced at the third Big W man as he joined the group.

Billy de Groot was an orphan, a shirttail cousin that the Warrender family had taken in some years back. A gangling eighteen-year-old, he wore two six-guns crossbelted and slung low on his thighs. Billy was very proud of those pearl-handled beauties. And of his friendship with his cousin Roger. He thought Roger was some shucks, a man to admire. But, then, Billy wasn't too bright. He eyed Tenney with stiff dislike, because the sheriff had cooled him in jail overnight a couple Saturdays since, when Billy had gotten drunk and shot up a saloon outside of Friendship.

Looking back at Trooper Yount, Tenney said, "Too bad about that storm. It must have raised hell with those tracks."

Trooper agreed blandly. "All kinds o' hell, I figured. So I didn't bother looking no more this morning. Rode to Big W to tell the Senator."

"Did you?"

"Didn't get to." A smug amusement touched Trooper's sleepy gaze. "Met his boy at the corral, and Roger says round up Soto and Billy and we would have a look right away."

Tenney's glance shuttled to Roger. He said thinly, "A look for what, besides stirring up a fracas?"

"For those beeves," Roger said sullenly. "All right, we could have sent a man to Friendship to fetch you. And wasted maybe a day, by the time he got there and you got here. Giving the Injun just that much longer to hide that cow or what's left of it wherever he's hiding the others. Christ, Frank, even his brand of penny-ante thievery can bleed a range. And Trooper's been missing cows on our top range for a month now. Tell him!"

"That's for certain." Trooper nodded. "Had my suspicions for sure, but jest one er two cows at a time, it's hard to be sure. They might of strayed some'eres." Heading off Tenney's next question, he added in the same bland voice, "Natchurly I reported my suspicions to the Senator a goodly spell back. He tol' me to keep a weather eye out. That I been doing."

"Convenient," Tenney murmured.

Roger reacted with a startled resentment. "What the hell does that mean?"

"It means he's covered with the Senator that far, anyway. All of you are."

"Are you suggesting that Trooper — or maybe all of us — set this thing up?"

"You tell me."

Roger scowled. He had a bullheaded way of refusing to think in advance about the possible consequences of his actions, then trying to bluff and bluster his way out of them. "Listen, Frank, now you be careful who you smart-mouth. You're not talking to some tank-town drunk on a Saturday toot. And being married to my sister doesn't give you any license to throw around wild accusations."

"Nor a license for you to take the law into your own hands. Or do you need a lesson in elementary civics? You have any complaints against a man, you bring 'em to a sheriff. In this county, damn it, that happens to be me!"

Tenney's glance raked the four of them with a bleak contempt he made no effort to hide now. Knowing only what he did of any of them, he could guess how this business had come to a head. Trooper, the old soldier and professional Indian-hater. Roger Warrender, headstrong and impulsive. Billy, his satellite. Tony Soto, always primed for a frolic or a fight with little thought for the consequences. A hand-picked quartet of ingredients for trouble if he'd ever seen one.

"Come on, Frank, you're a fair-minded chap." A small worry crept into Roger's look; his tone was placating now. "Why not hear a man out before you jump him? We didn't have a whole lot of choice."

"Suppose you tell me just what did happen. I'm really curious, Roger."

"Well, we came here, we called to this siwash, he came out of the house."

"He has a name: Jim Izancho."

"Iz— Christ, you expect a white man to twist his tongue around that? All right, he came out of the house, he had a rifle. Asked what we wanted. Just a look in his outsheds, I said. If he butchered any of the beef he took, he might have it stashed about. All he said was clear out. So I told Trooper to take a look in the tack shed. Then this siwash took a shot at us and we beat it for cover. He fired the first shot, by God!"

Tenney looked down through the screening trees at the house. It was dead quiet, no sign of life except the smoke furling from the chimney. Even from here he could see the slashes of fresh-splintered wood on the walls and puncheon door.

"So you proceeded to shoot his home to pieces."

"Damn it, I told you —"

"Roger, I'm telling you." Reaching for patience, Tenney kept his voice even. "See if you can wrap your brain around this: If you have reason to suspect a man of stealing, you bring your suspicions to a sheriff. If he investigates and finds sufficient grounds in your complaint, he — not you — goes to a judge, who writes out a warrant. He — not you — then serves the warrant on the accused party. You did just four things wrong, Roger. Let me explain it to you." Tenney lifted a hand and ticked off the fingers. "First, you went off on a cockeyed tangent with no real evidence. Second, you failed to report your suspicions to the law; that's me. Third, you trespassed on a man's land and didn't get off it when he told you. Fourth, you shot up his property. Even if you have all the damn proof in the world, you just don't do it that way. Does this make sense to you, Roger? Is any of it getting through to you?"

Roger flushed and started to reply, but Tenney cut him off flatly. "And fifth, for a maybe. Just maybe all the shooting you did hit some people in that house. I understand Izancho has a wife and kid. Just maybe you've killed someone. If you have, your asses are going to be in more hot water than even the Senator can bail you out of."

Roger paled a little then; he said nothing.

Trooper Yount clucked his tongue amusedly, shaking his head. "Jesus, what a mouthful! I recall me when all that legal

19

bullshit didn't cover no Indin. Ain't so sure it does now. Hell, they ain't even citizens."

"Some of 'em are," Tenney said coldly. "This is 1914, Yount. Not 1874."

"Why, hell, Sheriff, you lived here longer'n me. You know the score better'n me, for all your legal beaglin'. Folks hereabouts got long memories. They be minded to pay a man bounty on any red sons a bitches he fetches." Trooper's eyes glinted; he patted the old Springfield he held under his arm stump. "Me'n this little cannon was at Wounded Knee, dusted a couple o' them Sioux. Wouldn't mind retiring both of us with a 'Pache under our belts."

Roger had recovered his poise and some color; he managed a laugh. "You helped civilize 'em with a Krag in the Philippines, too, Trooper, right?"

"Sure's hell's hot I did. Gave them spicks in Cuba some whatfor too." Trooper grinned and winked at Soto. "No offense, sonny."

Soto gave an easy laugh. "That's all right. I like your eggs, old man."

Keeping his temper, Tenney said, "All right, I'll tell you deadeye dicks what. I'm checking on the situation in that house. Even if you didn't dust any Apaches, you're going to face some hefty charges if Izancho wants to press 'em."

"Hell, Trooper's right," Roger said cheerfully. "In this state, you won't find even a federal judge that won't back a white U.S. citizen against a Cherry-cow Apache."

"Maybe we'll see. A good chance Izancho's a citizen."

"How the hell would you know?" Roger's eyes narrowed. "What are you doing here, anyway, Frank? What brought you out here? You wouldn't be paying a little social call on his siwash?"

"Get out of here, Roger. Get out now."

"We're going. Fetch your horses, boys." Roger walked to his mount, picked up his reins, and swung into the saddle. He quartered around to face Tenney, grinning. "Hey. That'd make some sweet telling for the voters, wouldn't it? It should interest the Senator, too."

"You tell him," Tenney said gently. "I'll be coming to Big W first thing tomorrow to straighten your story out. Maybe to haul you to the cooler, too."

"You've got high-handed as hell since you started wearing that badge, Frank. But you don't run any more bluffs on me. You've stretched this one far as it'll go." Roger turned his horse away with a laugh.

Tenney stood watching the four men as they rode upward and vanished over the hilltop. He rasped a hand savagely over his jaw and swore once, bitterly. Then he looked down toward the cabin again. Still quiet as death. The Izanchos could only guess at why the shooting had ceased so abruptly.

Right now they'd be simply . . . waiting.

He felt a momentary qualm. This was sure as hell no time for a friendly visit. But now the visit had turned into a sheriff's business-as-usual; talking to Jim Izancho without delay was his duty. Just another damned job. And nothing would be gained by stalling.

Get to it, he thought. And started down the long incline.

As he neared the fringe of thinning trees where he'd be in plain sight of the cabin, Tenney felt sweat break on his body; his heart slugged against his ribs. Every gun in that house would be trained on him. Jim Izancho would see him before he could possibly recognize him. And what he'd see would be a white man making himself a clear target.

Maybe Jim wouldn't know him anyway. Christ! it had been fifteen years.

Tenney forced himself to keep walking steadily, resolutely. He had to get close enough to be heard before he sang out. If he tried sneaking in that close, from tree to tree, they'd spot him anyway. And promptly take him for an enemy.

The best approach was a bold one. The Izanchos would find that inexplicable enough to hold their fire. Probably they would.

Tenney dug in his heels on the last steep ascent, and then the slope tapered off and the last dense growth of pines was behind him. He continued at a steady walk toward the cabin, his flesh crawling with tension. When he halted at last, he was less than two hundred feet from it. The place drowsed under the hot sun. And that deadly silence held — not even a dog to pick him up.

He cleared the cotton from his throat and yelled, "Jim! Jim, it's me, Frank Tenney! I'm coming in, so hold your fire!"

After a moment, the cabin door creaked slowly open.

CHAPTER TWO

You remembered as vividly as yesterday how the friendship had begun. In the Fort Apache Indian Reservation. On a scorching day in the Arizona summer of 1899. With two boys who had little in common other than their age and a love of roughing it that was common enough to any boys their age, which was fifteen. The son of Lorne Tenney, subagent at the Indian Agency. And the son of Joe Izancho, known and remembered by his people as Skinazbas, a Chiricahua warrior who had been killed on Geronimo's last war trail.

Two boys, the Arizona-born white and the Apache Indian, tramping out for a day's hunt beyond the table bluffs above Fort Apache. You remembered toiling upward across the red, splintered rocks, whispering "hells" and "damns" as your hands grabbed for brief support at one oven-hot boulder after another. You remembered the wild laboring of your heart and lungs, your ringing ears and a drenching sweat that turned your shirt to a wet rag. Above all, you remembered your furious, puzzled envy of Jimmy Izancho, who climbed ahead of you with the ease of a mountain goat. And his faintly amused glance as the two of you stood at last on the summit of a huge hogback bluff.

But Jimmy merely said gravely, "It was a good climb."

Frank Tenney could only gulp and manage a nod.

From this eminence, the boys had a panoramic sight of the reservation. Its expanse dropped away from the Mogollon Rim to the northeast and embraced mountainous country of lush timber and flashing streams before dwindling southwestward into red-clay plateaus and ending at the Salt River, which divided the Fort Apache lands from the San Carlos Reservation. They could see only a fraction of the whole, but enough to suggest its wild and sprawling immensity. It was a land barely touched by whites, barely scratched by the Apache farmers with their sorry plots of corn and truck. ("Maybe we can make herdsmen of 'em, but not farmers," Lorne Tenney had said. "Washington sends agricultural experts to show 'em how to terrace their fields and rotate their crops, and they go right on stripping the topsoil for planting. A few strong winds and a few good cloudbursts do the rest.")

"Up there —" Jimmy Izancho swung a pointing arm toward a tall butte to the north "— is where boys of the *Be-don-ko-he* become men. I will go up there soon."

Frank Tenney sleeved sweat from his eyes and blinked at the bare-crowned monolith. It towered above every other height in the vicinity and it looked like almost a sheer climb. He said so.

"It is," said Jimmy Izancho. "On every side, if you wonder."

Again that amused, not unfriendly glance. He was polite toward his white companion, always speaking out of a calm reserve, and Frank Tenney knew he was still withholding judgment. Lorne Tenney had been assigned to this reservation six months past, but had brought his wife and son to Fort Apache less than a month ago. Much of the elder Tenney's work took him to the lodge of Jimmy Izancho's grandfather, head of a large clan, and so the two boys were frequently thrown into company. Neither had ever known a boy of the other race; thus a mutual curiosity seasoned their acquaintance. But, so far, little else.

Frank Tenney had the feeling Jimmy

Izancho was testing him in small ways each time they were together. And he'd half sensed, when Jimmy had suggested today's outing, that he might have a sterner test in mind. Frank felt more than a jab of resentment: what did it take to win this Apache kid's approval?

At the same time, he couldn't help rising to a boyish challenge. A touch of hostility stiffened his reply: "Is that all?"

" 'All'?" Jimmy Izancho lifted his straight brows. "No, there is a little more. If the medicine is to be good, you must work at it. You must stay on the butte for two days. You must eat nothing. You take only three swallows of water a day. You cast *hoddentin* to the four winds and pray. You carve a *tzi-daltai* from a piece of wood and ask the spirits to make it strong. Then you go down to the *ranchería* and ask the *izze-nantan* to pronounce a blessing. That is all."

Frank listened attentively. *Hoddentin*, he knew, was the sacred pollen of the tule rush that the Apaches sprinkled liberally at every ceremony — and ceremony surrounded every aspect of their lives. The *izze-nantan* was a medicine man. He wasn't sure about *tzi-daltai* but gathered it was a protective amulet of some sort.

"That's *all?*" Frank said. And tentatively

then: "It must get mighty cold up there nights. And hot all day. . . ."

"I think so."

"I know for a fact it's a sight harder to climb down anything than up it. And you fast for two days?"

"Fast?"

"Eat nothing."

"Right," said Jimmy Izancho, then turned on his heel in that sudden way of his. "Come!"

They descended the hogback's north flank on a less rugged slant, but so swiftly that it was all Frank could do to keep pace with his agile guide. Then it was up and down more treacherous slopes, where the Apache's curl-toed moccasins seemed to grip the rocks and yet barely touched them; he sprinted across the worst places, where Frank had to scramble wildly, his boots skidding on slick and broken shale. Several times, he fell, skinning his hands and knees. He wanted to holler at Jimmy Izancho to slow down, but clamped his jaw with a bitter pride and somehow held the pace.

They plunged into a shadowy ravine, where wind-twisted pines had taken a tenacious hold in the stony soil, assailing the boys with a smell of heat-baked resin. Jimmy led the way up its zigzag course at an easy lope that Frank tried to emulate. But his last fall had twisted an ankle, holding him to a half-limping walk now, and he soon lost sight of his companion.

The upward-twisting ravine ended abruptly on a high bulge of lava. When he dragged himself onto it, gasping and grunting, Jimmy Izancho was waiting. The Apache appeared to take no notice of Frank's condition; he gazed contemplatively into a vast gorge that seemed to yawn away from his feet.

"Down there," he said idly.

"What?"

"We will hunt there."

Jimmy Izancho gave a solemn nod downward, and Frank limped gingerly to the rim and peered down. Some terrific convulsion of ages ago had wrenched this mile-long fissure in the lava crust, splitting it almost a hundred feet across and a good hundred and fifty feet deep. Frank swallowed. The seamed and irregular walls of the gorge were nearly plumb-straight vertical anywhere he looked, tapering off toward the bottom in slides of collapsed rock.

"What's to hunt there?" He tried to sound casual.

"*Ka-chu.* You know the word? . . . Rabbit." The studied pause made it sound perilously close to an insult rather than a question.

Frank took another look. The floor of the gorge was covered with heavy chapparal that might be laced with rabbit runways, but you couldn't tell anything from here.

"Is it too steep?" Jimmy Izancho asked.

"Is it for you?"

Jimmy drew a finger across his cheek, pretending to think it over. "No-o, I don't think so. But I'm not a *pinda likoyee*."

White-eyes. Put that way, the Apache word for Americans was a definite taunt.

"Go on," Frank Tenney said grimly. "Let's see the color of your blood. I know what mine is."

"Enju." The soft Apache word held a spark of approbation. "Do what I do."

Both boys had knives, but Jimmy carried the only bulky weapons: a bow and quiver of arrows. He slung the bow over the quiver on his back, then spread-eagled himself belly flat on the rimrock and eased himself backward over its steeply rounded lip, his fingers and toes digging for holds along the rough rock. He worked gradually out of sight and then called from below: "Come!"

Without knowing what lay directly beneath, Frank followed his example. He scrabbled with his boot toes for slender holds on the rimrock, and then he could find none at all. Heart in his throat, he let himself down a few inches farther by handholds alone. Then a hand grasped his right foot, guiding it to a protuberance. He took a long blind step down with his other foot till it encountered a narrow solid ledge.

Frank watched Jimmy Izancho descend a couple yards to another ribbon of ledge. Now he was able to see where the Apache sought holds for hands and feet, but it meant staring down that nearly straight drop. Somehow he managed to emulate his companion, following him downward to the next stage and the next. Finally they reached a broad shelf halfway down.

"Rest," Jimmy said laconically.

Sweating but controlling his shakes, Frank sank to his haunches. Jimmy Izancho squatted down facing him. For the first time, a half smile touched the Apache's lips.

"I think you could climb to our manhood place," he said.

"I don't know."

"There's no water in your heart. That is enough."

After a moment's hesitation, Frank said: "Do you believe in all of . . . well, those old ways? I mean, you've been to the government school and all."

"Cow Bird, my grandfather, believes we

31

must do both if we want to survive. Practice your ways and keep our own." Jimmy Izancho shrugged. "I don't always know what to believe."

"Neither do I."

"Cow Bird says that will change. A man will find his way in time. It is hard to see sometimes, so I hope he is right." Jimmy rose to his feet. "Now we will go down and hunt."

The rest of the descent looked no worse than the part above, but Frank wondered if he could make it. His arms and shoulders ached from exertion; his legs felt rubbery when he stood. His hands and belly rasped nearly raw from scraping along rock. But he never hesitated. He followed Jimmy Izancho's lead, curving his numb fingers into cracks and around stony nubs, kicking for precarious footholds.

Twenty feet from the bottom, he froze against the wall. His vision was a spinning blur. He could no longer feel his fingers; he could see dark prints of wet slickness where they touched rock.

"Don't look down," Jimmy Izancho called from below him softly. "Your right foot . . . step down. Now —"

The shale outcrop collapsed as Frank's full weight came on it. His holds tore away.

Arms and legs flailing helplessly, he skidded face down past Jimmy Izancho. His body turned sideways as it jolted over a short straight drop. Then slammed to a jarring stop on a rugged spur of rock.

Red pain ripped his left arm; it exploded like a bombshell in his brain. He screamed. Blacked out for an instant. Then he twisted on his back, dragging his arm across his belly. The arm flopped grotesquely. A miniature river of shale splinters rattled down on him.

A momentary silence as he lay dazed. The hot blue sky pinwheeled; waves of pain rocked at the dim edge of his consciousness. Then another sound. It came from back of his head — a brittle burr of noise.

With a wrenching effort, Frank tipped his head to face back. From the tail of his eye he could just make out the rattlesnake. It was coiled on a shelf somewhat above and a little behind his sprawled body. He saw the dust-colored head flat and backdrawn.

Even if he weren't stunned by pain and shock, pure terror would have held him paralyzed.

His eyes moved to Jimmy Izancho on the ledge above. Jimmy's intent dark face, the bow in his hands, the arrow fixed and pulling back against the taut bowstring, rippled like heat shimmer in Frank's eyes.

The string twanged. The snake's thrashing body slipped from the shelf, slapping rock inches from his face before it fell past him to the gorge floor.

Jimmy scrambled down to the spur. There was just enough room for him to crouch by Frank's drawn-up legs. "Can you move?"

"I reckon."

Frank stuck out his good arm and Jimmy Izancho grasped it and hauled him to his feet in one strong pull. Somehow he mastered the pain and tightened his will around it as they half crawled and half slid the remaining yards to the bottom.

Leaving Frank slumped in the shade of a boulder, the Apache boy scoured up some straight sticks for splints. Then he took off his calico shirt and tore it into strips. He knelt beside Frank and said seriously, "Now it would be better if you know what you believe."

"Believe . . . ?"

"To set the bone I will have to hurt you. Maybe your Christ god can make you strong. You better pray hard."

"All right," Frank Tenney said. "I'm praying now."

He turned his eyes upward as Jimmy Izancho gently lifted his forearm, ripped the sleeve away and kneaded the flesh for the edges of broken bone. The jet of white-hot agony swelled to each beat of his heart. He heard the bones grind together. Felt the Apache's hands clamp and tense.

But he made no sound. Not till the hands gave a powerful tug. And then his scream died in mid-voice as he fainted dead away.

When he came to, he was stretched on his back. The broken arm was bulky with ravel-tied splints — the ravels torn from Jimmy Izancho's own clothing — and cinched up inside Frank's shirt. It hurt with a steady, sickening ache, and he knew that when he moved, it would hurt worse. Jimmy Izancho squatted in front of him, arms folded on knees, and he smiled just a little. But it meant a lot.

"It is a bad day to hunt," he said.

"Maybe another time," Frank whispered. "If we get out of here."

"That will be easy if you can walk." Jimmy pointed upcanyon with his chin. "There's a place we can climb out."

Frank extended his good arm, but Jimmy Izancho ignored it for the moment. Getting up, he strode over to the dead rattler and lifted it by the arrow that impaled its head. Then he pressed the arrow to the ground, set his foot on the shaft, and snapped it in half. Afterward he slipped the bow off his shoulder and bent it across his knee till the tough mesquite wood cracked and splintered. He flung the useless bow aside and walked back to his companion.

"Why did you do that?"

The Apache boy shrugged, but his mouth was flat with distaste. He reached down and grabbed Frank's hand and pulled him up. Then he said, "Those things are bad now."

"Why? Is the snake . . . uh, sacred?"

"Well, look, *sheekasay*. In your god teachings you got something called a devil. You don't worship it, do you?"

Still dazed, a little confused by the throbbing pain of his arm, Frank shook his head. "We aren't supposed to. Worship evil, I mean. Is that what *you* mean?"

"Evil. Yes, we worship that, too." Jimmy spoke carefully, choosing his words. "We think it is best not to make evil things mad. So we never kill a snake. Try never to," he amended. "We never touch again a thing we use in any connection with a snake."

Belatedly, Frank realized that the Apache had called him "brother" — *sheekasay*. To cover a warm flood of embarrassment, he blurted, "Do you believe *that*?"

Jimmy Izancho's taut face relaxed; again that suggestion of a smile. "I told you. I

36

don't know what to believe. Do you think I'm a fool?"

"Jeez, no!"

"Then, *sheekasay,* you see I'm too wise to take chances with my medicine. Come!"

That was the real beginning. During the weeks it took Frank's arm to heal, they spent a lot of time in each other's company at less vigorous pastimes. And afterward they climbed and explored and camped out and hunted together. From his Apache friend, Frank Tenney had gained insights and appreciations that still honed his outlook on many things.

What Jimmy Izancho took from their relationship, he was never quite sure. At times, Jimmy was lively and outgoing; at other times, he was withdrawn and brooding. These sharp turns of mood baffled Frank, with his phlegmatic and steady temperament. Yet they were alike in those ways that counted most with boys on the edge of manhood; he had passed Jimmy's "test." And so it had grown quicker and deeper, this friendship, than many between boys of the same race.

It was a short-lived time for both. In a few months, Frank's father had received an assignment to the Mescalero Reservation, far to the south, and moved his family there. The boys had promised to keep in touch, but neither was much for letter writing; their trickle of correspondence had lapsed after a year or so. And their paths hadn't crossed in all the years since.

Yet it had been an interlude, and one day in particular, that remained fresh in Frank Tenney's memory: the day that Jimmy Izancho had saved his life.

CHAPTER THREE

As he opened the cabin door and stepped out, Jim Izancho's dark face wore his familiar suggestion of a smile. Tenney felt a surge of quick relief; no amount of pleasure at seeing an old friend would permit that smile if any of his family had been injured. He came forward with a heavy Sharps rifle swinging in his left fist, but his right hand came out to grasp Tenney's as they met.

"Too long, Frank," said Jim Izancho.

"Too damned long, *sheekasay.*"

Jim Izancho's smile broadened, showing his square white teeth.

He'd grown to one hell of a specimen of manhood, thought Tenney. He had the great barrel chest and wiry legs of the Apache male but was far taller than most of his people; he stood a good six inches above Tenney's five-ten. Jim's build and carriage were those of the born and finely trained athlete; his movements had a fluid and graceful economy that bore out an incredible blend of speed and reflexes. The lean glide of muscles under his calico shirt just hinted at the mule-tough balance of strength and endurance that Frank remembered — that maturity would have increased.

Jim's glance flicked to the pine-clad slope. "Are those blue-ribbon Big W gents still up there?" he asked.

"Sent 'em packing out of here. Good thing for you I decided to pay my respects today."

"You took your time about it."

Tenney inspected the tone of his voice for an edge, but Jim Izancho's face showed only a quiet humor.

A face of chiseled angles, broad and hawk-nosed and heavy-cheekboned, it reminded Tenney of Geronimo's face in an oft-reproduced photograph of the Chiricahua war leader. Less stern, more prepossessing by white standards. But a face, Tenney suspected, that could turn fierce as flint at a shift of mood. And remembering the swift-reaching intensity of Jim's moods, he knew it would accurately reflect the man.

"Seemed a good day for it. As you used to say."

"It started out as one, anyway," Jim

Izancho said wryly. "But I reckon it hasn't turned out too badly when your one sociable caller happens to be the sheriff. For any white-eyes but you, I wouldn't have stepped outside just now on a bet."

He laughed then, clapped a hand on Tenney's shoulder, and propelled him toward the house. "Come meet the family. Grandpa you'll remember . . . old Cow Bird. He's living with us."

Rifle fire had pocked the cabin's peeled logs with fresh scars and splintered raw shards from the casings of the two front windows and the door, whose latch was shattered and dangling. A young woman was sweeping up broken window glass on the packed-clay floor as they entered.

"This is my wife," said Jim Izancho. "Sally, I want you to meet Frank Tenney. Best paleface friend a man ever had."

She set the broom aside and offered Tenney her hand, smiling. "I can't tell you how often Jim's spoken of you, Sheriff. Since we've moved here, of course. But long before that too."

Sally Izancho's skin tone and features showed her part-white blood. She was pert and pretty, slightly built, and she couldn't be much past twenty. Her blue-black hair was drawn to a tight, shiny bun; her eyes

41

glistened like warm tar spots. She wore a red calico blouse and a blue calico skirt, Indian colors worn in an Indian way; a belt of silver conches circled her narrow waist. Plainly she wasn't ashamed of her blanket heritage.

"Sally's a Navajo," said Jim. "Her mother was. Her daddy's a paleface stunt rider with Buffalo Bill's show. That's where we met. In London, England, believe it or not. Joe-Jim — come over here."

A boy of about four was sitting behind the puncheon table, only his round black eyes clearing its top. Eyes that were a bit leery as they studied the newcomer. But he promptly obeyed, wriggling off the chair and running over to them.

"This is our sole claim on posterity so far," Jim said. "Take your thumb out of your mouth and shake hands with Mr. Tenney. Can you say hello?"

"Hel . . . lo."

Tenney took the child's hand in his big hand, then turned it over. "Howdy, Joe-Jim. What's that in your hand?"

The boy's eyes grew rounder as he gazed at the coin Tenney had slipped into his palm. "That's a penny," he said soberly. And swiftly then: "Is it for me?"

"It sure is. It's for luck, too. An Indian-head penny."

"I'm sure you're a married man, Sheriff," Sally said. "Somehow it shows. Are you a father, too?"

Tenney nodded. "Pretty near. We're expecting our first in about six months."

"One in the oven, eh?" Jim grinned. "That's great."

An ancient Indian crouched in a corner of the room, huddled in a striped blanket. His face was a mummified brown mask; only his small eyes glittered with sparks of life.

Jim glanced at the old man, lowering his voice. "Likely, Granddad won't recall you. He's pretty old and . . . well, about all he does is sit in that corner. Want to speak to him?"

"Sure."

They went over to Cow Bird and hunkered down facing him. Jim said in Spanish, "*Abuelito,* Frank Tenney is here. You remember the young gringo I knew at Fort Apache — Frank Tenney?"

The old man's head slowly lifted. He stared at Tenney's face a long while. "*Si* . . . Tenney." Stirring the words to whispery sound, his voice was like a wind combing dead leaves. "I remember. You worked for the Grandfather of the United States. We drank *tulapai* in my lodge. Was that last year, Tenney?"

"It was fifteen years ago, Mr. Izancho."

"*Sí*. I remember." The old man's eyes slipped to blank focus beyond him. "You were a good *nantan*, Tenney. . . ."

Jim touched Tenney's shoulder and they rose, Jim saying quietly, "He thinks you're your dad. Same with me . . . sometimes. How about a drink, Frank? Too early for you?"

"I could stand one."

While Jim rummaged in a cupboard, Tenney sat down at the table, giving the single, large room a look-over. It contained no more than the rough furnishings that might be found in any cow-camp line shack, but showed a woman's scrupulously neat touch. Apparently only a few Big W bullets had found entry. A couple slugs had chewed up the tabletop. A big water *olla* suspended from a beam had been shattered, littering the floor with fragments. A rifle leaning against the wall by a window showed that Sally had shared the defense of their home.

Jim carried a dusty bottle and two tin cups to the table. "French firewater. Cognac from Paris I've been saving the last of for a special occasion." He filled the cups, handed Tenney one, and said, "*Salud*."

Tenney took the dark liquor in a swallow and let his belly absorb its soft fire before saying bluntly, "Jim, you want to prefer charges against those Big W men? You've plenty of grounds for 'em."

"Same old Frank. Right down to brass tacks." Jim Izancho's smile faded; he gazed thoughtfully into his cup. "What's their story?"

Briefly Tenney told him Roger Warrender's version.

Jim nodded. "Close enough, except I didn't shoot at anyone after I told 'em to clear out and they didn't. Fired over their heads, but that was all the excuse they wanted."

"Big W people ever give you any trouble before this?"

Jim stirred his head in negation, locking eyes with his friend. "You want to have a look around for those beeves they say I took? You won't need any warrant."

"No solid evidence. If they had any and got out a warrant, I'd serve it."

"I know you would. All legal and proper. I hear you're a pretty fair sheriff, Frank . . . fair's the word. But you would be. About those charges, now." Jim Izancho shrugged. "We're one Injun and his family in a country crawling with white-eyes. What kind of feeling will it breed up if an Apache prefers charges of any kind against white men?"

"There's still a lot of Wild West sentiment

in these parts, Jim. You answer it."

"Damn sore feelings. The kind we sure as hell don't need right now — on the edge of making a new life for ourselves. And those yahoos did us no real damage." Jim's glance touched Sally and Joe-Jim; his frown was slight, but enough to turn his face bone-lean fierce. "It's damn lucky for them they didn't. Thing is, what if they try the same again? Or worse?"

"I think I can guarantee they won't," Tenney said quietly.

"Can you?"

"I've lived in this county for eight years, Jim. Came here straight out of college. Practiced law till a couple years ago . . . when I got elected sheriff. I've learned all the open sores hereabouts and how to treat 'em before they get infected. It's part of the job."

"You know that young Warrender and his three chums?"

"As well as I know my own mother. They're the kind I keep a weather eye on. I think I clipped their wings just now. And I intend to make sure of it."

Jim was silent for a long moment, twirling the cup between his fingers. Then: "Wouldn't do your reputation a lot of good to jail some white men on my account, would it?"

46

"Not a whole lot, no."

Jim Izancho's scowl softened. "Don't take that wrong, Frank: I didn't mean — Ah, hell, maybe I did. It's hard for me to trust a white man any more. But scratch that. I don't want our friendship to get you in Dutch — in any way. All I care about is protecting my family. If the best way to do that is *not* press charges, well. . . ."

"It's up to you, Jim."

"I trust you, *sheekasay*," Jim said almost roughly. "Let's leave it at that. No charges lodged against that Warrender colt and his buddies . . . for now." He poured the remaining cognac into their cups. "Drink up. And while you're about it, tell me why it took you this long to get in touch. Did you just learn I'd settled here? Or did you think it was another Jim Izancho?"

Tenney grinned. "Not one or the other. Heard a month ago that old man Haskell had sold this chunk of land to Jim Izancho. The whole county was buzzing about it: an old-time cattleman like Milo Haskell selling a piece of his ranch to an *Apache* who planned to *farm* it."

Jim nodded wryly. "I can guess what they've been saying."

"And the word was you were the same Jim Izancho who broke all kinds of intercolle-

47

giate athletic records at Carlisle. So I knew it had to be you. Always made a point of following your exploits in the tabloids. Then there was that business with the Olympics a few years back. . . ."

Jim downed his drink quickly; his face hardened again. "Yeah. Wouldn't think they'd make medicine about that in a backwoods puddle like this."

"Fella, you made headlines all over. Even in a hick town like Friendship."

"Don't beat me over the head with it." A flat bitterness etched Jim's voice. "I've tried to live down the palmy days of Jim Izancho, All-American glory boy and prize fall guy."

Tenney gave him a sharp look. Then shrugged, letting the question that came to his lips die unasked. "Just as you say. Anyway — this place of yours is a long ride from town, and I've been busy as hell. It's a mighty big county to keep tabs on, and they don't allow me wages for more than three deputies. So I couldn't get out to see you till now." He grinned. "What's your excuse, Jim? Did you just learn I'm sheriff hereabouts? Or did you think I was a different Frank Tenney?"

"Right back at me, eh?" Jim laughed shortly. "I thought about looking you up, sure . . . the few times we've come into

Friendship for supplies. But, seeing how the good burghers there feel about the red brethren, I wasn't sure how you'd feel about renewing the acquaintance." He raised a hand. "Okay, I should have known better. But, then, I've been busy as hell too. Let me show you."

He rose from the table and Tenney followed him outside.

The Izancho cabin and outsheds were situated at the south end of a broad basin that was embraced by an arm of gentle hills on the eastern side and *mal país* badlands to the west. On its north and east flanks the basin was rimmed by sandstone cliffs. Pointing to the northwest, Jim said that a loop of the Santa Agrita River curved out of sight beyond a tall ridge there. It was the only place where his property touched the river. Several charges of dynamite set along a narrow spot in the lava rampart would open an *acequia* between the river and a deep valley that connected with the greater basin. Enough Santa Agrita water could be diverted through the valley to irrigate the basin's barren flats.

"I plan to raise alfalfa," Jim Izancho explained. "Going to run lateral ditches there . . . and there . . . and there." He pointed front and left and right with his chin. "I hope we can wind up this year with a cash crop. The Haskells have agreed to buy all the hay I can raise. We'll be off to a dandy start if we can get in a planting within the next month. And we can if the ditching is finished up soon."

Tenney could see that some ditching work had been gotten underway. "You doing all that by yourself?"

"A lot of it. Tom and Ed Haskell have lent me some Mexicans from their crew whenever they can spare 'em. Mexes don't waste much love on Apaches, but the Haskells pay their wages — and the Haskells'll be repaid when the crop comes in."

Tenney murmured, "M'm," scratching his chin.

Jim chuckled. "You're wondering why the Haskells haven't held onto this basin and done their irrigating and cropping."

"There's been talk, naturally. Everyone knows that old Milo's getting on in years — turned over the operation of his whole spread to his two sons. But nobody's sure what sort of deal you worked out with the family. The Haskells are a close-mouthed bunch."

"No great secret," said Jim as he related how he had first met Tom Haskell eight years ago, when both had been collegians training for the Olympics. Recently they'd had a chance encounter in Phoenix, where Tom was attending a cattlemen's convention. The two had discussed old times over a bottle, and when Jim had mentioned his intention to purchase land for farming, Tom had waxed warm about helping him implement his plans. Within an hour they'd hashed out a rough agreement and had shaken hands on it.

"Between you and me —" Jim flicked a grin "— I think Tom's kind of regretted his generosity. We never really were all that friendly . . . but you know what a few drinks and talking up old times will do. Still, he was as good as his word. Took the proposition straight back to his dad and brother."

"How did old Milo take to the idea?" Tenney asked.

"Not too enthusiastically, I gather. They're an impulsive crew — squabble among themselves all the time, Tom says. But if one argues for a thing hot enough, he usually gets the other two to go along. If a Haskell makes a commitment, the others feel obliged to honor it. Even to an Indian, seems like. So the deal was closed for this property — at the price Tom and I'd agreed on. Leaving me enough cash, with scrimping, to tide us over awhile."

As they talked, the two men idled along a half-dug ditch at a slow walk. The flats had an unpromising appearance, studded with broken boulders, patched with thickets of ironwood and mesquite and catclaw. But plenty of it lay open enough, Tenney thought, if you could get anything to grow on it.

"Kind of hard to picture you as a farmer, Jim," he said mildly.

Jim Izancho dug a heel into the bare earth; he shrugged. "A man can use up his options when he hasn't too many to choose from. Anyhow, I hope to run a few cattle before long if we can save up the wherewithal to buy 'em. They say we Apaches have to make lousy hoe men. Our ancestral memories or something. Your dad thought so, I recall. How is he, by the way?"

"Both he and Mom are fine. Pleased as punch about having a grandchild on the way. Dad's holding down a desk in Washington these days. Not too happy with it, but that's the price of getting kicked upstairs, he says —"

Tenney broke off. A dusty twist of movement under a creosote bush several yards away brought him to a halt.

He saw the dark diamond pattern and scaly coiling of the snake's body and heard the sharp, warning rattle. His mouth was suddenly dry, his hand clammy as it settled on the butt of his Luger.

Jim Izancho put out a hand and said, "Hold still. Back off."

They moved away and then swung to the right, giving the rattler a wide berth. Looking back, Tenney saw the reptile uncoil and slither out of sight. "I see you still feel the same about 'em," he muttered.

"So do you."

Tenney's heart was pounding; he knew from Jim's sharp glance that his face was stiff with reaction. "For a fact," he admitted. "They get me that way ever since . . . you know."

Jim nodded.

"In this job I've come damn close to buying it a few times. But I can't ever recall anything as close as that was." Tenney shook his head. "If you're going to settle here, I think you're crazy not to kill every one you see."

"White-eyes philosophy." Jim gave his enigmatic shrug. "Hell, the rattlers are thick as fleas in this area. A cow can't roll over without spooking up a couple."

"All the more reason."

"They're not the worst critters in the world, Frank. Leastways, they warn you."

"Not always, they don't."

"No, not always. Like humans, eh? Our lauded species."

He's really bitter, Tenney thought. Maybe with good cause. No point wondering aloud, though. Jim Izancho was plainly as moody a man as he'd been a boy; too easy to hit a sore nerve with him.

Abruptly Jim came to a halt. He scowled and looked down, kicking at a clod. "I've been thinking, Frank. Maybe that Warrender kid and his men weren't just hoorawing us out of pure meanness."

"What do you mean?"

"It could be a kickoff to something else . . . maybe the Warrenders have decided to put the heat on me. Did you know Senator Warrender has tried for years to buy this piece of Haskell range that touches the Santa Agrita?"

Tenney nodded.

Almost thirty years ago there'd been trouble between Milo Haskell and Stuart Warrender; old-timers claimed their quarrel had nearly exploded into full-scale range war. Warrender had claimed registered title to a jog of acreage west of the Santa Agrita, including this basin. Haskell, then a new-comer, had flatly contended that his own title covered the piece. After a lot of harsh cross-accusations and even a shoot-out or two between Haskell and Big W riders, both parties had agreed to accept mediation by the U.S. Land Office and to abide by its decision. A resurvey of the line had turned up an error in the original survey, showing that some witness markers had been wrongly placed. And the matter had been settled in Haskell's favor.

Warrender had then offered Haskell a good price for the disputed strip. Though he had no particular use for this arid section of range, Haskell had stubbornly refused to sell. Over the years, Warrender had repeatedly renewed his offer, doubling and then tripling it. But their old feud had never ceased to rankle feisty Milo; he was double-damned if he'd do any sort of business with Stuart Warrender, and that was that.

Their bone of contention had been rooted in the Territory's more lawless days — and Senator Warrender preferred not to discuss those times. But Tenney remembered that the Senator had once mentioned to him his reason for wanting to secure that strip west of the Santa Agrita. The river had its source in mountainous country to the north, part of the Sansone National Park, which extended to Big W's northern boundary. Snaking across the Warrender range, the

Santa Agrita provided a never-failing supply of good water year around. In more than one drought year it had been the key to Big W's survival as a cattle outfit. Haskell's smaller operation was confined west of the *mal país;* his cattle never ranged this far east.

Where the Haskell strip just touched a single loop of the Santa Agrita was the one place where Big W was vulnerable, the Senator had pointed out. Suppose that, one day, somebody decided to change the river's course at that point? It could be accomplished simply by blasting a short channel through the barrier ridge that formed the river's west bank along that deep valley. The Senator's concern that Milo Haskell might do it out of plain cussedness had long since eased. But suppose somebody else came into possession of the strip and wanted, for one purpose or another, to divert water onto that low flatland? Ranching, cropping, mining . . . you needed water for any of them, and no other source was available to this dry basin.

That worry had been an unceasing thorn in Senator Warrender's side for nearly three decades.

"I know the Senator feels he has a strong stake in this piece of yours," Tenney said.

"So you know about all that. Did you

know he's made me no less than four offers for it since the Haskells sold it to me?"

"I didn't know. It hasn't come up when we've talked."

"You know him pretty well, I take it," Jim said. "Well, I don't know him at all. He sent his lawyer with the offer to buy — a fellow named Burns from the firm of Hale, Addison and Burns. Each time, he upped the price."

"A generous one to start with, I'd wager."

"Sure. Mr. Burns couldn't understand why I wouldn't take it up. Got quite exasperated with me. Politely, I'll say. Said I was a mighty intransigent young man in view of my obviously impecunious condition. Something like that."

Tenney laughed. "It's no secret how much Senator Warrender wants this property, Jim. But he wouldn't lean on you to get it. Not as you suggest — by trumping up a clumsy rustling charge against you."

"That so? From what Tom Haskell's told me, he can be a pretty tough customer. Owns plenty of influence and didn't get it by playing pat-a-cake."

"True at one time, I grant you," Tenney said promptly. "In the old days Stu Warrender regarded this as his private corner of Arizona. Fought hard for what he got and played a tough hand all the way. But that was a long time ago, Jim, a time he wants to forget and wants other people to. Now, what about these offers of his? Was there some hint of a threat if you didn't sell? Any suggestion of it?"

"Nothing like that, no," Jim Izancho said stubbornly. "But that doesn't mean he couldn't find ways and means to crowd me. I'm not a big, white-eyed rancher like Milo Haskell. I'm just an impecunious siwash Injun. You've practiced law, you say? All right, you know how much legal weight any Injun's rights swing in the Arizona and New Mexico courts. Suppose Warrender decided to put a little pressure here, a little there. And maybe a more direct pressure on me. That play today by his kid and cowhands could be the start of something."

"Could be, but you're wrong. This was Roger's idea of a kid lark. He's still a runny-nosed juvenile who got spoiled rotten. One of the Senator's outstanding blunders and one he's painfully aware of. He'll be any-thing but overjoyed about what his son has pulled here."

"I don't know," Jim said slowly. "Warren-der is worried about me diverting water from the Santa Agrita. I told his lawyer the straight magoo about my plans, his first visit. Assured him my little irrigation project wouldn't use enough water to lower the Santa Agrita by a cow's piddle. But it didn't take worth a damn. Mr. Burns has made the Senator's displeasure very plain."

"Look here," Tenney said abruptly. "I'm calling on the Senator tomorrow — to discuss his son's little escapade. I'll talk to him personally about this. Get all the assurances of his honest intentions you want from his own lips. Senator Warrender's word is good as gold; even the Haskells tell you that. Fair enough?"

"You seem damned sure of Warrender. You have all that much voice with him?"

"Sort of. I'm married to his daughter."

Jim's eyes slowly widened. Just as slowly, his expression turned flat and guarded. "And you're pretty cozy in-laws?"

"He's a friend. This is on the q.t., Jim: I may be running for the state legislature this fall. To put it briefly, the Senator himself urged me to run and has promised me his full support. Financially and otherwise."

"In that case," Jim said in a colorless tone, "I wouldn't wax eloquent about our old times together if I were you. Not to your father-in-law, not to anyone. It would nicely cool your chances at the polls if it got public you and I were friends."

"Not 'were,' " Tenney said quietly.

Jim Izancho's face was a bronze mask.

"All right, Frank," he said. "All right. Just one thing. I've taken a lot of beatings in the white man's world . . . these last eight years. More times than I can stand to think about. You might call this a last-ditch stand. I'm going to make it right here and I'm going to make it good. Got to. For my soul's sake, if you want to put it that way. I'm not budging from this place. Not for hell, not for high water. And not for money. You just make that clear to Warrender, will you?"

CHAPTER FOUR

Leaning against a fence pole, Roger Warrender and his cousin Billy watched Tony Soto trying to curb the fractious pitchings of Roger's black mare Satana and not having much success. The horse had come high-rolling out of the pen and had tried at once to dislodge her rider, plunging up and down in a series of jolting pile drivers. Now she was switching tactics, twisting high and coming down with a sharp dip of her forequarters to one side or the other.

"Damn it, Tony!" Roger said sharply. "Don't let her sunfish on you. Knock her down!"

"Jeezos, I am trying, man!" Soto yelled as the horse's shoulder dipped hard to the right. "Can' you see I'm trying?"

Scowling, Roger took out a pack of Chesterfield tailor-mades, thumbed one free, and stuck it in his mouth. He didn't light it, just rolled it between his teeth and watched

Satana and her rider race around the corral, Soto fighting for control. As they tore past Roger, a burst of dust flew out between the rails, spattering his breeches and Cordovan boots. He swore, batting at his breeches.

Hearing the roar of a motor then, Roger straightened up and around.

A hundred yards away, a car was rolling up the long driveway that curved up from the road. Recognizing the vehicle at once, he felt a small heat curl the edge of his already vicious mood. Tenney was behind the wheel, and Bettina was beside him. Seeing Roger now, she waved at him.

He looked back at the corral, ignoring her. Sight of Tenney had stoked the simmering anger in Roger, and Bettina's being his sister didn't prevent some of it spilling over on her. God, it had been a sorry day when she'd married that shorthorn!

By now, Billy de Groot had turned around and was squinting at the car. "Say, Rodge," he said, "ain' that — ?"

"Yeah."

"Jeez. You reckon he come out here to comb us over again?"

"I don't know," Roger growled. "But I've had a bellyful of taking hard talk, I tell you that. First off him, then the old man."

Watching from the tail of his eye, he saw

the car pull up by the broad front veranda. The Senator and Roger's mother came out to greet the Tenneys as they stepped from the car, and all four of them went into the house.

Roger reached for a match, his scowl deepening. It had been a long while since Tenney and Bettina had come to the ranch for a visit; could be, this was just a family call. But that was unlikely, even though Tenney and the Senator had spoken at some length on the telephone last evening. Tenney had told Roger, after all, that he'd be coming out to discuss the Izancho business with the Senator. That was Tenney's way when it came to professional matters: having the whole thing out face to face.

Well, the Senator had sure as hell taken the incident seriously.

Following Tenney's phone call yesterday, the old man had summoned all four men involved — Roger, Billy, Tony, and Trooper — to his office and had given them a harsh dressing down. After dismissing the others, he had ordered Roger to remain behind. And had spent another half hour combing him over the coals. It was the worst hiding, verbal or otherwise, that Roger had taken from the old man since the time he was fourteen and had tied his sister's two pet cats together by the tails and tossed them into her room through the window. Hell, within recent memory he'd committed plenty of other escapades of which the Senator had heartily disapproved. Seemed he'd simply tested the old man's forbearance once too often.

That hadn't made the tongue-lashing smart any less. The sour burn of humiliation lingered this morning, so strongly that after readying Satana for a ride, Roger had gratuitously cut the mare with his quirt; she had promptly dumped him. So he had ordered Soto to ride her edge off.

The Senator had called Roger's action in hoorawing those Injuns totally irresponsible. Hell! Hadn't a concern for Big W been his sole reason? A big outfit like this couldn't just wink at every penny-ante thief who thought he could dip into Big W beef whenever the notion took him. Not and keep people's respect, it couldn't. Had to show 'em, too, that no goddam statute in a book would keep Big W from protecting its own.

Roger's hand shook a little as he snapped the match alight on his thumbnail and held it to his cigarette, glancing toward the house again.

Tenney and the old man would be hashing

the whole incident over once more. Discussing him as if he were a wet-eared kid. Roger felt a nudge of jealousy. Though Frank Tenney was only five years older than he, it was to his son-in-law and not his son that the Senator had lately given ear.

Naturally Stuart Warrender had his reasons, beyond any question of personal favoritism. He'd always been active in the Territory's politics, though his "Senator" was only a courtesy title, a respectful nickname he'd won by his long fight in helping bring Arizona to statehood. Now retired from the political arena, he was anxious to see the politicking tradition of his family carried on. The Warrenders had been gentlemen farmers in the East, and here they were gentlemen ranchers, but wherever they settled they had always strengthened their presence by capturing the plums of political office. It was part of owning influence and respect that the Senator took for granted, and having bitterly concluded that a capacity for public leadership had run dry in his own line — for Roger hadn't a jot of interest in taking up a public career — Stuart Warrender was willing to give all encouragement even to a family member by marriage. So he had sound reason for listening to, and respecting, Tenney's judgments.

Moreover, the Senator had been impressed by the fact that Tenney had talked Izancho out of taking the matter to court. Or so it was assumed: Tenney had merely said that Izancho wouldn't prefer charges. Something about that situation didn't quite meet the eye, Roger thought narrowly. Why Tenney's concern for that Injun? Had they some private thing going between 'em? What the hell could it be?

The mare had about pitched itself out by now, and finally she came to a lathered, side-heaving standstill. Stepping from the saddle, Soto said wearily, "Hokay, Rodge, she's all yours."

Roger dropped his cigarette, grinding it under a heel. "Changed my mind," he said abruptly. "I'm going for a drive."

Soto gave him an unbelieving look, then muttered, "Ah for the good chrissake," and spat disgustedly at the ground.

Roger's mood veered; suddenly he felt cheerful. "Come along if you want. You, too, Billy. Hell, it's Saturday. We ought to kick up some kind of excitement in town."

"Hey-ey," Soto said with a wide grin, then scratched his head dubiously. "I don' know. The Senator, he pretty mad on us. Maybe we better stick close to the place today."

"He didn't say anything about sticking close. Come on."

"Well . . . hokay. After I take care you horse and give her rubdown, I join you at the car barn."

"Garage, you dummy."

Soto, starting to strip the mare of bridle and saddle, paused and gave Roger a flat-eyed look. "Say, I ain' no horse. I ain' Billy, neither. You don' talk to me that way or I get mad."

"Just kidding, fella," Roger said with a brash grin. "Take it easy."

The big, three-stall garage was a little distance from Big W's old carriage shed but closer to the driveway. The garage was a new frame building; it contained a Rapid truck as well as the Senator's big, five-passenger Stafford and Roger's cyclecar. This was a brand-new Malcolm, and Roger thought it was sporty as hell with its sleek, low-slung chassis and cantilever springs and V-belt drive. You could nurse forty to fifty miles out of the light car on a single gallon of gas and it was so damn' maneuverable you could turn it almost like a cutting horse.

When they had it started up, Roger taking his place in the narrow driver's seat and Billy piling into the rear seat, they pulled out of the garage and braked up on the gravel driveway to wait for Soto. Listening to the motor idle,

Roger contemplated opening the petcocks on the engine in order to scare any horses along the road. But he remembered how the Senator had chewed him for spooking some of the ranch nags that same way.

Besides . . . Roger grinned and ran a hand fondly over the long-distance siren newly mounted beside the steering wheel. He hadn't tried this baby out yet and today would be a good time. Just a turn of the crank and if it sounded off the way it was supposed to, it ought to send half the horse-flesh in the county into a goddam panic.

Seeing Soto crossing from the corral to the bunkhouse now, Roger impatiently waved an arm at him and yelled, "Hey, Tony! Step on it! Let's get rolling!"

Soto vanished into the bunkhouse but reappeared a moment later, coming on the run with a bottle in his fist. "Damn it," Roger shouted, "don't be waving that thing out in plain sight! Stow it!" Obediently, Soto held the bottle under his jumper till he had reached the car and climbed in, wedging himself alongside Billy in the one-passenger back seat.

Roger sent the Malcolm spurting down the driveway, gravel spewing under the wheels as he swung onto the county road that led to town.

Soto tapped him on the shoulder. Roger glanced backward, returned Tony's grin, and took the proffered bottle. He downed a long, long swig of the fiery tequila and felt its raw force cauterize the lining of his stomach. He blinked and said, "Wooooof!" as he handed the bottle back. Soto laughed and patted his shoulder. Roger laughed too, feeling a great warmth toward Tony, who was a kindred soul with a good, healthy streak of wild in him, even if he was a Mex.

The road was nicely graded on the valley flats ahead of them. Roger let the Malcolm out at a reckless thirty miles an hour; the cold sear of wind made his eyes water.

A familiar sign grew into sight ahead; a crotchety neighbor had set it up along the roadside behind his fence. The sign had been shot full of holes by passing motorists and horsebackers but still bore a legible message in stern black letters: MOTOR CARS ARE THE CURSE OF OUR COUNTRY ROADS. As many times as he'd seen it, the sign always struck Roger as funny. He started laughing and couldn't stop.

Soto and Billy joined him, all three of them passing the bottle back and forth and laughing fit to kill.

Jim Izancho didn't go into the county seat,

Friendship, any more often than necessary. For one thing, most of the merchants didn't care for the Indian trade and made no bones about it. For another, the state of Jim's finances made it imperative to stretch his buying as fine as possible.

Mainly, he and Sally had fallen back on the ways of their ancestors for subsistence, and those ways had served them pretty well. Game was plentiful along the river bottoms; Jim molded and made his own bullets, saving the cartridge cases. Sally had a good-sized garden and a green thumb for it; she ground her own meal in a *metate* and baked her bread in a 'dobe oven. Gunpowder and bar lead, salt and sugar, a few other store-bought items, filled out their town needs.

Jim kept his trips to town down to one a week, and none at all would have suited him fine. Sally, he knew, looked forward to spending a day in town. Not that she ever complained of loneliness. But living in their remote valley was a sight different from what she'd always known, the life of a traveling show with its crowds and pageantry and excitement. It was good for her to get into town now and then, even a town that remained strange and unfriendly.

Saturday was always their town day, an adjustment Jim made for Sally's sake. He would have preferred any day of the week over the one on which the town was invariably crowded with white-eyes and their families. But he never betrayed that feeling to her, and this morning was no different. He hitched up the team to the spring wagon and, with Sally beside him on the high seat and Joe-Jim on Sally's lap, set out for Friendship.

There wasn't much of a road between their place and the county highway. Jim had graded the worst spots with a team-drawn scraper he borrowed from the Haskells, but it remained a bumpy and badly rutted trace that always turned to a potholed mire after a heavy rain. It was completely unnegotiable by any automobile, which was fine with Jim. He guided the team over it with a sure and careful hand, feeling no particular relief when the county road came in sight.

"Look!" said Sally to Joe-Jim. "See the telephone poles. Can you count them? One —"

"One," echoed the boy.

"Two —"

The angular march of wire-strung poles along the roadside was another view that gave Jim Izancho no pleasure. It was the only sign of habitation, aside from the county road itself, along this whole desolate stretch, and yet it annoyed him.

A wry smile touched Jim's mouth. In his travels he had seen the heart of white civilization, from its vaulting skyscrapers to the glitter and pomp of foreign courts, and those memories left him unmoved. Yet an ordinary line of telephone poles irritated him; it was too damned incongruous to this land. *Apache land,* he thought.

In his younger days he hadn't thought that way very often. He was first of all himself, Jim Izancho, and only incidentally a member of the *Shis-in-day.* The people. Or People of the Woods if you preferred. The Apaches. To be himself, a man in his own right, had seemed enough. But when you'd been gone from your people a long while, you came to realize how much of your strength was really a people's quintessential strength. Maybe it took "the slings and arrows of outrageous fortune" to turn a man's eyes inward and make him weigh the parts of his sum.

Yet his own way was still peculiarly that of a loner, Jim supposed. Even as a boy on the Reservation, he had spent most of his time far from the lodges of his clan. And had nurtured a secret contempt (whose memory now shamed him a little) for most of his tribesmen, steadily degenerating under the whites' rule. Theirs were the eroding ways of a defeated and beaten-down people. Very early, Jim had vowed that one day he'd strike out on his own, to his own self-finding as a man. It hadn't been necessary to love the white-eyes or their ways, which he'd regarded as slack and effete, to take a deep zest in the challenge of making a life among them.

Always, for Jim Izancho, there had to be the challenge.

Funny how ineradicable that need was to his whole nature, even after the disillusionments that had compounded one upon another during his years in the white world. Yet even now, carrying a black bitterness in him always, he could still rise to a strong challenge, in this instance to make a little farm work and pay. It had become as important to him as any greater goal on which he'd ever set his sights.

Jim turned the wagon east on the smoothly graveled highway, and now he shook the team into a brisk pace. Joe-Jim made a little noise of pleasure as they picked up speed.

Jim and Sally smiled at each other. Times like this, Jim thought, made everything worth it. So long as he could keep the resolution he'd made never to let Sally or the boy be infected by his own bitter depth of old angers, things might still work out for them. In spite of all else, he could still believe that.

Hearing the distant rattle of a car's engine far down the road, at their backs, Jim slowed the horses and pulled to the side of the road, gently sawing them to a halt.

As a mere precaution, he always stopped the team to hold it steady until a motor vehicle had gone past. Several years before, when he was breaking them in, a passing car would panic the horses into a run and he'd have the devil's own time bringing them under control. But as the numbers of automobiles had increased on county roads, the animals had gradually adjusted to the sight and sound of them, and Jim no longer had any real fear of their provoking an untimely ruckus.

The car was coming fast but slowed up as it neared them. Jim didn't look around; he kept a controlled rein on the team and waited for the auto to pass.

Then the car braked to a stop beside them, motor idling.

"Whatcha know," Roger Warrender said with a lopsided grin. "It's the Indin."

Jim looked at the three of them, not needing the evidence of the near-empty bottle in Tony Soto's fist to see they were all on a bender.

"Ho!" Soto hooted, making a loud smacking sound with his lips. "There is his squaw and papoose, too. Hey, ain' they one good-looking family?"

"Neat," Roger said. "Neat as a row o' pins. Sure be a damn shame if they got mussed up, now, wouldn't it?"

"Move on," Jim said stonily.

"What?" Roger cocked a hand behind his ear. "I hear you right, Indin? You tryin' to tell *American citizens* their rights on a *public American road?* That what you doin', Indin?"

"I've no business with you, Warrender. Go on."

"Oh, I dunno," Roger said happily. "I might just have some with you, now. Leastways some 'at didn't get finished. Right, men?"

Soto and Billy de Groot gave mighty whoops of agreement.

With a vicious abruptness Roger gunned the car forward. He sent it spinning down the road for fifty yards or so, then slammed the brakes and swerved off the road, churning up a vast plume of dust as he turned in a tight half circle. The light car leaped onto the road again and came barreling back toward the Izanchos, heading straight for the team.

75

Jim kept his thoughts cold: Hold steady now. It's a crazy game, is all. Just hold 'em steady and we'll be fine. . . .

He wasn't prepared for the sudden wail of a siren as it started up, rising at once to a keening shriek. The team horses promptly spooked, rearing and plunging in their harness.

The cyclecar roared by.

Jim had a glimpse of the reckless excitement in Roger's face as he furiously cranked the siren, but his mind barely registered the sight or the three youths' yells of derision. He was occupied with trying to fight the team under control. But it was futile; he knew instinctively that in a moment they would break and run.

"Get off!" he yelled at Sally. "Get off fast!"

She scrambled sideways on the seat, clutching the boy to her, intending to jump down. But her long skirt tripped her; she and Joe-Jim took a bruising tumble clear from the seat to the ground. Jim heard his son's short cry of pain.

The wagon leaped forward as the horses surged into the harness. Jim did not try to hold them; he kept a firm grip on the reins and did his best to guide the terrified animals. But they angled off the road at a pounding run. They didn't go far. One wheel bounced on a large rock and the whole side of the wagon rose clear of the ground. Feeling the wagon careen sidelong on two wheels, Jim sprang from the seat. He let his knees fold as his feet touched ground and then, letting his impetus carry him in a smooth roll, somersaulted twice and bounded back to his feet.

The wagon crashed on its side; the horses hauled it another three yards before its dragging weight forced them to a halt.

Looking back at the road, Jim saw that both Sally and Joe-Jim had gotten to their feet, apparently unhurt. He felt a swift wash of relief that dissolved almost at once in a rush of wintry anger.

Far down the road, the cyclecar had whipped around once more. They were coming back this way, letting the siren's wicked peal sound off again, this time as a gesture of triumphant mockery.

Jim moved quickly to the upset wagon and reached under the seat, where he kept both his Sharps rifle and his Greener shotgun. He never went far from home without one or both weapons; they were clamped securely to the sideboard by brackets of stiffened rawhide. Without a moment's hesitation, he wrenched the shotgun from its clamps and half broke it, checking the brass rims of the two loads. He snapped the breech shut and tramped back to the road in a few loping strides.

The car was quite close now, and deliberately he eared back the right-hand hammer and raised the shotgun and took aim. The siren quit abruptly; at the same time, Roger frantically applied the brakes. All three of the car's occupants instinctively ducked their heads, and Jim pulled the trigger.

The windshield flew apart in a blizzard of fragments.

Roger was still hitting the brakes, but the car's momentum was only partly checked. Out of control now, it veered off the road and jolted into a wind-scoured hollow. The wheels plunged into soft sand nearly to the hubs and came to a sudden stop, almost hurling Roger through the windshield frame.

The three sat dazed by the impact as Jim walked over to the car, not hurrying. He cocked the second hammer and pointed the Greener at the engine and let go. Fired point-blank, the full charge of double-ought buck tore the hood half off. It exposed enough of the mechanism beneath to assure Jim that he'd done it considerable damage.

Roger found his voice. "Why, you son of a bitch!" he screamed. "My God, you've wrecked my machine!"

Jim said nothing. His brain still swam with the high, wordless flare of an icy anger. Abruptly now, grasping the shotgun by its stock with his right hand, he swung it in a hard arc and let go, sailing it into the brush.

Momentarily the three men gawked at him. The invitation was as clear as any words could have made it, and he stood waiting. Roger, his eyes blazing with vindictive rage, piled out of the car, and Soto and de Groot were right behind him.

They came tramping up the short embankment and fell in abreast of one another as they reached the road. Jim stood in the middle of it, arms hanging loose at his sides, and they all came at him at once.

Jim barely moved a muscle till they were nearly on him. Tony Soto, to the left of Roger, was moving a little ahead of his companions, fast and graceful, a fighting grin on his mouth. Jim cut in under Tony's guard with one lightning-quick stab of his left hand, holding his fingers stiffened, and drove it into Soto's belly just under the breastbone.

Soto wheezed and reeled backward, his mouth popping open like a grounded fish's.

Roger tried to haul up short, but too late. Jim's right hand shot out and balled up the front of his Norfolk jacket and yanked him up on his toes. Roger got out a strangled yell before Jim's open hand slapped him once, twice, three times: three hard, flat blows that somehow conveyed the full sum of his contempt.

Billy de Groot had pulled up too, grabbing wildly for one of his two holstered six-guns. As he dragged it free of leather, Jim brought his right foot up in a side-lashing straight-legged kick without moving from the spot. The power of it sprang through the great muscles of his thigh and rippled down his corded calf and tensed ankle tendons into his arched foot encased in its heavy work shoe.

The square toe caught Billy's wrist. Bone snapped. He shrieked and fell to his hands and knees.

Roger brought his knee up for Jim's groin, but the Apache twisted his body enough to take it on the thigh. Momentarily off balance, he released his hold on Roger. In the same moment, Soto, his face twisted with pain, lunged at Jim from the side.

Jim caught his balance, swung on his heel, and sidestepped, all in one motion. One-handed, he seized Soto's arm and gave a hard, dexterous flip, at the same time ramming his foot between Soto's legs. Tripped and spun head over heels, Soto crashed on his back in the dust.

With Jim half turned away, Roger bent and scooped up a jagged hunk of baseball-sized rock and rushed at him, swinging it. Jim turned just enough to catch the rock against his spread right palm and wrench it away. His left hand closed over Roger's arm.

Roger howled as the crushing grip sent agony squirting through his arm. Jim jerked him forward till they were less than two feet apart. With the same fathomless contempt as when he'd struck Roger before, he dropped the rock and drove the calloused heel of his palm straight into Roger's nose. Cartilage crunched and blood spurted, and then Jim let go.

Roger took a step back. He dropped to his knees, cupping both hands over his nose. Little squeaks of pain trickled from his gaping mouth; he couldn't manage a louder sound without doubling his nasal agony.

Jim pivoted away, tramped into the brush, and retrieved his shotgun. He broke it, removed the spent loads and inspected the barrels for dirt. Afterward he dug two fresh shells from his pocket and breeched them, snapping the Greener shut.

As he strode back to the three youths, Soto climbed unsteadily to his feet, shaking his head to clear it. Billy de Groot was lying on his side, cuddling his broken wrist and moaning softly, tears cutting muddy tracks down his cheeks. Roger was still on his knees, his face pasty with shock and pain as he mopped gingerly with his sleeve at the blood pouring from his broken nose.

"You," Jim motioned with the shotgun at Soto, "and you," at Roger. "Get over to my wagon. Set it up."

"What?" A kind of glaze-eyed disbelief mingled with the agonized rage in Roger's face. "Go screw yourself," he whispered, "you goddam siwash —"

"Rodge," Soto put in softly, "I think maybe we do it, heh?"

Roger watched Jim's face for a long, careful moment, and then, without another word, eased laboriously to his feet. He and Soto moved slowly past Jim, heading for the wagon, and Jim followed them.

Stepping up by the team, Jim laid down his shotgun and took a firm grip on each horse's headstall, speaking quietly to them. He gave Roger and Soto the nod, and they laid hold of the wagon box at either end.

"Aw right, ready?" Soto grunted. "*Uno, dos, tres*. NOW!"

They heaved the wagon up and onto its four wheels.

"*Now* you have no more business with me," Jim Izancho said.

Picking up the shotgun, he motioned with it again, this time toward the road. Roger, snuffling against an unstanched flow of blood, gave the Apache a long look. "Oh, boy," he said. "You don't know. It's just started."

"Get walking."

Roger's glance shuttled toward his car and back to Jim. "I don't guess you're worth enough to pay for that. But, by God, you're gonna pay, all right."

Iron-faced, Jim said, "Get a horse."

Roger stared at him a moment longer, then dug out a wadded handkerchief and held it to his nose, giving Soto and de Groot a curt nod. Billy was weeping quietly, clutching his right arm above the broken wrist, as the three of them tramped away and started down the highway toward the Big W. None of them looked back.

Jim climbed onto his wagon and maneuvered it back to the roadside. He stepped to the ground as Sally and Joe-Jim came up. Giving them a sober study, he saw that his son's hand was freshly wrapped in a calico bandanna that was already stained with blood. Joe-Jim's lips were clamped fiercely shut; his eyes were tearless.

83

"He gashed his hand on a stone when we fell," Sally explained. "It will need stitching."

"All right. We'll see a doctor in town."

She laid a hand on his arm. "Jim. Don't look that way. Please."

He tried to relax the flat muscles of his face. "I'm sorry, Sal. Are both of you okay . . . otherwise?"

"We're fine. It's just a little cut Joe-Jim has."

She kept her gently insistent hold on his arm, her eyes worried and a little frightened by what she saw in his face.

"That's right," he said quietly. "I'd like to have blasted them. It was all I could do not to. Those white sons of bitches."

"The one was a Mexican, wasn't he?"

"Him, too."

"Don't, Jim," she said in a hushed voice. "Don't. Please!"

She knows, he thought. For all his trying to show her only his gentle part, to hide the bitter violence that always lurked so near his surface, she had seen it; she knew. Perhaps she always had known.

"It's all right, Sal." He slid an arm around her waist, giving her a quick hug. And spoke with real gentleness then, forcing himself to smile. "You know? This was what Frank said wouldn't happen. Said he wouldn't let happen."

She did not smile. "Jim, the sheriff is your friend. You must go to him about this."

"Why?"

"So he will hear the truth from you. Those three will tell something else."

"I mean why, what good will it do, what can he do about it? It's a goddam siwash's word against three whites. Or two. Whatever."

"Jim. . . ."

"All right." He gave a resigned and weary nod. "I didn't say I wouldn't see him."

CHAPTER FIVE

"All this dust," said Bettina. "Lord, but I wish we had a closed car."

Tenney, occupied with steering the Buick Ten back down the highway toward Friendship, gave his wife a brief glance.

She made a pretty picture in the prescribed motoring ensemble for milady this season. The striped rubberized auto coat, designed to repel both rain and dust in an open car, hid the faint signs of her pregnancy. Bettina's shining brown hair was pulled back in a fashionable pug and topped with a wide-brimmed hat fastened down by a silk scarf. Tied in a big, floppy bow under her chin, it matched the cornflower blue of her eyes.

"Damme," he murmured, "but you do remain a fetching baggage."

"Really?" She looked straight ahead. "I don't know how I manage it in all this dust."

Tenney realized that her voice had a distinct edge. Another glance showed him a tightness of discontent marring her full mouth. He could guess what was wrong, but he only said mildly, "All right, Betts. Get it out."

"I think you know."

"Look, I didn't tell your pa I wouldn't run, did I?"

"You as good as said it." Abruptly she looked at him, letting out her anger now. "How *could* you, Frank! Weeks ago, when Daddy asked you, you said yes, you were interested in trying for the legislature. You *know* how hard he's been working to pull strings on your behalf — while you've done virtually nothing. Then you say a thing like that to him!"

"Betts," he said patiently, "all I said was —"

He broke off with a frown, mentally reconstructing his talk with the Senator. It had begun cordially enough, with Stuart Warrender agreeing that Roger and his companions had stepped out of bounds yesterday and telling how he'd made his displeasure clear to the four of them.

"When I take that piece of land," he'd added casually, "I'll do it lawfully. Not under a shoddy pretext, like trumping up a phony charge."

Not quite sure he'd heard right, Tenney had said: "You don't mean you *are* thinking about running Jim Izancho off his property?"

The Senator had shown an easy smile. "I'd not put it that way, Frank. Oh, I fully intend to oust this redskin. But all legal, with ribbons on it. Izancho's not a U.S. citizen, right? He's an Indian, a ward of the government. That makes any right of his to buy or sell land anywhere pretty tenuous at best. Fact, he has no damned rights at all except on a federal reservation, and those are strictly defined. I have lawyers working on that angle right now, preparing a brief for a federal hearing on my behalf. If it goes the way I expect it will — you know how even federal courts in this state feel about an Injun's so-called rights — I'll have that boy where the hair's short. And if he declines to move then, *I'll* move him."

As he'd spoken, the Senator had kept those colorless, show-nothing eyes of his on Tenney's face, watching for any reaction. Keeping his expression mildly dubious, Tenney had said quietly, "Disproving his title wouldn't give you that right, sir. Title to that piece would revert back to Milo Haskell. And Haskell might tell Izancho to stay on anyhow — just to spite you."

The Senator had produced a cigar and

clipped the end, still watching Tenney's face. "That would be too bad," he'd said gently. "Izancho intends to divert the Santa Agrita into that dry basin. Don't think for a moment I'll let it happen."

That flat declaration, Tenney knew, had been both a question and a warning to himself as sheriff. Warrender wanted to handle the problem by legal means, but he might overstep legal bounds if he had to, and he wanted to be sure of his son-in-law's stance if it happened.

Tenney had been tempted to pick up the challenge — except it would have served no purpose. He knew what the Senator did not: that Jim Izancho's pride wouldn't permit him to remain on that land if his title was voided. Nor would he accept the Haskells' charity if they offered it. Yet — hoping to avert even a legalistic brouhaha — Tenney had considered marshaling Jim's own arguments concerning the Santa Agrita diversion. But Warrender, he'd known, would be fully aware of those arguments and be utterly deaf to them.

So he'd tried another tack: "Well, I tell you, Senator. You could just be grabbing a wildcat by the tail. Izancho's not your run-of-the-mill siwash. He's something of a celebrity."

"I'm aware of that, Frank. But, from all I've heard or read, he's dragged his colors through a bit of mud. I don't think his kind of notoriety will count for much in the court of public opinion, do you?"

"Maybe not." Tenney had played his final card: "There's one other thing, though. Jim Izancho has his citizenship."

The Senator had paused in the act of striking a match. Then he'd chuckled and lighted his cigar. "That's absurd."

"Absurd or not. You've heard of the Dawes Act?"

"The so-called 'general allotment act' of 1887? Yes, of course. What of it?"

Both Bettina and her mother had been paying close attention to the conversation, and at this point Eleanor Warrender had put in quietly: "I have never heard of the Dawes Act, Frank. Perhaps neither has Bettina. Would you tell *us* about it?"

Tenney had explained that the Dawes Severalty Act had been pushed through the U.S. Congress by "friends" of the Indian who had insisted that assimilation of the redman into American culture could be most quickly achieved by doing away with outworn customs and attitudes to which most Indians clung. Reservation life tended to maintain traditional tribal ways; it fostered indolence. The key to transition, they had declared, was to make farmers of the savages. The Dawes Act had authorized the allotment of reservation lands into individual parcels, bestowing on each Indian a piece of tribally owned land whether he wanted it or not. To ensure that the transition wouldn't be too abrupt, the land was to be held in trust for a period of twenty-five years, during which it would be ineligible for private ownership or sale. At the end of that time a patent in fee simple would be given the individual — and with it would be awarded all the rights and duties of citizenship.

The Senator had made a brusque gesture. "What's that got to do with Izancho? Get to the point, Frank."

"Well, Jim Izancho was three years old when that act was passed. His father was killed just a few months later, raiding with Geronimo, and Jim's grandfather, Cow Bird, who was head of their clan, saw that a piece of land was set aside in Jim's name. The trust period ended two years ago. And that makes Jim Izancho a landowner and U.S. citizen."

Stuart Warrender's eyes had hardened. "You must have had quite a talk with that Injun yesterday."

"I did," Tenney had said promptly. "Always followed his athletic career. Izancho's an interesting fellow, Senator. An American original — almost. Nobody you can compare him with except maybe Jim Thorpe."

No point in mentioning that his knowledge of Jim Izancho's reservation allotment dated back to their boyhood time together. Jim had given him good advice, he wryly knew, in suggesting that he keep their friendship under wraps.

Even so, the Senator had eyed Tenney with displeasure that was tinged by a faint suspicion. "Any 'rights' of his," he'd declared flatly, "would rest on damned tenuous grounds, it seems to me. Izancho hasn't lived on any reservation in years . . . couldn't have done a thing toward tilling or improving his parcel."

Feeling a quickening irritation of his own now, Tenney had answered bluntly: "That could be, sir. You might still take the question to court. Things being as they are, you might even win. Too bad Izancho won't sell out to you. But even if he would — he's an educated man. You'd have to pay him a hell of a lot more than twenty-four dollars."

A slow flush of anger had started up from the Senator's collar. He had opened his mouth, then abruptly checked his speech.

Moving to the oaken sideboard, he had poured two glasses of whiskey, then had walked back to Tenney and handed him one.

"I would at that," he'd said almost jovially. "You know, Frank? It's nonsense, of course, but Roger had the notion you and that Indian are friendly."

"If Roger ever thought too hard," Tenney had said flatly, "he'd have a headache for a week."

A muscle had flicked in Warrender's jaw, but he'd had full control of himself now — even gave an indulgent laugh. His son-in-law's bluntness might be hard to swallow at times, but it was a quality the Senator could respect — and he had a strong reason for not wanting to feud with Frank Tenney. "Agreed . . . reluctantly. But what I'm getting at, my boy, is that with election time coming up, you can't be too careful. You know how people hereabouts stand on the Indian question."

It had only nettled Tenney further. He'd taken his drink in a swallow, then had looked Warrender squarely in the eye. "I don't know as there's any question in my mind, Senator. And I don't know that any damned office under the sun is worth that kind of price."

A few moments of tense, cold silence had followed. When the Senator had spoken again, it was on a complete change of subject, and his manner had been distant and formal, just short of chilly. Shortly afterward, the Tenneys had taken their leave, and nothing at all had been resolved.

Silence held between them as they continued down the highway.

Tenney supposed that Bettina had reason to be mad. On his part he didn't feel angry, only perplexed and a little sheepish. He wished he could keep their marriage clear of his public life, no easy thing when your father-in-law was also your political sponsor.

Moreover, Bettina was ambitious for him, and he knew that his back-talking her father annoyed her far less than his potential refusal to run for higher office. She'd assumed almost unquestioningly that he would run, and he'd let her believe it, because it was easier to vaguely hedge when you were still undecided. Tenney's present line of work satisfied him; he hadn't reached a point in his career or his thinking where he was prepared to decide whether or not he wanted to move on and up. But a dissatisfied wife made a large difference; it could push a man into a course for which he had no real heart.

Was he letting that happen? Tenney wasn't sure. Ambition was a contagious thing; if a man had a kernel of it in his system, it would be damned easy to let himself be flattered into a wrong choice by those who figured they knew what was best for him.

Tenney leaned forward, squinting his eyes. Up ahead, three figures were trudging along the road. Someone's car must have broken down. When they were a little nearer, he recognized Roger and Soto and de Groot; he slowed down, pulling to a stop abreast of them.

Bettina gave a little exclamation of shock.

Roger's nose was mashed to a pulp; blood coursed in half-scabbed rivulets down either side of his mouth. Billy de Groot's face was streaked with tears and he was bent painfully over his right hand, cuddling it against his chest.

Red-faced and sweating with this unaccustomed exertion, Roger burst out hotly: "That goddam Indin friend of yours wrecked my car! He shot it to pieces!"

"Make sense," Tenney said curtly. "What happened to you?"

"We were driving to town and we met that goddam Indin —"

"Izancho?"

"The son of a bitch had a shotgun and he let it off at us just like that, no warning at all! Then he jumped on us like a goddam wildman!"

"You're saying one man took the three of you apart. Is that right, Roger?"

"For no goddam reason at all! My car's in the ditch back there and it's all shot up, go see for yourself!"

Tenney eyed him for a long moment, then said quietly, "Roger, you're a damned liar. . . ."

Bettina was furious as they drove on.

She let him know it too, spilling out a torrent of stored grievances along with the immediate ones. Why had he taken this irrational dislike to Roger? Why assume because her brother had committed a few past mistakes that he was always in the wrong now? Why make those hurt boys walk clear back to Big W when he could have given them a ride?

Tenney held a grim silence till they reached Roger's disabled Malcolm. He stopped, got out, and made a careful inspection of the scene, including the road itself for some distance either way. He found two places where a car had swerved off the road and turned around in sweeping circles, the wheels digging deep, wide furrows in the off-road ground.

He pointed these out to Bettina.

"What of it?" she said coldly.

"Nothing — yet. Just remember what you saw. I'm going to get Jim Izancho's story."

"Which you'll unquestioningly accept, I suppose." She looked at him with finely pursed lips. "You know, Frank, I think Roger had a good question. Why all this bleeding-heart partiality for poor Lo?"

"Don't call a man that, Bettina. He has a name."

"Poor Lo the Indian. What's in a name?"

Resignedly, Tenney started up the car.

The town of Friendship had come to life in the 1870s as a mining boom town. When the first big silver strike was exhausted, it had continued a middling existence in the heart of this mining and cattle country, never growing bigger or smaller. Friendship was an American backwater, not really isolated but well out of any mainstream current, and the twentieth century had hardly touched its placid, semirural ways.

The town sprawled like a tired dog in the May heat, the cottonwoods that lined its unpaved side streets drowsing in a flinty dance of sunlight. The Tenneys' whitewashed frame house was close to the eastern outskirts, and Tenney let Bettina out at their front gate. Not saying a word, she marched up to the porch, unlocked the door, and let herself in. Tenney put the car in the old buggy shed that served as a garage, then headed downtown on foot.

It shouldn't take long, he bleakly reflected, for news of that highway run-in to get around. No matter how it had really happened, it could lead to more and worse trouble easy as falling off a log — unless he took steps at once to wrest out the truth, then took a fast stand on the matter. First he meant to check on whether Jim Izancho had come to town after his clash with Roger. If not, he'd saddle up and ride out to see him.

Tenney had turned onto Main Street at the corner of the mercantile store and was heading toward the courthouse when Dilworth Mudd came quartering from across the street. Dilworth, a middle-aged man with protruding teeth and hair like matted straw, was turnkey at the county jail, and he looked mildly excited.

"Frank, hey! I was headed for your house. Hoped you'd be back from Big W by now."

"Anything wrong?" Tenney asked.

"I reckon not yet, but you best hurry. They's an Indin in your office. Biggest, meanest-looking buck I ever seen."

Tenney smiled. "I think I know him, Dil."

"Do tell." The jailor scratched his chin. "Well, I was sweeping the place out when this Indin come straight in and plunked hisself in a chair and says he'll wait for you till you show up, and by God that's all he'd say. So I come a-looking for you. You best get a move on."

"Why?"

"I just now seen O.D. headed for the courthouse. You know how O.D. is. He sees that Indin sitting in your office, ain't no telling what he'll do."

Tenney went on at a fast walk, then quickened to a run. Dil was right: if Oliver Dempster Bangs and Jim Izancho had a difference of opinion, it would take about a minute or less for it to flare into trouble.

The courthouse was a blocky, three-story brick building at the street's northern end. It was set back on a patch of lawn fronted by old cottonwoods. Bypassing the sidewalk, Tenney cut across the grass to the side entrance that led to his basement office. He loped down a flight of stone steps and hurried through the basement corridor, his boots echoing on the concrete floor.

The door of his office stood open, and now he heard O.D. drawling ominously, "Buck, I will give you one more chance to say what you're doing here. Then I am gonna —"

99

Tenney stepped into the room.

Jim Izancho was sitting on a bench against the wall, his arms folded, and O. D. Bangs was standing in front of him, hands on hips, leaning pugnaciously forward.

O.D.'s glance shuttled to Tenney now, and he said severely, "Frank, you hadn't ought to leave this here office unlocked like you do. It's got so any kind o' trash that wants to walks right in when they take a mind."

Tenney nodded in dry agreement, looking at O.D. with a mental shake of his head.

O. D. Bangs was a real case. Night deputy for the sheriff's office, he was a solidly built young man of twenty-six. He wore his yellow hair and mustaches long. He wore a fringed buckskin coat and a huge white Stetson, and on his boots he wore big, dragging rowels weighted with miniature dumbbells. Billy de Groot had emulated O.D.'s habit of toting a pair of Colts cross-belted and slung low on his thighs in tie-down holsters, as he fancied the old time gunfighters had worn them. For all that he looked and acted like a bit player from one of the Selig two-reel Westerns, of which he was a rabid fan, O.D. was a capable deputy, Tenney had to admit. You needed to swallow twice to keep him down, but he was dependable, performed his duties to a T, and was only about one third as dumb as he looked. He had enough pure guts for two men and the gall to match.

"It's all right, you can go," Tenney told him. "Hello, Jim."

Jim Izancho nodded and didn't otherwise stir a muscle. O.D. scowled and started to say something; Tenney cut him off flatly: "You here to see me about anything, O.D.?"

"No, I just dropped by. But Jesus, here's this siwash just sitting like he owns the place and he won't say a goddam word."

"Mr. Izancho's got business with me. We've talk to make, so if you don't mind —"

O.D. lounged to the doorway, then turned and said with a gibing grin, "You sure he can talk?" And swaggered out.

Tenney took off his cap and long car duster and hung them on a hook. He removed his tie and collar and dropped them on his desk, afterward settling into his swivel chair with a grimace of relief. Looking at Jim Izancho, he said simply, "I met Roger and his chums on the road."

A corner of Jim's mouth lifted faintly. "Was I to blame?"

"That's what Roger says. The tracks where he turned his car a couple times say different. Want to tell me about it?"

Jim did.

Tenney propped his feet on the desk and crossed them, then leaned back and folded his hands behind his head, squinting thoughtfully. "I don't think you have to worry, *sheekasay*. Oh, it'll be an Indian's word against white men's, so Roger will try to brazen it out; as for Billy, he'll stick fast on whatever Roger says. About Soto, I'm not sure. . . ."

Jim Izancho smiled grimly. "He's a Mex; there's your answer. I never met one that didn't hate Apaches. Why not? We gave 'em hell for more centuries than anyone can count." He looked squarely at Tenney. "Just say how it will go, Frank. Do I get arrested?"

Tenney moved his head in negation. "Not by me. If the Warrenders got out a warrant, it'd go to court. But it won't. Those wheel tracks bear out your story and you've two witnesses to 'em: my wife and me."

"Think you said she's a Warrender."

"Right down to her soles. But she won't lie under oath. Bettina won't lie, period. Not even for her kin, and the Senator knows it."

Jim was silent for a moment; he set his hands on his knees and gazed at them. "Better than I came here looking for. Maybe I wouldn't have come at all if Sally hadn't insisted."

"Sally's smart."

"And I'm a red-headed fool," Jim said quietly. "I came near to putting those guys under for good. My boy hurt his hand falling off the wagon —"

"Serious?"

"Just a cut. Directly we got to town, we took him over to that doctor's, what's his name, the young one."

"Courtland."

"Yeah. I left Sally and the boy at his place and came looking for you." Jim raised his eyes. "Frank, they could have gotten badly hurt. It's pure luck none of us were. I never was a patient fellow, you know . . . not a very good Apache that way. But I can hate like one."

The hands clamping Jim's knees were corded with tension, Tenney saw, and now he realized the contained depth of his friend's rage.

"I wish I could give you some kind of assurance against the future," Tenney said slowly. "But afraid I can't, after all's said. I just came from a talk with my father-in-law."

"And?"

"I guess you never really know about a man. The Senator's hungrier than I thought."

Tenney told of Warrender's intention to

take Jim's land claim to court and his own invoking of the Dawes Severalty Act. "I don't know how much it counts for, but I hope you've got citizenship under that act, Jim. Fact is, I wasn't really sure."

"Neither am I. Try to establish it either way and you'd sink in a bureaucratic bog of red tape." Jim laughed and shook his head. "The Dawes Act. That goddam chestnut! You have any idea what the real purpose behind it was?"

"I always figured it was to absorb the Indians' own identities. And maybe to weaken their political muscle by breaking down their tribal cohesion."

"Right. And by carefully making no allowance for children unborn. Our land — for as long as tongues will twist and whiskey will flow." Jim's face grew serious. "If he can't move me by screwing my title, what then?"

"I can't say for sure how far he'd go, Jim. All the way, so he threatened. Maybe it was just talk. Or a bluff he hoped I'd pass along to you."

Again a long silence, and Jim said gently: "All this is putting you on a mighty tough spot, *sheekasay*. I'm sorry for that."

Tenney shrugged. "Just say it goes with the job."

Jim laced his fingers together and leaned

forward, resting his elbows on his knees. "I could move on, couldn't I — and it would solve all our problems. But I've moved on for the last time, Frank. No more of that. No more." He paused, frowning as if with the effort of shaping his feelings to speech. "It's not just that. I'd been bumming around for years. Everything I'd turned my hand to had soured on me one way or the other. For Sally's sake, for the kid's — not to say my own — I had to stop somewhere and settle down."

Tenney hesitated before saying, "If it comes to the worse, there's always that allotment land of yours back at Fort Apache, Jim. Yours free and clear now, to do with as you please."

Jim Izancho's eyes kindled; he shook his head quickly and vehemently. "No. I won't go back, Frank. Not ever. It's not just foolish pride. Oh, hell, maybe that's a part of it; I suppose it is. But that damn reservation . . . no son of mine's going to grow up as I did. Sure, I could have sat and stagnated. But I was ambitious. And that's the price of progress for an Injun. You attend a white man's school, wear white man's clothes, chop your hair off white style."

Tenney said pointedly, dryly: "And off reservation?"

Jim gave a strained grin. "*Touché*. But it's not the same. At least, off it, you decide for yourself. Even if my citizenship's valid, that Dawes thing doesn't cover my heirs or descendants. Joe-Jim would be another reservation siwash, living in squalor, filth, disease. Do you know what their mortality rate is? Their rate of alcoholism? You get a dream budded and it's dead." He snapped his fingers. "Like that." A painful pause. "You know something? I never did go through the Apache manhood rite. I never took that climb to pray to the winds and make my medicine."

Tenney scowled at the toe of his boot. "Look, pal, if it's none of my business, say so. But what about that Olympic thing?"

The big Apache rose and began to pace the room in a restless circle, his tread as springy as a cat's. He said nothing for a half minute. Then: "All right, you've followed my so-called career. You know how I chalked up a fancy record in sports at the Indian school in Carlisle, Pennsylvania. Jim Thorpe came along a few years later and shaded me, but not by much. I was that school's black-haired boy and there were all kinds of pressures on me to train for the Olympics.

"Well . . . I balked. Athletics was never

that big a part of my life. What the hell does being a prize athlete amount to? A bunch of trick reflexes, for Christ's sake. I had more important things to prove. I'd done damn well scholastically, and I *was* proud of that. I wanted to find out what an Indian could do with a good education. In your white world, first of all. Later on, maybe I'd come back to the reservation and try to use all I'd learned to help the People."

Again the wry, painful grin. "Trouble was, I was *too* full of ideals back then, Frank. They gave me a lot of grease about how much good I could do my people as the nation's first record-breaking Indian athlete. All right, it was grease on the old ego, too. So I went into training, accompanied by a big-ass fanfare of national publicity. They hired a whole battery of press agents to keep the ball rolling . . . you know how effectively. It got so I couldn't turn over in my sleep without setting off seismic tremors. And — Hell, you know the rest."

Tenney grunted. "What I know is what the newspapers said."

"Well, they didn't exaggerate any. They told what happened, and a few of 'em even gave my side of the story. Trouble was, nobody ever believed my side. Sure, I got in a brawl in a whorehouse and the cops got called and I got thrown in a drunk tank. But the way it all started was, I got slipped a mickey finn in a saloon where I was having a beer, *two* beers, with a gent who called himself Otis."

"I never heard that part of it, Jim."

"It got told in a press release, but damn few of the tabloids picked it up. It's good old yellow journalism that sells papers, right? Making out that the current pride of the Indian race was a drunk, a brawler, and a whoremonger, man, that was rich."

"What happened in that saloon?" Tenney asked.

Jim let his shoulders lift and fall, wearily. "I'd been out jogging around the cinder track by myself when this young guy came up and introduced himself. Said he was Bob Otis, a reporter for the Kansas City *Star.* Said he'd traveled a long way just to see me and would I give him an interview. Seemed a personable chap, and I had a terrific love affair going with the press — then. Was doing my damnedest to oblige all its minions. Otis suggested we talk over a drink and said he knew a nice quiet place for it, so we went to this across-town saloon. On my second beer . . . bam! the roof fell in.

"When I woke up, I found myself in this cat house — but didn't right away realize where I was. When I tried to get out of the place, a pair of house men, ex-pugs they looked like, jumped me and there was a free-for-all. Meantime, the madam phoned the bulls. I was too groggy from that mickey to put up much of a fight, and the cops threw me in the wagon and hauled me in."

Jim pulled up facing a wall papered with WANTED flyers; he stared at it pensively. "You can guess the rest. When my story was checked back, it fell through at every point. The barkeep at that saloon vowed he'd never seen me in his life. The madam claimed I'd come into her place drunk and started a ruckus. And the Kansas City *Star* had never heard of a reporter named Bob Otis. Neither had anybody else. It was a nice frame, *sheekasay* . . . so damn pat you'd think for that reason alone somebody'd have suspected that I'd been had."

"Had by who?"

"Your guess is as good as mine. Lots of folks didn't like a redskin outshining white men at white men's sports. A few hundred of 'em wrote and told me so. Better I bite the dust, like a good Injun should. So a few of 'em got together and fixed it." Jim shrugged. "That's my guess, anyway. No master conspiracy. Just the down-home folks showing their vote."

"And naturally you were disqualified from the Olympics competition."

"Naturally. Couldn't have a lowdown siwash like me representing all them down-home folks." He gazed contemplatively at the flyers on the wall. "Of course James Francis Thorpe made it a couple years ago . . . all the way to the Stockholm games. Then they disqualified *him* on the grounds he'd played semipro baseball in 1911. Yep. And they took away old Jim's trophy and his gold medals and they erased all his Olympics records clean off the books. They just plain don't like a gen'man of color, any complexion, walking off with their lily-white laurels. As Jack Johnson and old Jim and me all found out. Yessuh."

"A lousy deal," Tenney said. "But that was quite a few years back, Jim."

Jim nodded, dropping on the bench again. "But people never forget a thing like that. I was a national scandal. All the prominent Indians came down on me harder than the whites, it may not surprise you to hear. What could I do? I drifted here and there. Held and lost a score of jobs. Drank and fought. Mostly drank. Went slightly worse than the tabloids had made me out. Then Buffalo Bill Cody spotted me playing Chief Wahoo, complete with 'ughs' and pidgin

English, in a medicine show where I was making five bucks a week and all the booze I could drink. Having some intimacy with the curse of barleycorn himself, the old colonel on a whim took pity on me, hired me away for his Wild West circus, dried me out, and halfway straightened me up. Then I met Sally . . . and everything changed."

Tenney smiled. "Worth keeping straightened up for."

"Oh, sure. And fighting for. You know," Jim added almost cryptically, "my father was killed just before Geronimo surrendered to General Miles, in eighty-eight. My old man, you might say, was the last Apache. He was one of those who never gave up. Grandpa always said Skinazbas was a damn fool to throw his life away. I can't even remember him, but I allow he was my kind of fool."

Not quite sure what to read into those words, Tenney only nodded and said, "Believe I owe you a drink."

He dug a bottle of whiskey out of a cluttered drawer in his desk and was rummaging around in it for a couple glasses when the phone on the wall gave two long rings and two short ones. Tenney lounged to his feet, saying dryly, "I'll give you one guess," and lifted the receiver from the hook.

"Sheriff Tenney."

"Frank, this is Stuart Warrender. Roger and the boys are back . . . and they've told me what happened. Did you call Roger a liar?"

"Well, Senator, I'd lay odds that's about all he told the truth about."

"Frank" — the Senator spoke crisply and distinctly, but his voice quivered with a chill restraint — "I want that Indian arrested."

"Take it you're not interested in how he tells it."

"Not very." A pause. "You mean you already have him in custody?"

"Not exactly. He got to my office before I did."

"I see." A longer pause. "All right. How does he tell it?"

Briefly Tenney told him Jim's version, and about the corroborating wheel tracks.

"Frank," Warrender said impatiently, "that Injun assaulted and injured my son. He broke Billy de Groot's arm. He wrecked an expensive car. And he could have killed somebody with that shotgun of his. Now, I don't give a good goddam if the boys did hooraw him a little bit. There was no call for all that. I want Izancho arrested for assault and battery and for property damage. Roger and I will be in this afternoon to prefer charges —"

"Senator," Tenney said.

"What?"

"I'm not going to arrest Jim Izancho."

Warrender's voice crackled at him. "Just what the hell are you about, Frank? I thought we had an understanding."

"So did I. Seems we were both wrong. One more thing, Senator . . ." Tenney hesitated then, but a distaste for his own hypocrisy was suddenly rank in his mouth; he needed to spit it out. "For once, Roger was right. Jim Izancho and I were boyhood friends. He saved my life when I was fifteen years old."

"Ah!" Warrender's voice shook with the depth of a suppressed anger. "Then, you've not been entirely honest with me, Frank, have you?"

"I'll apologize for that," Tenney said quietly. "But I stand by every other damn thing I said. What it all adds up to is, Jim Izancho's in the right."

"You know that, do you? Same way you know he didn't steal those cows of mine?"

"That's right, Senator. I know him. As well as I know that pride and joy you sired."

After a pained silence, Warrender said icily, "Very well. *Now* we understand each other. But you'll damn well arrest that siwash if I have Judge Coombs get out a warrant. It'll be your job to serve it, like it or not."

"Agreed," Tenney said. "It'll be my job to serve one on Roger, too, if Izancho swears it out. And I'll put all the weight this office has behind getting that warrant made out." He cocked an eye at Jim Izancho. "What about it, Jim? You willing to sit in jail a spell?"

Jim rose and came over to the phone. After adjusting the mouthpiece to his height, he said into it, "Sure. If Roger is."

Tenney tipped back the mouthpiece and said mildly, "I guess that's it, Senator. You can drag this into court, but it might be embarrassing as hell. Because then your own daughter would have to take the stand and testify those wheel tracks were as noted. And you know damn well she will."

A long pause on the wire.

"Frank," Stuart Warrender said then, "you could have gone a long way. You're young, you're cool, and you're tough, and I believe you're ambitious. You could have had the Warrender fortune and contacts behind you. But you'd make a rotten legislator. Because you're stupid, Frank. So abysmally goddam stupid it turns my stomach."

A heavy click as he brought the receiver down. Tenney hung up and looked at Jim Izancho.

"Man, what you just did —" Jim shook his head, slowly and wonderingly. "That's about the dumbest thing I ever heard of."

"Then, you and the Senator and I all share one point of agreement," Tenney said dryly. "Care to split a bottle with a goddam fool?"

CHAPTER SIX

The gash in the little boy's hand was deep but not serious, Dr. Courtland had assured Jim and Sally. He would clean it and stitch it up. In a week the hand would be as good as new. The Izanchos had inspected the cut and changed the bandage every day for five days. To all appearances it was healing up cleanly. There was no swelling or inflamed tissue or fever, none of the ordinary signs of infection, that would have showed otherwise.

It was well into the fifth day before they began to suspect something was wrong. Joe-Jim wasn't his usual, bright-eyed self that morning, but his temperature was normal, and neither Jim nor Sally was unduly concerned. By late afternoon, though, he was complaining of "hurts"; he was stiff and sore all over, particularly around the mouth, and he was having trouble swallowing.

Still the Izanchos took no particular alarm. They put their son to bed and agreed that if he wasn't better by morning, they'd take him to the doctor. Yet Jim Izancho felt a deepening unease without quite knowing why. He continued to worry the matter in his mind as they ate supper.

It was the grandfather who gave the answer. Ordinarily, old Cow Bird so totally ignored the currents of their lives that you wondered at times if he was even vaguely aware of what passed. Tonight, however, he did not retreat to his usual corner after rising laboriously from the table. Instead, he shuffled to the bunk where his small great-grandson lay. Jim and Sally watched attentively as he touched the boy's face and chest, and then Jim rose and went over to him.

"What is it, *Abuelito*?"

The old man grunted a brief reply in Apache, and Jim, rusty in the old tongue, couldn't easily sort out the sense of what he was saying. When he did, the shock held him mute for a moment. Then he looked at Sally.

"Grandpa says it's lockjaw."

"Lockjaw," she whispered. "Oh, God, Jim, *how?*"

"That cut, I reckon. No other way the infection could get in." Jim shook his head with a swift, savage anger. "I should have known!"

"How could you?" Sally's eyes glistened wide in the rush of her fear. "Jim, how *can* you be sure?"

"He's showing all the symptoms. It just never occurred to me that might be it — never knew anyone who came down with it. But I've read about it. Sal . . . even if we're wrong, it's nothing to take a chance on. I'm getting Joe-Jim to town right now."

"I'm going with you."

Jim shook his head impatiently. "I've got to make time, honey. For one thing, it'll be dark soon; for another, the faster we get him to Courtland the better. I won't take him in the wagon; I'll carry him on old Blue. Wrap him in a blanket while I saddle up, all right?"

A few minutes later, he led the saddled mare to the front of the cabin, threw the reins, and stepped into the lamplit room. Sally had bundled Joe-Jim in a quilt, and now wordlessly she placed him in Jim's arms. The boy's eyes were clear, not a hint of fever in them, and you could tell he was scared but meant not to let on by an eye flicker. Jim looked at him and at Sally and felt a surge of pride, quick and fierce and possessive, in them.

"Don't worry, honey," he said. "It's hardly got started. The doc will get it checked all right."

She nodded gravely. "What do they do for it . . . lockjaw?"

"Oh, there's different things. All kinds of drugs and serums, I hear." He voiced the lie casually, a stopgap for her rising fear and not his own; he'd never heard of an effective treatment. "Just sit tight. I'll be back as soon as I can. Likely not before morning, though."

Sally held the boy while Jim stepped into the saddle, then passed him up. Cradling the quilted form in the bend of one arm, Jim spoke quietly to Blue and drummed his heels on her flanks, putting her in motion. He looked back once at Sally framed in the lighted doorway and felt a thickening of his throat. It was all there, he thought, in that cabin and in his hands, all that meant life for Jim Izancho.

The sun's last flare had flattened above the western hills, and already the afterglow had begun to fade. It clung awhile longer to the high places, and Jim put Blue to a quick canter as he climbed the south ridge, following the wagon road. After the ridge dipped off, he settled into a slower pace, for a fuzzing dusk had filled the low spots.

After a steady two miles, Jim's quickening impatience pushed him into picking up the gait again. The road was still badly rutted, but it held to fairly even flats now, and the turnoff to the county road wasn't far ahead.

Early dark had mantled the landscape by now, but ahead of him the telephone poles stood in high relief against a cobalt sky, marking the road to Friendship. For once, Jim saw them with pleasure. He urged Blue forward at a trot now, but he had forgotten the last potholed stretch just before the turnoff; it was invisible in the darkness.

Suddenly one of Blue's forehoofs plunged into a hole, slewing her off balance. Only Jim's catlike reflexes enabled him to kick free of the stirrups and spring sideways as the mare's forequarters collapsed. He landed precariously on his feet, stumbling wildly. His effort to stay upright was successful, and then he turned swiftly to Blue, seizing hold of her headstall as she staggered up.

She was limping. It was obvious before she took two steps.

"Daddy," Joe-Jim said in a pained, husky whisper that wrenched at him.

"It's all right, Joey. You stay quiet."

Silently cursing his luck, Jim laid his son on the ground and hunkered down to inspect the mare's right front leg. The sensitive tips of his long fingers told him the trouble at once: a pulled tendon. Blue would not be carrying him anywhere for a good time to come.

Jim lost no time deciding what to do. Blue was the only saddle mount he owned. He could return to his place and hitch up the team and wagon, but it would sacrifice precious time. With the town road just ahead, he might as well proceed on foot, carrying Joe-Jim. Also, with any luck he might flag down a passing motorist, though it seemed a dim hope. This lonely road wasn't heavily traveled even by day.

He took the time to tie Blue in a pocket of brush; he threw off the saddle and slipped her bit. Jim had a strong feeling for horses — another of his un-Apache traits — and he disliked leaving the mare this way, but there was no choice. He'd pick her up on his way back, probably in the early morning.

Jim set out on the dark road whose dusty ribbon was etched by a faint starshine. He tramped steadily toward town, now and then shifting into the effortless jog trot by which Apache runners used to cover well over fifty miles in a day.

But those old-time boys hadn't been handicapped by the fifty-pound burden of an ailing child; they had packed only a horsegut water bottle and light weapons. Jim Izancho was a powerful man, and even at thirty, his athletic years well behind him, he was in superb trim. But his training days had taught him better than to crowd his body beyond a reasonable limit; it only wore a man down the faster.

So he continued to jog and walk, jog and walk, at the same mile-eating pace, and felt no strain at all. Yet he chafed silently against the minutes and miles that seemed to run on forever.

Then a fresh panic seized him as he felt the stiff, wrenching contractions of muscle start up in his son's body. Combing his memory frantically, Jim remembered from his reading that motion or noise could trigger off that kind of reaction in a tetanus sufferer. That it was, in fact, the next agonizing stage of the infection. Yet Jim had no choice but to keep going. The boy could no longer stifle his anguished groans, and Jim set his teeth and steeled his mind against the sounds.

God, if he could only go faster!

Civilization hadn't dulled the keenness of Jim Izancho's perceptions. His all-sense alertness had been ingrained by a kind of boyhood education that his brief sojourns at a government school hadn't provided; the desert wilds had been his real schoolyard. Even in his driving anxiety, his eyes and ears and tactile sensibilities never ceased to probe the restless night, with all its sounds and smells and odd touchings of sensations.

He'd been on the county road for maybe twenty minutes when he picked up the rattle of a motor along the road behind. The car was still far away, yet he identified it almost at once from the engine's sound. A Ford Model T — a battered old clunker of a one, he guessed.

What was the difference, he thought blackly: he'd get no ride off any white-eyes.

But the fine edge of a rising desperation had already crowded Jim to decision. He continued walking. When the clatter of the Tin Lizzie was loud at his back, he halted in the middle of the road and turned, waiting stolidly with his feet braced apart. He stared into the bobbing glare of the car's acetylene-gas headlamps and waited for it to slow. Which it finally did, its high, buggylike shape bouncing to a stop just twenty feet short of him.

He heard a hand brake ratchet up, throwing the Ford's engine into neutral, and then a man's tight, hard voice: "Who'n hell are you? What you want?"

Jim tramped around to the driver's side and said flatly: "A ride to town, if you're going that far. My boy is sick. He's damn sick. Lockjaw it looks like, and he needs a doctor fast as I can get him to one."

The man's sullen, country face was squinched up suspiciously as he tried to make Jim out better, and now he said abruptly: "By God, it's an Indin!"

"What?" The woman beside him leaned over to peer past him. "Oh, God," she shrilled softly. " 'Tis an Injun sure enough. Jase, now you drive on straightaway. For God's sake, drive on!"

"Mister," Jim said quietly. "Listen, will you please? I'm not asking for —"

The man's right hand came quickly up; cold light glimmered along the barrel of a heavy Colt. "All right, Indin, you scaring my wife," he said softly. "Just you back off then, hear?"

Jim stood motionless.

The man thumbed back the hammer. "Goddammit, I'll blow your ugly head clear off!"

Jim took a step back, then another. The brake rasped off; the car lurched forward.

He stood for a long moment, watching it retreat down the road in a silvery moil of dust. He had not sweated from exertion, but now he felt sweat oozing from every pore. Slowly his lips peeled back off his teeth.

He started walking again.

★ ★ ★

Night deputy O. D. Bangs gave a grunt of relief as he signed his name, completing the odious chore of filling out a report on a couple drunk arrests he'd made earlier tonight. He hated any and all paperwork. Besides giving him a mild headache, it didn't square with his romantic conception of his own job. Nevertheless it was a part of that job, and O.D. performed it with the same painstaking care that he did any side of his work.

After impaling the report on the paper spindle, he straightened a kink out of his shoulders and leaned back in the swivel chair, yawning and stretching his arms. He glanced at the big clock on the wall of the sheriff's office. Midnight on the dot. Six hours to go before his shift was up. This nightwatch was a first-rate pain in the ass, and O.D. was profoundly glad that the county board had voted to pay Tenney wages for another deputy, who would take over the night shift starting next month.

It would release O.D. for daywork. Which was when things generally got popping, by Christ. When they happened at all.

Yawning again, O.D. opened the left bottom drawer of the big desk and thumbed through a stack of pulp magazines he kept there. He pulled out the latest issue of *All-Story Cavalier Weekly*, which was running a new Zane Grey serial. O.D. had read the first installment only four times. He had to read any Western story at least six times before it commenced to pall on him.

O.D. was thoroughly lost in the exploits of *The Lone Star Ranger* when a mild noise made him glance up in surprise. A man was standing in the open doorway; he had softly cleared his throat.

O.D. was promptly rankled by three things: First, the man had moved so silently that O.D. hadn't heard him. Second, he had caught O.D. entirely off guard. Third, the son of a bitch was a goddam Indin. The same one O.D. had seen in this office last Saturday, and he was carrying a bundle of some kind, a quilt wrapped around something else.

Leaning back in his chair, O.D. cocked his right boot on the desk and said nothing at all, arrogantly eying the redskin over, head to foot. Jesus, the son of a bitch was as big as he was ugly. After a quarter minute of silence, O.D. barked, "Aw right, buck, what is it? Say your piece and clear out."

"I want to see Frank Tenney. Is he around?"

"Goddlemighty," O.D. said disgustedly.

"You know what time it is?"

"I don't have a watch."

Son of a bitch was deadpan as hell. Like all of 'em O.D. had ever seen. God, it made you wonder if they had any brains behind their faces. "Jesus —" He snickered and shook his head. "There's a clock on the wall, chief. See it? It says past twelve o'clock. That's midnight, okay? Hell no, he ain't around, he's at home. You think he stays up twenty-four hours waiting for Indin callers?"

"Can you tell me where he lives?"

"Sure I can, but I dunno's he'd thank me for telling you. You go rousting him out o' bed and I'm like to catch hell."

"That won't happen," the Indian said tonelessly. "Frank Tenney and I are friends."

A sudden moan came from the bundle he held. It startled hell out of O.D.

"What's that?"

"My little boy. He's very sick."

"Yeah?" O.D. began to grin. "Well, Tenney may be a friend o' yours, but he ain't no medicine man. Hey, I tell you what. I'll get a rattle and a bunch o' feathers and meet you outside o' town. We do big dance to spirits, gettum little chief all well. How's 'at sound?"

The Indian didn't twitch an eyelash. Yet something changed in his face, and O.D. didn't like the look of it. He chuckled to cover a sudden uneasiness and — not being sure just how chummy Tenney and this siwash were — made his voice as amiable as he could.

"Ain't got much sense o' humor, have you, chief? Well, heh heh, that's fair enough, Indins ain't s'posed to have. Live and let live, I say. To each his own. You go down to Plum Street, that's two blocks south, and turn right. Third house on your left, big white wickiup with a willer tree in front, that's Frank's place —"

O.D. blinked. The Indian had gone out the doorway as noiselessly as he'd appeared. With a faint grunt of annoyance, O.D. picked up his magazine. But it failed to engross him as before. Presently he returned it to the drawer, settled back in his chair, and laced his hands behind his head, his eyes speculative.

Most folks around Friendship would have laughed if you'd told them O. D. Bangs was a young man with ambitions. O.D. was only languidly aware of that general opinion. The fact was that he'd give his eyeteeth to step into Frank Tenney's boots. Sheriff Oliver Dempster Bangs, of Buck County. Damn, if

that didn't have a nice jingle to it! But, for
O.D., it had always had a hopeless sound,
too. Tenney liked his work and people liked
Tenney. He could continue in the office till
kingdom come, it had seemed.

Only, maybe not, thought O.D. Not if old
Frank kept up this newfound habit of chum-
ming with redskins. It wasn't one calculated
to win him any applause at the polls, that
was sure. And county elections were coming
up this fall. Just about anything might
happen between now and then. Like, say,
folks getting a whole new slant on Tenney
and on O.D. himself.

O.D. began to chuckle dreamily in his
throat. And went right on chuckling for
some time.

Slacked in his easy chair, Frank Tenney
scowled at his newspaper. He had read the
front-page headline and the article beneath
it three times over, and still it eluded his full
concentration.

Ordinarily his attention would have been
grabbed and held by a news item about a
Congressional leader's warning that Presi-
dent Wilson's action in sending a U.S. naval
force to Veracruz was pulling the nation to
the brink of a war with Mexico. Because
Friendship was situated as close as it was to

the border, this could be a matter for sharp concern. Yet Tenney couldn't dredge up enough interest to make the information more than half register.

He dropped the newspaper on his knee, scraped a palm across his jaw, and stifled a yawn as he glanced at his wife. Bettina was seated on the sofa, knitting squares for an afghan. Her lips were pursed tightly, her movements jerky and bored and irritable.

"Betts, you shouldn't knit in that light. Want me to move the lamp closer?"

She didn't look up from her work. "There's quite enough light, thank you."

That does it, Tenney told himself grimly. Now you can stay shut up and not feel bad.

Amazing what a breach even a small difference of opinion could open between two people with strong feelings for one another. And this wasn't a small one. It simply hadn't been forced into the open before.

The quarrel went deeper than his espousal of Jim Izancho's cause against her father's. He'd explained his old friendship with Jim, but the telling had failed to engage Bettina's sympathy. What she regarded as his misdirected loyalty didn't rankle her half as much as what she termed his "lack of ambition." His clash with her father on the phone had cleanly severed any hope of a glowing political future — that was how Bettina had seen it. And she was likely right. But her irritation had pushed him into flatly declaring that no political future could ever weigh all that importantly in his scheme of things. Then the quarrel had turned heated, finally breaking off in a chill silence that had held between them since supper.

Tenney, usually slow to wrath, felt a growing restless anger that nearly matched Bettina's.

He was partly to blame, he knew, for his failure to declare to her a good while ago that as yet he wasn't truly sure what he wanted. Bettina had her reason for feeling misled. All the same, he'd been a good husband and a fair provider — and would do his damnedest to be a good father. Shouldn't there be a reasonable limit on what a woman might rightfully expect of her man? . . .

There was a muffled knock at the outside door of their enclosed veranda.

Bettina said, "I'll get it," and rose quickly as if the mere act of answering the door were a release from tension.

Tenney looked back at his newspaper. Bettina opened the front door and went out to the porch. He heard the veranda door creak open and then the sharply imperative lift of her voice: "Frank . . . Frank!"

Ten minutes later, Jim Izancho's little son had been installed in the Tenneys' spare bedroom. Bettina was busy seeing to the boy's care, while Jim sat on the horsehair sofa in the parlor, his big frame hunched forward, elbows on knees, as he quietly talked and Tenney listened.

After finally arriving in town with Joe-Jim, he had gone directly to young Dr. Courtland's house, where the doctor had his office. But the house had been locked and dark, and no amount of pounding at the door had brought any response. Next Jim had tried the home of Dr. Eustace Beatty, the town's only other physician, only to be told by Beatty's wife or housekeeper — whoever the woman was who had answered the door — that the doctor was out for the evening. Without saying any more, she had slammed the door in his face.

"So then I went to your office and found out from that Montgomery Ward deputy of yours where you lived." Jim smiled tiredly, shaking his head. "I hate like hell to keep fetching you my troubles, Frank."

"What friends are for. Not to mention sheriffs." Tenney tugged his lower lip, frowning. "Jack Courtland left yesterday on a fishing trip, I happen to know, and he won't be back till Friday. But maybe —"

He broke off as Bettina entered the room. Her sleeves were rolled up and her face was grave, but she gave Jim a tiny and impersonal smile.

"I'm no physician, Mr. Izancho, but I did what I could. I know the main thing to do with lockjaw is get the patient's muscles to relax — so I gave your son a sedative I sometimes take for my insomnia. And it seems to be working. I have him all comfy now, so if you want to look in on him again. . . ."

Jim got up, his face working faintly. "Thank you, Mrs. Tenney. You've been very kind."

Silent as a shadow, he left the parlor. Bettina began rolling down her sleeves. Tenney rose and went over to her, laying a hand on her arm.

"Betts. Thanks."

She showed him the fraction of a prim smile. "What did you think? That I'd turn away a sick child?"

"No," he said gently. "I never thought that."

Bettina's face softened; she came up on tiptoe and brushed her lips to his.

Tenney smiled. "How do you think the boy will be?"

"It's way too soon to tell. The relaxant is

doing its job for now. I guess we keep our fingers crossed."

He rubbed his jaw, scowling at the pattern of the carpet. "It's a damn disgrace when a man can't get a doctor for his kid because they're Indians."

"Frank, I wouldn't argue that. But what can you do?"

"Try to raise Beatty myself. Likely he's at hizzoner the mayor's house with the usual Wednesday-night poker cronies. Generally their games go on half the night."

"Lovable Doc Beatty," Bettina said with a wry smile. "Let's see, it's about one o'clock. How many sheets to the wind would you guess he is by now?"

"Maybe I'll get lucky."

Tenney walked into the hallway where the telephone was, lifted the receiver, and spun the crank to get Central. When a woman's slightly bored voice answered, he said, "Midge, this is Frank Tenney. Get me Mayor Wills' home, please."

The mayor himself answered the phone, his voice mildly slurred. Sure, he could put Doc on, no problem getting him away from the game; he'd been losing all night. Tenney braced himself for the worst, and his heart sank when Beatty's voice came over the wire.

"Tell me one thing, Doc," he said coldly. "Just how high are you riding?"

"Don't take that impudent tone with me, young fellow." Dr. Beatty rumbled with drunken dignity. "What is it you want?"

"There's a sick boy at my place. He's down with lockjaw. Can you come right away?"

"Didn't know you —" Dr. Beatty hiccoughed gravely. "Didn't know you had a boy, Sheriff."

"He's the son of a friend."

A long pause.

"Doc?"

"Eh . . . yes, I hear you. My wife called a while ago and said a siwash Injun with a sick kid was looking for me. To forewarn me, you know. It wouldn't be that kid?"

"Suppose it is?"

"I don't treat siwash Injuns. Not even friends of sheriffs. Just a policy of practice."

"Doc —"

The doctor hung up.

Tenney stared at the receiver in his hand, then slowly replaced it on the hook. A faint sound at his back brought him around. Jim Izancho was standing there. Light from the parlor only dimly penetrated the hall; Jim's face was in shadow. He said nothing at all, but Tenney knew he'd heard enough to understand.

CHAPTER SEVEN

It was dark under the pines, where the light of a crescent moon hardly reached. Coming down the steep and rugged slope on foot, the three men groped and stumbled and cursed. Even by daylight and if they'd been sober, and if each of them hadn't been lugging a five-gallon tin of kerosene, it would have been a tough descent to manage.

Roger, leading the way, had drunk enough to make him start feeling a little queasy now. But he would have cut his tongue out before admitting it. He could hear Trooper Yount's stiff tread and labored grunts just behind him, and the softer sounds made by Billy de Groot bringing up the rear. Both were having a hard time of it — Trooper with his one arm, Billy with a broken arm.

By the time they reached the base of the slope, Roger was gulping heavily and covered with sweat in spite of the night's coolness. But it was easier going now, the pines thinning away to show the open flat beyond and the blocky shapes of the cabin and outsheds. Roger halted and set down his tin of kerosene, then sank onto his haunches. Trooper and Billy glided up on either side of him and hunkered down too. Digging a flask out of his coat pocket, Roger took a big pull at it and shut his eyes for a moment.

It seemed to pacify his stomach. Able to trust his voice now, he murmured, "Well, they're all abed. Not a light showing. Hope you birds are still game."

Billy gave a nervous giggle. Trooper merely grunted.

"Right." Roger passed the flask to them and waited till it came back to him. He took another large swig and said, "Got it all straight? I take the house. Billy, you light up the barn. Trooper, all the smaller outbuildings. We have to work fast, and for Christ's sake don't make a lot of noise. Then we get our asses back here and watch the fun."

They split apart now, and Roger watched his companions fade away into the tree shadows to his right, carrying their kerosene tins, both of them a little unsteady but moving surely enough. Now Roger left the trees and skirted deep to his left, coming around back of the cabin. He moved with exaggerated care, aware of how drunk he was. Yet his brain and actions were knit by a thread of purpose. . . .

Not that there was anything very complicated to it. All they had to do was burn the son of a bitch out. And nobody else, whatever he might suspect, would know anything for sure. Nobody except Tony Soto.

Today, Roger and Billy and Tony had been behind the stable passing a bottle back and forth when the notion had come up. It would be so damned *easy*. The siwash didn't even own a dog. They could sneak in and do the job and clear out and who could prove a thing? Soto had chuckled over the idea as much as the others. Maybe it had even been Soto who'd brought it up, during the run of booze-fired talk; Roger couldn't remember any more. But abruptly, when he'd realized Roger was dead serious, Soto had backed off fast, saying, "Listen, man, I don' do nothing like that. Sure, I lie about what happen when the car is busted up. Tha's so your pa don' fire me. But now I keep the nose clean so I keep the job. *Sabe?*" And Soto had walked away.

That was okay, so long as he kept his mouth shut. Roger hadn't the least worry that Soto might say anything to anybody: on the contrary, he'd lie his head off to shun any implication that might connect him with his business. Let Soto get goosy about anything, that's how he always reacted.

Roger hadn't been daunted. He and Billy had let it be known they were riding to town for a nightlong drunk, and had saddled up and set out on the town road. However, they hadn't gone far when they'd turned north, toward Big W's top range and the Lost Valley line shack that Trooper Yount held down alone. And had packed along plenty of bottled goods in their saddlebags. Given Trooper's usual thirst and his hatred of Injuns, Roger hadn't reckoned he'd be hard to persuade. And he'd been right.

It had been late afternoon when they had reached the line shack and a little after dark when, laden with three tins of coal oil taken from Trooper's supply lean-to, the three of them had set out across country for the Izancho place. It was a long ride over rugged terrain, with only a sliver of moon and Trooper's knowledge of the country to show the way. Anyway, they hadn't been in any hurry, wanting to be sure all those red nits were in their blankets and sawing wood by the time they got there. So the three had passed the bottles back and forth, keeping their zeal steadily fired but not getting so drunk they couldn't maneuver.

All in all, though, it was Roger's will that

had regulated the other two. Purpose burned like a sullen coal behind his liquored senses. Even whiskey hadn't dulled the steady pain of his nose. That Indian had mashed it as you'd squash a bug under hand. And he'd done it so damn easily!

Roger touched the bandage that covered the broken member; he winced and swore. It was going to hurt like hell for a long time.

Purposeful as Roger's rage was, there was nothing particularly calculating in it. He was sore as hell and he wanted to hit back, that was all. Maybe Izancho being a son-of-a-bitching siwash full of educated airs who was trying to play white man made it a little easier to contemplate burning him out. Hell, any white man worth his salt would get pissed at something like that.

He moved carefully and silently through the deep shadows back of the cabin, then stopped to listen. The cabin was quiet in the night. It should be a snap, but you couldn't be too careful, dealing with a passel of these red nits. There were, anyway, four of 'em in the cabin, even if only one of 'em was really dangerous.

Roger sidled to the cabin wall and re-moved the cap of the coal-oil tin. He moved slowly along the wall, holding the can tilted so its contents gurgled softly over the logs.

After soaking the back wall, he worked along each side wall halfway to the front, spilling the kerosene with a patient care till the tin was empty.

He struck a match on his thumbnail and cupped its flare between his palms, then touched it to the notched end of a log. The damn stuff took like tinder, fire sweeping along the rear wall so swiftly it half alarmed him. Roger retreated at a stumbling run, the empty tin swinging from his hand.

Heart pounding heavily, he regained the trees and crouched close to the ground, watching gouts of fire leap from the barn and other buildings. Good timing! The whole goddam place was turning to a torch at one time. He heard a pounding of feet now, and a moment later Billy and then Trooper dropped down beside him.

"Look at it," Trooper said huskily. "Jesus, look at 'er go, will you! Green wood and all, I didn't reckon she'd burn thataway, but goddammit she's a hummer!"

"Been a dry year," Roger muttered. "That pine pitch damn near explodes when it gets going."

"Rodge," Billy said in an awed voice, "you reckon they will get out all right?"

Roger chuckled, unscrewing the top of his flask. "They will, when it gets hot enough in there. That's why I left the front way open for 'em. The door's clear right enough. Don't worry."

He took a deep jolt of the fiery liquor and gave a momentary thought to how the Senator would take this incident. But he already knew. The old man would be pleased. He'd suspicion what had happened, but he wouldn't ask a lot of questions, not when it was more convenient not to.

Roger took another pull and swiped a sleeve across his mouth, passing the flask to Trooper. God, the flames were spreading like fury, already enveloping the roof, and still there was no response from inside the cabin. A first twitch of nervousness jerked at his mouth. Hell! Were those Injuns dead to the world? Goddam house was burning up right over their heads and still they. . . .

Abruptly the cabin door was flung open. Two figures stumbled out. The tawny flow of light showed them to be the woman and the old man. She had both arms around him, desperately holding him upright as she braced herself against his stumbling weight. The woman didn't stop when they were safely past the fire's scorching aura. Half dragging the old man, she staggered on across the clearing and into the trees beyond the firelight.

Roger waited tensely for the big Injun himself to come out, but there was no sign of him or his kid. Flames were showing inside the house now — and even if he'd delayed to gather up some belongings, he wouldn't remain inside this long.

Trooper said softly, "Somep'n's way wrong here."

"Obviously," Roger snarled.

His fingers beat a nervous tattoo on his knee. Where the hell was that Injun and the kid? For that matter, where were the woman and the old man? The pine shadows had swallowed them and the woman hadn't reappeared, as one would expect, to attempt the rescue of prized things from the flames.

Because she knew the men who'd set the fire might still be about and she wouldn't risk running into them? Sure, that was it. She'd stay where she was, back in the trees, her and the old man. But where, goddammit, was that big Injun and his kid?

There was a sudden commotion among the trees on the tall slope at their backs. A pounding of hoofs, then the feral whickering of a horse. The sounds came from where they'd left their mounts tied a little way upslope. And that had been Satana's fierce whinny, Roger knew. Something had upset the mare for sure . . . maybe a lion.

The thought hadn't spent its shock along his nerves before Roger leaped to his feet. "Come on!" he yelled at his companions. They turned for the slope and started up it at a driving run, weaving between the pine boles in a scrambling haste.

The exertion rapidly sobered the three men; they were prepared for almost anything as they came piling into the clearing where they'd left the horses. In the dim moonlight it took several moments to piece out the scene before them.

A woman's still form lay on the ground, twisted at an awkward angle. Satana stood a few feet away, side-shuffling wildly as she yanked her head against the halter that tethered her to a tree trunk. She quieted as Roger approached. With shaking fingers he lighted a match and bent over, holding its flare close to the Indian woman's face.

A wide, deep gash lay bright crimson across her forehead and scalp, yet there was practically no bleeding. Roger groped frantically for her wrist and could locate no pulse. Then he tore open her blouse and felt for a heartbeat.

Nothing.

"Godalmighty," he whispered.

Trooper said roughly, "Lemme see," and stooped beside the body. After a moment he grunted, "That's one dead squaw. Stone dead, for sure."

Roger felt his head spin dizzily; a dry scum filled his mouth. He had to swallow hard to keep from being sick.

Trooper rocked back on his haunches, saying musingly, "What I reckon happened, she come up straightaway through the trees here and come purely by chance on our hosses. Could be she tried to get on one, so's she could go fetch some help. Or mebbe she just figured to untie 'em and drive 'em off. Set us afoot. Either way, she picked herself a dandy. Way I figure it, that Injun smell must o' got this mean cayuse o' yourn riled. She just naturally reared back and stomped 'er."

He straightened to his feet, stretching his arm. "Well, there's one red louse ain't gonna hatch no more nits."

Billy said in a thin, high voice, "Where's that old boy? What happened to him?"

"He gotta be close around," Trooper observed. "It don't figure she would just leave 'im."

Roger remained as he was, numbly crouched on his heels, staring at the dead woman. He was dully aware of Trooper tramping around the clearing's edge, poking into the shadows. And presently Trooper gave a flat grunt and said, "Over here."

Woodenly, Roger got to his feet and, Billy trailing after him, walked over to where Trooper stood. Dimly seen, the old Indian sat on his hunkers just inside the trees. The three men stood looking down at him and he looked back at them, his face a seamed, unchanging mask.

Trooper broke the silence. "Well, who's gonna do the honors on ole Gran'paw here? You wanta or should I?"

"What?" Roger said shrilly. "What do you mean?"

Trooper let the rifle in his hand slide down till its butt rested on the earth. He eyed Roger with a kind of sleepy-eyed amusement. "Now, what you reckon I do, boy? I mean, we have dusted ourselves a redskin and old Gran'paw here has seen our faces."

"Christ, Trooper! It was an accident —"

"Sure 'nough it was." Trooper's voice held a grin. "But it's what *we* done got this here squaw killed. Now, you looky here, Roger. I don't know how much savvy ole Gran'paw's got left in his bean, but could be he got enough to say what happened to-night. Might even be he can tell one white man's face from another. Like yours and young Billy's and old Trooper's, say. Now, you got any smarts atall, you can see we just gotta dust ourselves another 'un and then cover up how it all happened."

"God!" Revulsion crawled in Roger's mouth; he tried to spit it out with the words. "How can we do that?"

"Easy as falling off a log. We just take both the bodies down and dump 'em in that shack you set afire. Won't be enough left for anyone to tell the real what-for o' things."

"I mean, *how can we kill this old man?*"

"Oh, that. Why, shit, son, that's easier yet. Ain't no fuss to killing an Injun or a nigger. Any man's been there'll tell you. Me, I was at Wounded Knee, but that wa'n't nothing. Why, goddam, in the Philippines what we useta do, we would round up a passel of them Moros 'n' make 'em dig a big pit and put all the sons a bitches in it and then just plug away. Boy, I been there and you can believe what I say. Killing an Injun or a nigger feels like when you stomp a snake. What it is mostly, it's a pure relief."

Roger's mouth half opened, but no words came out.

"Looky here, boy," Trooper's voice hardened now. "We come here to lay a few fires. Burn out that goddam 'Pache and put the fear o' God in him. That's one thing. Killing's another, way the law looks at it. Ain't but one way to cover our tracks. I told you

147

what that be. Now, you figure on what happens iffen we don't.''

Roger's brain was in a sick whirl. He knew the gnawing fright of a trapped animal. But every weighing of one element against another tipped back to the cold truth of Trooper's words.

"A course," Trooper said meditatively, "anybody can tell the house didn't get fired accidental. Not with all them outsheds gone up too. But ain't no help for that now."

Roger managed to say thinly, "What about Izancho and that kid of his? What about them?"

Trooper shrugged. "Well, what about 'em? They ain't here, that's all we know. All that matters, too. This ole boy's the only witness." He clamped his rifle under his arm stump, laying his hand on the metal-shod butt stock. "Tell you what, now. I can do the job and I can do 'er nice and quiet." He grinned. "You boys just turn your backs and swallow spit."

For a moment, Roger only stared at him. Then he turned blindly and walked a few yards away. Billy held close beside him, trembling, his eyes wide and watery. From behind them came the flat smashing impact of a blow. Then another. And Trooper's soft grunt of satisfaction.

Roger scarcely heard the last sound. A rush of hot fluids boiled up from his stomach and he fell to his knees, retching.

CHAPTER EIGHT

Jim Izancho spent the night on a cot in the room where the Tenneys had installed Joe-Jim. He slept the sound sleep of a healthy and tired man till the first peach-colored streak of sunrise touched through a window against his eyelids. Then he came awake as a dog wakes, all his senses ready. He rose at once, his big frame uncramped by his exertions of the night before, and looked long at his sleeping son. He touched the boy's forehead and found no heat, and then remembered that fever wasn't a characteristic of lockjaw.

Momentarily Jim debated. Joe-Jim seemed to be resting comfortably. Meantime, Sally would be worried sick, and the sooner he got home and partly relieved her concern, the better. He would bring Cow Bird and her back to Friendship and set up a camp just outside of town, so they could remain near Joe-Jim till he was well.

There was no sound in the house. Frank

and his wife weren't up yet, and Jim was impatient to be on his way. Quietly he went out to the kitchen and after a minute's search turned up a pad and pencil. He jotted a note of explanation and thanks to the Tenneys and left it in plain sight on the table, then made a silent departure by the back door. At the livery stable he roused the dozing night hostler and rented a horse. . . .

The heat of a new day lay on the morning land like a dry quilt by the time Jim swung off the highway onto the bumpy trace that led to his place. He paused long enough to pick up Blue from the brush pocket where he had left her tethered. Considerate of her limp, he went on slowly.

A pungent sharpness touched his nostrils. Just the faintest whiff of a smoky something, and it didn't come from someone's breakfast fire. The odor was heavy and rank with char, as of wood burned in quantity and still faintly aflame. Distinctive and recognizable . . . but puzzling as hell. No hint of smoke on the sky, which ruled out a forest or brush fire.

Still idly puzzling, Jim rode on. He crossed the pine-covered crest where the switchbacks ran down to his layout. And then he stopped. Dead still.

Only a few wisps of smoke still peeled off

the cabin's smoldering remains. Jim's consciousness encompassed the sight and the fact in one instant. And left him too stunned even for a start of surprise. The scene simply shocked his brain and body into utter immobility.

Then he pushed the livery nag down the hill at a run. The horse was still running when Jim dropped off it, hitting a full-stride run of his own as he touched the ground. He came to a halt in the yard just short of the blackened jackstraw tumble of the house logs.

And let out a great shout from the pit of his fear: *"Sally!"*

Silence answered him. He called out again and again, turning to face in all directions. Shouted till his voice hoarsely broke.

For the second time in less than twelve hours, Jim Izancho felt the grip of a clammy terror. For the first time, he lost control of himself.

Laying hold of a charred timber, he wrenched at it with all his giant strength, hauling it free of the rubble. In a frenzy of effort he dragged free one burned fragment after another, heaving them aside as he burrowed blindly into the hot ashes.

He didn't notice when his clothes began to smoke. Not till his left sleeve suddenly burst into flame did Jim come to a murky realization that the heat was past bearing. He staggered backward out of the cloud of soot his exertions had stirred up, coughing and retching. Fell to his hands and knees, half overcome by ash and smoke. Instinctively he batted at his sleeve, beating out the flames. Great blistered weals had formed on his hands and arms and legs. The searing agony of it shocked him back to a half sanity.

Jim raised his head, wagging it slowly from side to side. His eyes swam with a haze of pain and streaming tears. Somehow through their watering, and following a thread of returning reason, he managed to make out the heaps of char that marked the sites of the other buildings.

God oh God.

No accident . . . the whole place was fired deliberately.

Sally . . . Grandpa!

Did they get caught in it or not?

The volley of odd and inchoate thoughts beat against Jim's brain as he climbed to his feet, his muscles numb against the agonized stretch of scorched flesh. Yet the core of his nervous system was insulated by shock from any real consciousness of pain. His body functioned in the way expected of it; that was all.

And gradually as he forced his legs to move, his mind began to budge too. Sluggishly at first and then wildly as the questions welled up and funneled into a hard focus.

What had happened? He could be sure of nothing save that fires had been started. Jim's thoughts touched briefly, impatiently on the possibilities, then thrust them away. No answers — yet. Nor reason for them unless they held a hint of Sally's fate . . . and Grandpa's.

That came first.

Their bodies were part of the burned rubble or they weren't. No way of making sure till the intense heat had abated.

If they'd escaped from the blaze, where were they? The fires must have been set hours ago, in fact not long after his departure. If the two of them were okay, surely they would remain close by. The old man was too feeble to walk far and Sally wouldn't have left him.

Suppose they went horseback? They could have taken the team horses. Jim had blinked his eyes fairly clear, and now he stumbled toward the pole corral, under the trees a little way off. Before he reached it, he saw that the animals were still inside it, and he came to a befuddled stop.

Yet his thoughts were sharpening by the moment, growing cold and keen, and then one answer dawned on him. Christ! As a boy, he had become a tracker next to none other in the Fort Apache band. He had honed to a fine edge the kind of skills and instincts that a man never lost.

He might forget them for a while. In the occupations of a different life the edges might rust a little. But they could be honed anew.

Moving with purpose now, Jim went over the bare dirt of the yard again and again, being careful to scuff up no more sign than he'd already disturbed. And bit by bit, giving his pulse an unsettling jolt with each fresh revelation, he began to unriddle the story.

All the sign was there, plain and unmistakable. Three men had been there. One of them was Trooper Yount; Jim recognized his slight limp. Another had worn fancy riding boots like Roger Warrender's. The third man had small feet, as small as Billy de Groot's. What the three of them had done and how they had done it were just as clear. Jim found the three empty coal-oil tins back in the brush.

Most important, Sally and Grandpa had gotten safely out of the burning house. She had supported the old man across the yard to the edge of the timber.

Hope flared in him and so did a wildness of impatience. But it was harder to follow track across the springy needle carpet beneath the trees. Jim climbed the steep pine slope slowly, tracing the signs of Sally's and Cow Bird's ascent. And with a rising anxiety, the tracks of the three pursuing men. For Sally and Grandpa had left signs only of their ascent. The men had gone up and come down. On the descent they had been carrying a heavy object or objects. . . .

At the summit of the hill he read the last vestiges of the story. And in them he found what, by this time, he had almost known he would find.

By early afternoon the ashes of the house had cooled enough for Jim Izancho to exhume from them the remains of his dead.

He buried them in the white man's way. It had been so many years since he had believed in anything at all that it didn't seem to matter. He felt no urge toward ceremony, red or white. But after laying his wife and grandfather to their last rest under a pine-sheltered knoll, he felt the first vague stirrings of sensation behind his numbness of grief. And oddly those stirrings whispered of the old ways, the rituals of tradition, the need for reverence that was due the dead.

He got a handful of ashes from the house site and mixed it with a handful of dirt. Beginning at the southwest corner of each grave, he sprinkled the dirt and ashes in a circle around it. As he did so, he muttered prayers to the gods who held up the four corners of the earth, petitioning them to ease the path taken by the souls of his beloved and his grandsire into *o'zho*, heaven.

And through a long day he chanted the death lament, submerging his own being and all of tearing grief in the narcosis of its rhythms, dulling and salving them. For as the Old Ones in their wisdom had known, in any other direction lay madness.

The shadows grew long and went unnoticed by Jim Izancho; he barely heeded the hazing of twilight into darkness. His mind was adrift in a confusion of memories and emotions of which he tried not to make sense. He could lightly bear the pain of flesh; anguish of soul was another thing. And in the ether of ritual lament there was no room or desire for reflection. He felt the slow wearying of his body, the weakening of his voice in chant, and yet he cudgeled himself onward.

Jim never knew when, utterly spent, he slept at last. When sleep did come on him, long after midnight, it was the deep and exhausted slumber of a man drugged past dreaming. He lay all night on the grave of his wife, his fingers dug into the mound of earth.

Morning came and wakefulness, and with it a razor freshness of grief. But lamenting would help no longer; he had done his lamenting. The need to do and move was on him now, and if the inner hurt was still too great, there were other ways of dealing with it. The agony of his burns was not severe enough. He cut switches of mesquite and lashed his blistered flesh with them till it bled.

That did the work. Narcotized pain with a pain that was almost equal but excruciatingly different. Now he could goad his punished body to do what must be done and not be turned aside by any softness of spirit.

Jim had the clothes on his back and a few pocket items, of which the only useful one was a large jackknife. There were other things he would need. Not many, but a few. He would get them as they were required. His first fact was to turn loose the four horses, the team animals and old Blue and the livery horse. For his purposes now, a horse would only prove an encumbrance. These tame nags would find their way to one habitation or another. Nothing else of value remained to him here; the few personal items he might have valued had been burned up.

Fleetingly he thought of Joe-Jim. He had to quietly harden himself against the tenderness such thoughts aroused. Later he could safely think of his son. But not now.

And Frank Tenney . . . had he anything to say to Frank? Jim considered the question as impersonally as if Frank were any other sheriff.

No. He didn't feel the least temptation to give up any part of the course of action that was framing in his mind. It was as if the soul of Jim Izancho had been stripped to the gaunt bone. As if all feeling but one had been flailed out of him. And that one nestled like a live coal in his brain, hot and consuming.

That was all he wanted. That one, wolfish hunger and the cold clarity of sense and thought to feed its urges.

Signs he'd found at the top of the hill had been confused enough that he couldn't be sure how Sally had died. But in spite of the condition of the bodies, the way of his grandfather's dying had been sickeningly plain. His skull had not been crushed by a fall or other accidental means. No mistaking the evidence that death had been dealt by at least two blows, separate and deliberate.

On the exact nature of Sally's death Jim could only speculate. While his frenzied thoughts were chilling back toward patterns of reason and letting him speculate more coldly on the matter, the more terrible those speculations became. At last, with an iron effort, he shut them off. But a horrendous conviction was seeded by now, reinforcing his grim intent. . . .

He was almost equally sure about the men's identities, but on this point Jim was taking no chances. After departing his place, he took up the trail of the three men. Through a long day, he painstakingly tracked them. He found where they had split apart, one going east and the other two southwest. He followed the lone horseman to the Big W line shack held down by Trooper Yount. Afterward, he tracked the duo of riders deep into Big W range. By then it was growing dark and Jim quit the trail, satisfied. The goal of those two riders was obviously Big W headquarters.

Three men. At least three who were directly responsible. And a great ranch. And a man that men called "Senator."

But all of it could wait. He felt no need for hurry. On the contrary, he felt a kind of deep and ghastly calm. A desire to plan with care, to shape the weapons of death and terror, and to savor their shaping to the full.

The next morning, Jim Izancho came to Squaw Peak. A lofty and isolated promontory, it was as awesomely rugged as it was precipitous. An experienced climber might ascend it. So might a powerful and athletic man with nothing but determination to feed his purpose.

Sometimes Jim had idly thought that Squaw Peak would be ideal for the manhood rite if he ever felt inclined toward the consummation of it. Always, in a corner of his mind, he had felt a strange, abiding lack, like a scar on his manhood, in never having taken the traditional and ultimate step of *Shis-in-day* puberty. Always, too, he had countered that nook of nagging emptiness with the same argument: The whole business was so damned silly — hoary and meaningless nonsense fit for the mentalities of children or savages.

Even now, as he set foot on Squaw Peak's lowest slope, he argued with himself. *Why?* You don't believe in anything. Man is up from dust and he goes back to dust. There's nothing else. You know that. So why this goddam rigamarole?

Maybe there was a psychological nexus to the thing. Yes — that made sense. Like the chanting at graveside, it exorcised the negative. Only, the negative wasn't a passel of diabolical spirits. Just a freight of insupportable garbage that you absorbed lifelong — a sorry hash of upbringing and experience.

But why, then, couldn't a man just say the hell with it? To that he had no answer. Except to plod on and upward.

Jim had eaten practically nothing in two days. He was not aware of hunger but had scoured up a few edible roots and tubers to help keep up his strength. Already lightheaded from the stresses of grief and lack of nourishment, he was in no condition for a grueling climb or the fasting that would follow.

Yet he fiercely welcomed the prospect. No need to think . . . now. Only climb. Go up and up and up. Think of nothing. . . .

The lower, south face of the escarpment wasn't so steep as it was simply treacherous. A slanting mass of rubble, it cascaded away under his driving feet. Jim slogged against it with an insensate doggedness, stumbling and falling. His heavy work shoes made him awkward. But, once he reached the solid rock above, no matter that the going was much steeper, he swung upward with the grace and ease of a mountain ram. He still wished, though, for a pair of the stout, curl-toed Apache moccasins he had worn as a boy.

He paused only once, above the rubble where several stunted and twisted pines grew out of a rocky crevice. One of the trees had been killed by lightning long ago; it was split and blackened from crown to roots. Wood on which lightning had seared its electric dance was as sacred as any object that Usen had placed for men's use. This Jim knew from tellings of the People that were age-old, and for once there was no impulse in him to doubt or to ridicule. From the dead tree he wrenched a flat splinter about three inches long and an inch wide, and shoved it in his pocket. Then he toiled onward. . . .

As he climbed, the cliff grew increasingly perpendicular, the holds for hands and feet harder to locate. In the fierceness of his striving, Jim felt a terrible relish in this rugged ascent where a single misstep or insecure hold would plunge him hundreds of feet to an instant death. In his present state of mind, in fact, he was only a hair's breadth from inviting such an end. Only that spur of cruel purpose kept the thrust toward life burning and tingling through his brain.

The strain ate at Jim's muscles; he was pouring sweat and his whole body was trembling. By now he was working upward by slow inches, sometimes supporting his whole weight by the grip of one hand or the brace of one foot on a shallow protuberance or fissure. His chest and belly were scraped raw by the rasp of rock to which he clung, and his fingers left prints of red on the cliff face. His ears sang with the dense rhythm of his blood. . . .

At last he dragged himself painfully onto a ribbon of ledge. He lay on it face down for a minute, then drew himself to a sitting position. His legs dangled over a sheer drop, and he gazed down it almost indifferently.

Taking out the sliver of pine and his jackknife now, forcing his numb hands into motion, Jim began to whittle at the soft wood. As the shavings dripped away, the splinter quickly assumed the shape of a man, short-legged and with no arms, flat on both sides. On one side he carved two parallel zigzag lines running up and down; on the other side he etched two crosses.

Afterward he pulled out a folded bandanna and carefully opened it, revealing a handful of dried cattail pollen that he'd gathered in the river bottom the day before. Properly gathered by a woman and blessed by an *izze-nantan*, a medicine man, the pollen was supposed to be transubstantiated into a powder of miraculous properties. (Maybe it was no good this way, but in his fog of weariness Jim decided it was the thought that counted.)

He sprinkled some of the *hoddentin* on each side of the wooden figurine — investing the zigzag cuts with the power of lightning, *ittindi*, and the crossed lines with the force of the black wind, *intchi-dijin*.

He threw a pinch of powder before him, another over his left shoulder, and one over his right, and yet another behind him.

"Be good, O winds!" he chanted.

He cast a pinch of *hoddentin* above his head.

"Be good, O *ittindi!*"

Step by step, thus, Jim Izancho called blessings on his *tzi-daltai,* his protective amulet, exhorting the gods of earth and sky to strengthen his medicine and protect him against the weapons of his enemies. The light faded and darkness came. So did the night chill and a searching wind that cut him to the marrow, but he never ceased his prayers.

Sitting on the ledge through the night, he

slipped in and out of a half trance till he no longer knew where he was. The empty gulf beneath and the one above him were as a single black abyss where his spirit wandered and touched the *chedens,* the ghosts of the Old Ones from the sacred corners of the earth. To him they whispered the lore of old and gave him promises of aid:

Brother, long ago we came from a place of cold to this land. We found a people living in cliffs and them we fought and drove toward the ocean. For many years were we masters of this land. Then the pinda likoyee *came and with his numbers broke our power. Yea, the white man is stronger than we till the day of our glory comes again. Brother, we will sing our war songs again. But you will sing them now.*

The touch of the *chedens* was like a benediction, full of a strength that armored his soul. When it returned to his body as a first ray of dawn struck the high place, it was not the hint of coming sun that put a warmth in his flesh. Jim ceased his chant. He opened his eyes, blinking, and then he stood up on the narrow shelf. He gazed contemplatively downward at the descent that would be harder to manage than the upward climb had been.

It would be as nothing. The weakness of body, the cramps of muscle, and the slight dizziness — all were as nothing. The whisperings of the *chedens* still made a prickle of static heat along his veins. Now he was a man. No warrior yet — but a man fit to blood his enemies.

He began the descent.

As he climbed down the last few yards to the base of the promontory, Jim heard a warning burr that pulled him up short.

Almost bemusedly his gaze sought and found the flat rock, ahead of him and a little to his left, where the huge rattlesnake lay coiled. Then he moved off a little way and found a dead mesquite tree, from which — with a couple twists of his strong hands — he broke off a long wand that was forked at one end.

A light, speculative smile touched Jim's lips as he slowly sidled back toward the rattler. In close now, he made a swift feint that provoked the reptile into striking. He drove the crotched end of his stick back of its head, pinning it hard to the ground.

There was an evil *cheden,* a devil, in the rattlesnake. As a boy, he would never have provoked it except in the direst need, as when he had saved young Frank Tenney's life. Now, perhaps, he was less skeptical than he had been a day before. But, buoyed by a strong medicine, he felt unafraid.

Even a devil had its uses.

Jim's smile widened as he watched the reptile's furious writhings. Odd how it was such a universal thing — that fear and revulsion which the snake inspired in humans. Didn't the white-eyes, too, have a devil they sometimes associated with a serpent? . . .

CHAPTER NINE

Trooper Yount was in a foul mood as he returned to his lonely shack from a day of riding line. It had taken him half the day to drag a Big W cow and her calf free of a deep, wide mudhole in the Santa Agrita bottoms. Apparently the calf had gotten bogged down first and the cow in trying to approach it had mired herself as well. Roping them out had been a hard, awkward, dirty job, as it always was, and the sun was low by the time Trooper finished up.

It was close to dusk when he reached the line camp and turned his mount into the corral. His dog, tied to a stake in the yard, slunk out of Trooper's path as he limped toward the house. The animal had gotten more than one kick for failing to move fast enough, and Trooper had never needed even the excuse of a bad mood to fetch him a hard one.

He'd gotten the ginger-colored mongrel

from a Mex farmer when he was a pup. The dog had been evil-tempered from the first, and that was fine with Trooper. He hadn't acquired the cur for company, merely to alert him to any prowler — lion or bear or human. The camp being where it was, way to hell and gone from much of any place, having a good mean dog on hand had seemed a sound idea. . . .

Trooper banged into the house, lifted a half-full bottle of whiskey from a shelf, uncorked it, and took a massive slug. The liquor tendriled powerfully through his belly and brain without improving his mood in the least. He set about fixing supper while he polished off the bottle. When it was empty, he set it aside with a dozen other empties that were stacked in a neat pyramid in one corner. After he had twenty or thirty bottles collected, he'd take them to a nearby canyon and amuse himself using them for target practice.

Like many middle-aged bachelors who were set in their solitary ways, Trooper Yount was careless about his person but compulsively tidy about his quarters and his belongings. He kept the cabin's two rooms scrubbed and swept; he was extremely fussy about having "a place for everything and everything in its place."

Tobacco and whiskey were Trooper's sole indulgences, and he never stinted on them. Before shoveling his steak and fried potatoes from the skillet onto his plate, he broke out a fresh bottle. He'd brewed up a pot of coffee, but ignored it for now, filling his cup to the brim with whiskey. Awkwardly he cut his steak into small pieces, no easy task for a one-armed man. Afterward he carried his food and booze to the table and was sitting down to eat when the dog began an uproarious barking.

Swearing, Trooper got up and went to the door. He opened it and peered out. Dusk had blurred into first darkness and he couldn't make out much of anything. He took his bull's-eye lantern from a peg by the door and lighted it and went outside. The dog's racket subsided to a steady growling.

Trooper prowled around the tack shed, woodshed, stable, and outback, finding nothing amiss. The horses, when he approached the corral, acted a little skittish, but more'n likely that damn dog had set 'em off.

Cursing in a monotonous mutter, he walked back to the house, aiming a kick at the dog in passing. The mutt avoided it with the celerity of long practice. Entering the cabin, Trooper sat down and attacked his meal, wolfing down mouthfuls of beefsteak and spuds with small swigs of whiskey. Taken like this, the booze was quickly absorbed by the grub and didn't hit a man's brain with half the force of straight slugs. Trooper was an old hand at spacing his drinks with meals. Knew how to get him a healthy glow that would last late into the night, yet enable him to greet the next morning in a black mood but not too hung over.

Having finished supper, he carried his dishes to the wreck pan and put on a kettle of water to heat. He was reaching for the bottle to refill his cup when the dog's wild barking started up once more. Trooper slammed open the door and glared at the darkness. He bawled, "Shut up, you sonuvabitch!" And as the dog tapered off to a growl, listened intently for any sound that didn't fit the night's usual pattern.

He heard a soft wind combing the dry grass. That was all.

Hell. There wasn't a goddam thing out there.

"You start up over nothing again," he said in a loudly ominous voice, "and I'm gonna knock the living shit outa you."

The dog fell completely silent.

Trooper closed the door and filled his cup

again. When the water was hot, he poured it into the wreck pan and added a little cold water. He went at his few dishes and utensils with a dishrag and a bar of strong yellow soap, pausing now and then for a sip of whiskey. Afterward he dried the dishes and put them away, wrung out and hung up his dishrag and towel, and carried the pan of dirty water to the door.

He had to set the pan on the floor in order to lift the latch. As he did so, the dog broke out again, now with a frenzied, gnashing fury. "That does it," Trooper muttered. Striding to the woodbox, he caught up a hefty length of stovewood. Then he opened the door and with a savage curse flung the heavy chunk into the darkness toward the barking.

It struck. The dog gave a startled yelp, followed by another burst of raging barks.

And suddenly then, a complete silence.

"All *right*," Trooper growled. He picked up the pan of dish water and flung its contents outside. Then he paused to peer into the night, listening to the low moan of wind. He couldn't make out a single other thing now, sight or sound, and he wondered if he'd seriously injured the mutt. Ah . . . the hell if he had!

He closed the door and dropped the night

bar into place. Belatedly he remembered that he hadn't fed the dog today. Hell — let him go hungry. Serve the sonuvabitch right.

Trooper stamped over to the stove, slung the pan on its wall hook with a clatter, again filled his whiskey cup, and poured coffee into another cup. Slacking back into his chair at the table, both cups in front of him and whiskey bottle at his elbow, he felt his spirits lift almost at once.

This was *his* time of day, by God. When his duty by big-ass Big W was done and he could give himself to a rosy euphoria of idle memories and musings.

It didn't matter that most of his life, since he'd come squalling into the world one winter night in a Georgia sharecropper's shack, had been one sad misery after another. All the memories took on a pearly glow when he was moderately in his cups. He could repetitiously muse on them by the hour and never tire of it. Even his years in the service (which in the field had been largely a history of forced marches and cold camps, blazing heat or icy drizzle, bouts with typhus and dysentery and yellow fever) had a glamorous tinge of their own. . . .

Trooper's revery ended on his first brittle awareness of a *sound* . . . a sound that made his scalp prickle.

At first the noise had probed but vaguely at the edge of his blurred mind. A strange note on the wind, perhaps. Now, abruptly, he realized it wasn't the wind. It seemed to swell and ebb on a minor key like the luting, faltering cry of a hurt animal.

The dog? Goddammit! He must have fetched the beast a really hard one.

Swearing continuously, he rose and moved a little unsteadily to the wall where his lantern hung. He lighted it, then raised the bar and pushed open the door. Now the sound came to him far more clearly. And quite suddenly, for a reason he couldn't explain, he wasn't sure it was the dog at all.

Trooper stood undecided for a moment. Then he moved back from the doorway, set his lantern on the floor, and went to a shelf where a Colt .45 lay wrapped in its shell belt. It was a cursing, awkward chore to get the belt buckled around his middle. But to venture outside he'd have to carry the pistol holstered; he could manage only the lantern one-handed.

Holding the lantern high, he stepped out the door and slowly crossed the yard, straining his eyes into the wavering pool of light. The dog had been staked out near the tack shed. When he was about six yards from it, Trooper saw the animal sprawled on its side in the wind-bent grass. He swore with an unbridled viciousness, knowing from the dog's inert position that it was dead.

An instant later, he saw something else. A sight that brought him to a dead stop.

Standing upright in the dog's flank was a feathered arrow. Jesus! That's what had killed him, not —

Trooper was taking two more steps forward even as the thought chaotically formed. And in the same moment felt a sudden blow in the calf of his left leg. Not a particularly painful blow. Just a quick one accompanied by a needle-like stab that startled hell out of him.

Trooper grunted his surprise and fell back a step. He swung the lantern around as he peered off to his left.

What he saw froze him to the marrow with a thrill of pure terror. A huge rattlesnake back-drawing to coil, hissing furiously now. Trooper let out a hoarse yell, almost dropping the lantern as he stumbled backward.

The snake remained where it was, coiled and hissing. Never taking his eyes off it, Trooper carefully set his lantern on the ground. His flesh was shrinking and clammy with a paroxysm of fear and revulsion; the spot on his leg seemed abruptly to writhe with maggots of fire. It was all he could do, still half fuddled with alcohol, to draw his Colt and thumb back the hammer and steady the weapon.

The gunshot pounded against his ears; the stink of cordite shocked him halfway sober.

The rattler's headless body thrashed bloodily in the grass. Trooper stared at it with squinted eyes and a rush of terrified realization. Why did the end of the reptile's tail seem oddly fixed to the spot? And why hadn't it given a burr of warning?

His tottering legs took one step. Another. And he saw. A sudden and violent compounding of the terror that already possessed him made Trooper sway dizzily.

The rattlesnake's tail was bound by a cord to a stake driven in the ground. It had been tied purposefully at a spot next to the faintly worn path that led from the house to the tack shed.

And its rattles? There were none. *The row of bony buttons on the snake's tail that should have chattered an alarm was missing!*

Trooper let out an inarticulate croaking noise; he stumbled backward. Tripped on the lantern and nearly fell. Then he turned and legged it toward the house at a limping run, the oblong of lamplit doorway picking out his way. Even in his frenzy of panic, his flesh ached with the agonized expectation of a bullet in the back before he reached safety. . . .

He plunged inside, slammed the door, and dropped the bar.

Another terror, deeper than any fear of the unknown nemesis who had rigged that trap, took a grip on Trooper. He dropped on his butt on the floor, tearing wildly at the leg of his Levi's. Then with a curse he yanked out his hunting knife and ripped his pants leg to the knee. The tiny, oozing punctures showed livid just above the top of his half boot.

God, *what?*

Cut.

Yeah — cut deep and wide. Get out all the goddam poison you could before the sonuvabitch got spreading. Shuddering and biting his lip, he crisscrossed the affected area with savage strokes of his knife. Careful! Jesus — hit that big artery and you'd really have something. . . .

Staggering to his feet, he got a towel and mopped at the streaming cuts. The skin around the bite was already turning a dis-colored purple, by which he knew the venom had been absorbed to that extent. Sweating and shaking, he tied another towel around his leg above the place and rammed a ladle through it, twisting for a tourniquet.

Trooper's heart was pounding wildly, whether from fear or the poison taking hold, he didn't know. What now? God — a lone man who got snakebit far from any kind of help was in a serious way. Ride to Big W? Out of the question. Not with that snake-trap sonuvabitch prowling out there in the dark. Besides, he recalled some army medico saying that violent exertion would make the venom work faster. Same medico who had said that taking liquor would have the same adverse effect. . . .

Hell with that newfangled bullshit, Trooper thought. His old pappy had sworn by both tobacco and whiskey for every ailment from goiter to gallstones and he'd lived to eighty-seven. Trooper limped to the table and seized up the bottle and took a long pull from it.

Clutching the bottle, he crossed painfully into the back room, where he had his bunk. He felt nauseated and a little weak, his pulse had begun to race, and now there was no doubt of the poison's effect. Drink and rest . . . that was the ticket. Goddammit, in his time he'd taken worse in his system than rattler pizen and he'd tough out this siege, too, without a lick of help.

Drink and rest. And sleep.

The room's single window was hinged to its upper frame so it could be propped open with a stick. Trooper had left it that way this morning and now, seeing it still gaping wide, he swore at his carelessness. Quickly he shut and locked it and pulled the frayed flour-sack drape across it.

He moved unsteadily to the bed, blinking against his blurring sight. His muscles were weak and trembly; he felt near to vomiting. He collapsed across the varicolored blanket that covered the bunk.

Lamplight from the front room reached only faintly into the back one. And the blanket's colors and design were just similar enough to a diamondback's markings that his watering eyes failed to see the second rattlesnake, coiled at the foot of the bunk. Until, that is, he caught the sudden hiss and movement.

Trooper screamed and scrambled sideways, grabbing for his holstered pistol. But too late as the rattler struck.

The note Jim Izancho had left in the Tenneys' kitchen said he'd be back later that day with his wife. When they hadn't shown up by late afternoon, Tenney began to wonder. By evening he was puzzled enough to wonder aloud to Bettina, who was preoccupied with seeing to the little boy's comfort. Anyway, he said, Jim and his wife should certainly be here tomorrow; maybe they were delayed by something else going awry, like the old man taking sick.

Next morning, Tenney drove to Galeytown, a village on the western line of his county, to make the regular monthly check with one of his deputies who was posted there. He didn't return home till late the following day, and when Bettina told him Jim and Sally Izancho had still failed to appear, he began to feel a genuine worry. There was more than one reason for concern. Jim's little son was no longer resting comfortably. His body was seized with spasms, he was in considerable pain, and he kept calling for his dad and mother.

By the next morning, when the Izanchos still hadn't turned up, Tenney decided to wait no longer. He got his horse from the livery and rode out to the Izancho place. Arriving there shortly before noon, he was stunned by what he found.

He wasn't enough of a tracker to decipher the trampled sign around the heaps of blackened rubble. All he could be sure of was the obvious. Something had happened to Jim, his wife, and his grandfather. A number of widely separated buildings had been burned, meaning the fires had been set deliberately. Only the corral remained intact, and the horses were gone. Soon, by a hit-and-miss search, Tenney found the empty kerosene tins and shortly afterward the knoll with its mound of freshly turned earth. Against temptation and a flood of horrendous speculations, he did not dig into the mound. He headed back for town to get shovels and witnesses.

Going to his own home, Tenney put together a small supply of food and a bedroll while he told Bettina what he had found and that he'd probably be gone overnight. Afterward he rounded up his two deputies in Friendship, O. D. Bangs and Bob Threepenny. Armed with shovels, the three men rode back to the Izancho place.

It was late afternoon when they arrived. In less than a half hour they had exhumed two charred bodies, of which just enough remained for Tenney to identify them as Sally Izancho and Cow Bird.

There would have to be a coroner's inquest. But, for now, Tenney was damned if he'd remove these two from where they had been so carefully laid to their final rest (by Jim, he was sure). What would be the point? The old man's skull had been crushed; that was obvious, but how in hell could a medical examiner tell anything else that was useful from corpses in this condition? If the county court issued a directive that they be brought in for examination, he'd do so — but not till then. At Tenney's order, both bodies were returned to the earth and the grave filled again.

O. D. Bangs was in a considerable excitement. He barely troubled to conceal his pleasure at having the monotony of his job livened by a double murder. It was one of the times Tenney had to swallow harder than usual to keep O.D. down. Ignoring his deputy's speculations, keeping most of his own thoughts to himself, he told Bob Threepenny — who was a full blooded Pima Indian and a fair tracker — to see what he could make of the sign.

By sundown, after painstakingly covering all the ground in a wide radius of the place, Bob was reasonably sure of several things: At least three men were responsible for the atrocity and it had been committed before Jim Izancho had returned home last night. The prints of his heavy work shoes overlay the other discernible tracks, and these had been made by cowmen's boots, except that one fellow evidently had worn fancier riding boots. It seemed likely, therefore, that Jim himself had unraveled enough sign to draw conclusions of his own.

Knowing his Apache friend's woodcraft, for he had seen enough instances of it in their boyhood, Tenney guessed it wasn't unlikely that Jim had also drawn some accurate conclusions about the general physical characteristics of those three men. But Bob Threepenny's abilities weren't sufficient, as Bob readily admitted, to fill in the brushstrokes that tightly. One of the cowboot fellows did have smaller feet than the other, and the latter apparently had a gimpy right leg. That was all he'd say for sure.

Darkness was closing down, so Tenney and his men prepared a sketchy supper and made camp on the spot. They roused out at first dawn. After a hasty breakfast, Tenney put Bob Threepenny on the trail. Could he follow those three riders . . . and could he get an idea where Jim Izancho had gone?

Bob did his best, but picking up sign on the dusty, grassless area around the Izancho place was one thing; following it across needle duff and rocky stretches was another. Within the hour, after covering less than a hundred yards, he admitted his bafflement. Tenney, usually stolid, felt his patience fraying. They were only wasting time. Roger Warrender wore riding boots, Billy de Groot had small feet, and Trooper Yount limped.

Damned skimpy evidence, but those fellows and Tony Soto sure as hell had a motive — and who else did?

With that, Tenney made the decision to press a direct and immediate confrontation with each of them. The line shack held down by Trooper Yount was a good deal nearer than the ranch headquarters, where he might expect to find the others. And as Trooper was alone, Tenney could deal with him and not worry about interference.

Even so, as he and his men forded the Santa Agrita and pushed west toward the Big W line camp, Tenney tasted the bitter knowledge that fixing guilt on any one of them wouldn't merely be difficult: it might prove impossible.

Motivations be damned! Who'd care? Decent and respectable folks, people who wouldn't waste a shred of liking on Roger or his buddies, would nevertheless find perfectly acceptable even the flimsiest alibis they might offer. Damnation! Even if you turned up enough to hale the bastards into court, even if a logical case could be built against them, what chance was there of a conviction?

What chance — when both victims were Indians?

But these bleak considerations touched

only the surface of Tenney's worries as he rode through the sun-washed morning. The big question that loomed in his mind was: *What had happened to Jim Izancho?*

If Jim knew only as much as Bob Threepenny had managed to uncover (and Jim had probably uncovered considerably more), he would be fairly certain of the murderers. Certain enough to move on that evidence alone. For, knowing Jim and his close-to-surface rage as well as he did, Tenney hadn't a jot of doubt that Jim would take the meting of justice into his own hands. Or anyway, try like hell to. . . .

The three lawmen rode through a break in a screen of tall timber and came into a small valley, where the line camp was.

The place had a strangely quiet and deserted feel to it as they neared it. At first Tenney was unable to fathom why, and then it came to him. Trooper had a dog that always set up a lusty alarm at any visitor's approach.

O.D. echoed his own thought: "Say, I wonder where's that mean mutt of ole Trooper's?"

Tenney raised a hand to halt the others.

"Maybe that means something," he told them. "Maybe nothing. Only, let's be sort of circumspect, boys. O.D., come with me.

Bob, you have a look around the corral and sheds."

Bob Threepenny nodded and swung away from his companions.

Tenney and O.D. rode up to the door of the cabin and swung off their horses. O.D. made an ostentatious point of unlimbering his right-hand six-gun, and Tenney gave him a warning look. But Tenney himself snapped off the thong on his Luger holster before he stepped onto the porch and rapped at the door. When there was no answer, he knocked again.

Still no response.

Tenney tried the latch. It wasn't padlocked, yet the door refused to give. The solid rattle it made against the jamb indicated it was barred from the inside. How in hell could that be if Trooper wasn't home?

O.D. said excitedly, "Barred, huh? We bust it down?"

"Door with a heavy bar won't bust too easy, Oliver," Tenney said dryly. "There's a window in back. We'll —"

"Frank . . . you better get over here!"

That was Bob Threepenny's quietly urgent call. He was standing over by the tack shed, looking down at the ground.

"Go around back," Tenney told O.D. "See if you can force the window. Break it if you have to, take a look inside, but don't go in alone. Understand? Wait for us."

Even before he reached Bob Threepenny, Tenney saw the dead dog on a patch of bare earth, an arrow protruding from it. But he was standing at the Pima's side before he saw, in the tall grass at Bob's feet, the twisted body of the big diamondback, its head blown to a pulp.

"That's something, ain't it?" Bob said quietly.

Tenney nodded in fascination, barely noticing the faint tinkle of glass as O.D. shattered the window at the rear of the cabin. It was something, all right. A rattler divested of its rattles and fastened to a stake by its tail. But what in hell . . . ?

"Hey, Frank!" O.D. yelled. *"Hey, Frank!"*

Tenney and Bob Threepenny exchanged glances. O.D.'s voice carried a note that went considerably beyond his usual excitability. The two men had their guns out as they headed for the house at a run. . . .

CHAPTER TEN

"*Luna del sangre,*" Tony Soto said musingly. "There is blood on the moon tonight."

Hay crackled under Billy de Groot's back as he shifted uneasily. "What? What's 'at?"

Soto took a pull at the bottle, then passed it to Billy with a laugh. "Hey, *hombre*. Drink up. Your nerve, I think she need it." He nodded upward at the moon swimming in a reddish veil of clouds. "It's something the old ones tell. When the moon is so, they say, it means one will die."

Billy drank, blinking against the liquor's burn. "They's one dead already," he muttered. "Trooper —"

"Christ's sake, will you knock it off?" Roger snapped. "Just knock that crap off."

Soto hiccoughed and grinned. "Scary talk, ain't it, Rodge?"

"Old wives' bullshit is what it is."

"Sure, tha's what it is. But she get under a fella's skin, hey?"

Roger decided that Soto was feeling cocky and smug because he thought he hadn't a goddamn thing to worry about. After all, it wasn't Antonio Soto who had burned the Apache out and killed his squaw. Antonio Soto had righteously declined to have anything to do with the foray and so was in the clear. Goddam smart-ass greaser, Roger thought morosely.

The three of them were sprawled in a mound of hay at the front of an open-sided hay shed. From here they had a panoramic view of Big W's headquarters. Off to their right, the lights of the big house sparkled. Way to the left and somewhat downslope of the house but still well above the barns and sheds and corrals, the bunkhouse lights shone. The moon shed its ghostly and tranquil glow across the whole scene.

Roger took the bottle from Billy and swigged deeply. One of the ranch dogs barked, sending a cold ripple along his spine. The night had a chill to it, but that wasn't why Roger shivered. All the same, he'd rather be out here than in the house.

Being afraid was rather a novel experience for Roger Warrender. In his school days, being bigger and stronger than most kids of an age with him, he'd always been the bully rather than the bullied. Later on, Warrender money and influence had cushioned any consequences of his various hell-raisings. The killings of the squaw and the old Indian had changed that lifelong state of affairs. The Senator would be inclined to brush aside his burning out that Apache; Roger had been well aware he was on safe ground there.

But murder. No. Indians or not, Stuart Warrender wouldn't condone cold-blooded killing.

Roger's horror at Trooper's ruthless disposal of the old man had worn off swiftly. Afterward, his sole thought had been to cover up his own part. Throwing the bodies in the fire wouldn't wholly divert suspicion from Trooper and Billy and him even if the corpses were consumed beyond determination of how death had been meted. So, before the three of them had parted company four nights since, they'd agreed on a story. Trooper would simply deny any knowledge of the arson and double killing and swear he hadn't seen hide nor hair of Billy and Roger since the day they'd shot up the Izancho place. Since Roger and Billy had left the Big W together that night, they would have to alibi one another. Saying they'd intended to ride to town, but as they'd had bottles in their saddlebags, had decided to stop along

191

the road, climb off their horses, and get drunk there.

A thin excuse, for sure. But what the law might think hardly worried Roger. Hell! Let Frank Tenney try to prove a damned thing. Given the climate of public opinion hereabouts, only the most solid and irrefutable evidence would satisfy any court. Trouble was, the Senator could draw the same inferences Tenney would. And what the Senator might do about it on his own hook was *damned* worrisome.

Roger had quietly sweated out three days and nights of waiting for the ax to fall. The fact that it hadn't done so almost at once had increasingly puzzled and worried him. The ordinary currents of country gossip had brought word to Big W that Jim Izancho had taken his ailing child to Friendship and, so far as anyone knew, had returned to his home next morning. If Izancho had reported to Frank what had happened, that damned suspicious nature of Tenney's should have brought him pouncing on Roger and his friends right away.

So Roger had been braced for Tenney's coming. But there'd been no way of preparing himself for the horrifying shock he'd received when Tenney and his deputies had arrived at Big W headquarters this afternoon. They had brought Trooper Yount's body with them. And with it Tenney's careful and graphic description of what the evidence told about Trooper's dying. Through it all, Tenney had never taken his eyes off Roger.

Roger had been petrified as much by the appearance of the body as by Tenney's story. Probably this was all that had kept him from losing both his self-control and the contents of his stomach. As it was, he supposed he'd lost most of his color as Tenney told about the rattleless rattlers, one tied outside and the other to the framework of Trooper's bunk, and how Trooper had managed to kill both snakes but the venom of the second bite had finished him, a work doubtless accomplished by the rattler tied to the bunk, for the night bar had been on the door and Trooper's body lay twisted on the floor. . . .

"Jeezos, tha's some way to die, hey?" Soto said reflectively as he lighted up a cigarillo and tossed the match away. "She's painful as hell, I'm bet."

"Watch where you throw your damn matches," Roger snapped. "You set this bunch of hay on fire, that'll be all we need. The old man's pissed as it is."

"Hokay, Rodge. But that Apach', he's one cute fella." Soto jerked out a chuckle.

"Having rattlers do his dorty work! Ain' no better way to scare the shit out of a guy you don' like. Leave it to an Injun. Tha's an old Injun trick, you know; taking off the rattles. Not Apach' so much, but Injun. A Sioux fella I meet once, he tell me the Crows use' to do that to their enemies. The Crows, they trap a whole den of rattlers an' take off the rattles and let 'em go in the enemy camp. Boy, that is some dorty trick."

"How they do that?" Billy asked with a kind of morbid fascination. "Get them rattles off, I mean?"

"Ho, that ain' nothing." Soto waved his cigarillo, dropping a scatter of sparks in the hay. "What you do —"

"Will you *watch it* with that damn thing?" Roger snarled.

"Sorry, Rodge. What you do, you take a good hold on the last button on the tail and give a good twist and off comes the whole set of rattles. Is simple."

Roger took a nip from the bottle, muttering, "That Apache son of a bitch must be crazy. Jesus, he's got to be! What he did to Trooper. . . ."

"Sure, I guess he crazy all right," Soto agreed cheerfully. "But who get him that way, heh? You tell me. Who?"

"Listen, Tony, don't be so damn smart-ass! *You* may not be in the clear so far as that Apache's concerned. You were with us the day we shot up his place and he might just figure you were along the other night. . . ."

"Huh. I don' think so. He know his enemy, that one."

But the lilting note had ebbed from Soto's voice. He got up and stepped out of the shed, stretching his arms. "Is late. I guess I hit the blankets, not the hay. I tell you, boys, I think I sleep with gun under pillow. Maybe you do the same, hey?"

"Hell," said Billy with juvenile bravado, "ain't no Injun gonna come into the ranch looking for us."

"Cómo no?"

"Jeez, he ain't *that* crazy."

"Billy, I hope you right." Soto yawned and dropped his cigarillo to the ground, scuffing it out. *"Buenas noches. . . ."*

When Soto had left for the bunkhouse, Roger and Billy finished off the bottle. Afterward, the two made their way toward the big house, a little unsteadily. Billy hung close to Roger's side, chattering a blue streak. Ordinarily Roger would have ordered him to shut up. For once he let Billy rattle on, knowing he was trying to exorcise a real or imagined terror.

Even dulling his faculties with liquor

hadn't wholly allayed Roger's own nervousness. He still felt queasy when he thought of Trooper. That Apache could have shot Trooper easy as not. Instead he'd contrived an elaborate and frightful trap. It took a lot of hate to kill a man that way. Enough so there was plenty left over to vent on anyone else who'd put a canker in his craw.

Meantime there was the Senator to be uneasy about. Even now Roger felt a reluctance to return to the house and a possible collision with his father. He'd rarely seen Stuart Warrender's wrath at full tide, but it was nothing a man wanted to run afoul of.

Today he'd seen the Senator's anger blaze out at Frank Tenney. The explosion had come after Tenney had made no bones about inferring that Trooper and Roger, and possibly Billy or Soto, too, were prime suspects in the murders of Sally Izancho and the old man. But Roger hadn't been deceived by the Senator's heated repudiation of Tenney's suspicions. That bitter quarrel of a week before was still fresh in memory, and Tenney's blunt accusation had rubbed salt on its rawness. A man of the Senator's pride and temper could react in only one way. And having hotly defended his son and the others, he couldn't bring himself — yet — to question Roger's alibi more closely.

But Roger was bleakly aware that this was only a temporary reprieve. The scene at the dinner table had made that clear enough. The family had eaten in a silence chilled by Stuart Warrender's forbidding manner. Roger had been glad to get out of the house and find a brief refuge in the hay shed with Billy and Tony. The three had discussed how Tenney had toughly questioned them, overriding the Senator's objections. Frank could be a hard-nosed bastard when it suited him, Roger thought narrowly. Right now he didn't have enough on them to haul them in, but by God if he ever did it would mean a real third degree.

Jesus. It might come to that if the Senator learned the truth.

Roger figured he could keep doggedly lying if he had to. But a weak sister like Billy was bound to crack under a little grilling. If only their goddam alibi didn't sound so flimsy! But what better one could they have offered? Insist that you'd been in town that night and Tenney would want to know where and then check for witnesses. . . .

One of the two dogs tethered near the veranda began to bark savagely as they neared it. Roger cursed the animal into silence. Fuddled as he was with drink, he thought the shadows around the house held a flow and swell of menace. As he and Billy entered the parlor, he was relieved to see that although a low-turned lamp was burning on a taboret, his parents had already retired. At least he needn't worry about a confrontation with the Senator tonight.

Parting with Billy at the door to Billy's room, Roger let himself quietly into his own room. After taking care to lock the window and draw the shade, he woozily undressed and extinguished the lamp and crawled into bed. He went to sleep almost at once.

He wasn't sure what awakened him. Perhaps it was a vague awareness in the currents of sleep that a dog was barking outside. Or maybe he only dreamed it. Roger groaned and turned over. It was the abrupt cessation of the barking that rang a dull alarm in his drugged brain. Was that a sound of something outside fumbling at his window? He struggled toward wakefulness. . . .

Suddenly glass shattered. Broken shards jangled on the floor. And something else, a bulky object of some kind, landed with a crunch among them.

Roger raised himself on his elbows, muttering, "What is it?"

A draft swept the room. He could hear the painful slugging of his heart in the darkness. He strove to penetrate it, but all he could see was a dim square of shade-covered window across the room.

Then he heard the soft rustlings and hissings that made his skin crawl and his blood freeze. *Oh Jesus!*

Except for being partly drunk, he probably wouldn't have moved at all. He would have thought to yell for help. Instead he fumbled for the lamp and box of matches on his bedside stand. Those furious sibilances and dry, unseen stirrings seemed to crash like surf against his pounding ears. He got the wick trimmed and peered with straining eyes as the wavering glow spread through the room.

Oh . . . God!

Three of them that he could see. A collapsed canvas bag lay under the window; a rattlesnake was crawling out of it. Another diamondback was coiled beneath the window. The third and biggest one had already slithered halfway across the floor to his bed.

Roger measured the distance to the commode, where he kept a pistol. But nothing in the world could have made him step barelegged onto that floor. *God, one of them he hadn't seen might have crawled under his bed by this time!*

What he could do, it occurred to him quite suddenly, was yell for help. His first shout fizzled in a throaty clot of phlegm. He gagged it free and let out a piercing screech. Then another.

But the household was already aroused. Footsteps in the hallway. The door of his room was flung open. His father stood there, a gaunt and high and nightgowned form in the wavering light, his white shock of hair disheveled. There was a big Colt revolver in his fist.

The Senator's blue eyes blazed; he swore.

On the heels of his oath came the roar of his six-gun. The gun blasts rocked and echoed thunderously in the room.

A slug's impact sent the biggest rattler spinning across the floor. And the snake by the window lashed in a bloody dissolution. The Senator's first two shots did as much. His next two went wide of the mark. The rattler that had partly emerged from the sack tried to recoil in a hissing paroxysm of fright. The Senator's fifth bullet demolished the pitted wedge of its head.

The first snake was injured but still active. The Senator dropped his pistol and seized up a hand-carved armchair that stood near the door. Swiftly crossing the room, he swung the heavy piece down in a crushing blow. Then he looked at his son.

Roger stared at the twitching, dying serpents, wondering if this was a nightmare, after all, a drink-induced hallucination from which he might awaken any moment.

Now a different sort of noise cracked his alcoholic fog. It was the voice of Billy de Groot, from the adjoining room. He was giving out scream after scream in a high, wordless rhythm. . . .

Billy's window hadn't been broken. He'd left it unlocked. It had been gently jimmied open, and the bag — this one containing two rattlers — had been dropped quietly inside. When the shouts and shots had awakened Billy, he had leaped out of bed in the dark. One of the reptiles had struck him.

It took a while for the commotion to die down. The gunfire had brought several of the crew to investigate; the Senator told them to make a thorough search of the whole ranch headquarters. Within minutes the men were fanning across the place with guns, lanterns, and electric torches. All they found were the bodies of two arrow-killed dogs. At the Senator's order, others of the crew searched the house from end to end for more snakes. None turned up.

The Senator had dispatched the two rattlers in Billy's room. Like those dumped into Roger's, they were found to be rattleless. The canvas containers that had held both sets of snakes were secured at the mouths with drawstrings that the prowler must have loosened just before dropping the bags through the windows.

"Diabolical," the Senator kept muttering. "Absolutely diabolical."

Roger, still in the grip of a marrow-icing fear, thought that was the understatement of a lifetime. God . . . that Apache must have been prowling nearby the whole time he and Billy and Tony had been in the shed. He must have watched them disperse to the bunkhouse and the house. And by the lights that were extinguished in two windows he would have picked out the locations of Roger's and Billy's rooms.

Goddlemighty!

It would have been so damned *easy* for the son of a bitch to take their lives in any of several different ways. That was what really stuck in your craw! He'd chosen to menace them in this fashion, knowing it was a way that might fail to kill. Knowing, too, with all the cunning of his savage soul, that it would strike a terror to his victims' guts that no other means might have accomplished.

The effect on Roger's mother was almost

catastrophic. Gentle and retiring, Eleanor Warrender had merely moved in her husband's wake for thirty years. She was so high-strung as to be unnerved by the most trivial family crisis, and tonight's incident had left her virtually prostrate.

When the excitement had tapered off, the crew returned to the bunkhouse except for several men assigned to patrol the yard for the rest of the night. Billy had been treated with the anti-snakebite apparatus that was kept on hand, and the Senator saw to it that his wife was well sedated with a dose of nerve pills. He ordered the stolid Mexican housekeeper to put her to bed and then to clean up the mess in Roger's and Billy's rooms.

Afterward he turned grimly to Roger. "Come to my study," he said crisply.

This was the moment Roger had dreaded. As he followed his father into the privacy of the oak-paneled office-study, he had the thick, defeated sense of a man maneuvered into a corner.

The Senator closed the door behind them and faced his son.

"Now, sir" — he spoke with a kind of deathly calm — "I want the truth. No more of your damned lies."

Almost mechanically Roger assumed a

startled and righteous look. He began to shake his head. "I don't —"

The Senator struck him with a clenched fist. It wasn't a very hard blow. Merely a quick, contemptuous one that caught him on his pudgy left cheek with an impact that half swiveled his head. And left him blinking with pain and anger and humiliation.

"Pa. . . ." His voice dwindled under his father's stare.

Senator Warrender's hot eyes cooled with the knowledge of victory.

"Now," he said calmly and very softly, "we'll have the truth. I will stick by you. Did you think I wouldn't? Whatever else you may be, such as a blundering blot on my name, you're my son. Also, the damage is done — you can't mend broken eggs. But." The Senator raised a finger almost under Roger's nose. "There is this: If you lie to me again, I will make you sorry you ever saw the light of day. Now. Out with it all, and don't neglect a detail."

CHAPTER ELEVEN

The small bedroom crawled with a dry, sour heat. Tenney watched with only a half attention as Dr. Jack Courtland took the sleeping boy's pulse. The rest of his mind was on the clatter coming from the kitchen, the angry rattle of pots and pans as Bettina prepared supper.

Family loyalty. What a set of damned blinders it was!

Not that he'd been in the least diplomatic in his handling of Senator Warrender's feelings at Big W yesterday, Tenney had to admit. He'd been exactly as roughshod with the Warrenders as though they weren't his in-laws (and influential ones at that). He'd been as savagely blunt with them as he would be with any stranger he was sure had broken the law but couldn't be brought to trial for lack of evidence. And then Mrs. Warrender had gotten to her daughter by phone before Tenney had returned home.

Bettina's whole first impression of what had happened was hopelessly colored against her husband.

Another quarrel had ensued. And the twenty-four hours that had elapsed since hadn't been enough to abate the heat it had generated. Tenney had just returned from a long, hot, punishing, and wholly discouraging day in the saddle, leading a hunt he'd been certain would be fruitless. It was almost a dead certainty that nobody who wasn't as desert-wise as Jim Izancho was going to locate him before he was ready to be found.

Dr. Courtland, a studious-looking young man with a deep widow's peak, straightened up from his examination. He studied Joe-Jim Izancho with pursed lips. "I think he's passed the crisis, Frank. Those relaxants seem to have turned the trick. It was a mighty near thing with him."

Tenney nodded morosely. "And a damned good thing you got back yesterday."

"Hell," Courtland said with his wry, quiet smile. "Your wife's been doing all for him any sawbones could. Relaxants and soporifics are the ticket. All I did was continue the treatment with supposedly more efficacious drugs. Not really much else you can do for tetanus but wait it out. Latest thing I've read on the subject is the British Army's come up with a kind of serum they're testing. Some positive results, but no very conclusive ones so far. Nothing like a war, or the prospect of a war, to hasten the course of medical progress. Humanity is full of delicious ironies."

"Jack, you're too young to be cynical."

"But not too inexperienced, I'm sad to say." Courtland slipped the stethoscope off his neck and placed it in his black bag. "What a day! I'd invite you to offer me a drink, but I have other calls to make. . . ."

Tenney saw Dr. Courtland down the hallway and out to the front door. As he closed it behind the doctor, Tenney had a renewed awareness of Bettina's noisy activities. It was time to mend the breach or at least attempt a truce. He walked back to the kitchen and paused in the doorway, taking in the odor of roasting beef from the big Monarch stove.

"Smells good," he began. "It's been a long while since —"

Bettina swept by him on her way from the stove to the sink, not even glancing at him. He felt a hot-cold rush of anger as he couldn't remember feeling it. Without a word, he turned and tramped out to the hallway, pausing only long enough to whip his hat off a wall hook before slamming out the door.

She could slop the hogs with her damn roast for all he cared!

Tenney hadn't reached the end of the block before a guilty awareness touched him of how juvenile he was being. It wasn't the first time Bettina had turned a cold shoulder to his initial effort at making up, and that largely for the sake of not granting him forgiveness too easily. A little sparring usually brought her around. But he wasn't in the mood for going back and apologizing. Not just yet. He was dirty and hungry and tired, and his temper was riding an unusually fine edge. Right now, more than anything, he wanted a drink. Maybe several drinks.

As he came onto Main Street, where lights were starting to bloom in the windows as twilight deepened, he saw Bob Threepenny idling along on his rounds and crossed the street to intercept him.

"Evening, Frank. Had supper?"

"Not yet. How are things?"

"Quiet as a rattler with no buttons." The Pima smiled faintly. "And that's no joke."

Tenney had ordered his deputies to keep particularly close watch on the stores during their nightly rounds. Several shopkeepers had complained that a few nights ago their places of business had been broken into and some articles of value stolen. A Winchester rifle and a shotgun and some ammunition, a hunting knife, an ordinary kit bag, a length of pipe, a coil of wire, some canvas tenting, a quantity of grub, and, oddest of all, a cured deerhide.

Tenney hadn't been sure the break-in artist was Jim Izancho, but the theft of the tenting material would now seem to confirm it. Those voluminous canvas bags that had been dumped into Roger Warrender's and Billy de Groot's rooms last night had been crudely fashioned, according to the description, though effectively serving their purpose: to hold rattlesnakes.

Tenney and his deputies had learned of the midnight visitation when they'd encountered a couple of Big W hands on range this afternoon. Roger had escaped damage, and the snake-bitten Billy would apparently survive. Meantime, said the punchers, they were out by orders of Senator Warrender on the selfsame task that engaged Tenney and his men: to run down Jim Izancho. Other members of Big W's crew were out searching in pairs also. And the Senator's orders, if they spotted the Apache, were to shoot him on sight.

Tenney had felt a brief irritation with Warrender's failing to notify his office of the incident. Yet he couldn't really blame the Senator for feeling as he did or even for taking the law into his own hands. This was still a country where the law was expected to place a broad interpretation on a man's rights. Izancho could be shot for trespassing, if nothing else.

Tenney's glance moved up and down the street. "Where's O.D.?"

Bob Threepenny nodded toward the Lady Gay Saloon, across the street. "Believe I saw him pop in there a few minutes ago."

"Well, he's going to pop right out again."

Tenney angled across the street to the saloon and went in through the swing doors.

The place was fairly crowded for this early in the evening and for a weeknight. As he moved to the bar and signaled for a whiskey, he had no difficulty picking up O. D. Bangs. The deputy's brash voice dominated the room. He was sitting at a table with three other men, and several more were gathered around, listening. O.D. was wholly involved in his favorite role, being the center of attention. Whiskey-flushed and happy, he was summing up Jim Izancho's recent activities from his enviable position as an "insider," and with a considerable zest and detail.

". . . and by God we ain't caught hide nor hair of the son of a bitch yet. Him covering all that ground on foot, too. Ain't that a caution?"

"Hell, that ain't nothing for a 'Pache." Another drugstore cowboy putting in his two cents' worth. "Your old-time 'Pache runners used to jogtrot a hunnerd mile or so in a couple days. 'Sides, this 'un was a Olympics champ."

"No, he wasn't," O.D. came back promptly. "He got hisself disqualified . . . ."

While he was talking, a trio of cowhands had entered the place and bellied up to the bar near Tenney. They paid the sheriff no attention, though he knew all three better than he cared to. They were Big W men who'd more than once cooled their heels in jail for starting a barroom ruckus. Their leader, Big Bull Anders, a massive and kettle-gutted fellow with sly, pale eyes, ordered drinks by silently raising three thick fingers while he listened to the talk.

Catching O.D.'s eyes now, Tenney motioned to him. O.D. got up and swaggered over to the bar, not in the least abashed as he plunked his empty glass down alongside Tenney's full one. "Drink up, boss. I'll order 'nother for us."

Tenney said, "No. You won't," and took his drink in a swallow, feeling it hit his empty stomach like hot lead. "Did anyone ever tell you," he said thinly, "that you talk too damned much?"

O.D. managed to look slightly ruffled and mildly injured at the same time. "Shuckins. What's wrong with spreading the word? Folks oughta know what's up."

"I'll tell you what's wrong" — Tenney lowered his voice — "slow and quiet, so you'll grasp the idea. Lots of people hereabouts are old enough to remember when just the whisper of an Apache rising was enough to send the whole Territory into jitters. There are at least two men in this room who fought Apaches. Others who lost relatives at their hands. And it's happened in recent years, not right around here but other places, that a few young Indians will get hold of some liquor and go on an overnight rampage that scares hell out of everyone. People in Arizona and New Mexico feel more strongly about Indian threats than any place in the Union. And not without reason. After what's been going on, they'll be sleeping with guns by their pillows and shooting at shadows. Spelling out the details of an atrocity makes it just about twice as bad. Does what I'm saying fall anywhere inside your grasp, Oliver?"

O.D. took no offense. He grinned lopsidedly. "Sure. You reckon I'm dense?"

"I wonder. You were told to patrol the east side of town, not drink up a storm and shoot off your mouth."

"Shuckins, Frank. The Pima's on the job, ain't he?"

"As long as Jim Izancho's at large, you and Bob will both be making rounds at the same time every night. I'll relieve each of you at intervals, as I told you before. All clear?"

"Surest thing you know." O.D. waggled a finger at the bartender. "One for the road, hey?"

"O.D.," Tenney said quietly. "I'll say it once again: no more drinks. Then I'll start kicking ass."

"All *right!* Jeez. . . ."

O.D. swaggered out, not too unsteadily. Tenney frowned after him. O.D.'s cocky bravado was an old story, but this was the first time it had ever caused him to neglect his duty.

Tenney turned a brooding attention to the mutter of conversation in the room. He knew from the low-pitched talk and several covert glances in his direction that the local grapevine had conveyed its predictable fund of information. By now, everybody and his brother knew he and Bettina had been caring for the fugitive's child and, by way of the Warrenders, of his old friendship with Jim.

It was Big Bull Anders who chose to make an open point of it. He banged his glass on the bar for a refill, then said loudly, "Jesus Goddlemighty! Things've come to a pretty pass when one siwash Injun can get away with shit like this one's done."

"Goddam right," offered one of his two companions, an unwashed puncher named Milt Isley. "That red bastid is like a crazy wolf. Oughta pizen-bait him like one."

"Sure thing," put in white-whiskered Harve Millet. "Treat 'em like varmints. I allus said we shoulda wiped 'em out fast as they gave 'emselves up back in the eighties. Women, too. Get 'em where they breed, I allus said. Tell you, boys . . . my pappy carried to his grave the scars he got when Mangas Coloradas' bunch burned him out in sixty-one."

"Hey, Tenney!" Big Bull shoved his bulk past his friends and pushed along the bar toward Tenney, halting a couple yards away. His ham of a fist engulfed the glass it held. "What's this I been hearing you and that 'Pache is old buddies?"

Tenney scrubbed a weary hand over his face, motioning the bartender for a refill. He let his glance circle the room. Everyone had fallen silent, just watching now. He spoke softly. "When we were kids, right. It doesn't mean I condone what he's done. Or what was done to him."

"That right? How come you keeping that siwash kid at your place?"

"The boy's been sick. Dangerously sick. No other place to put him. That's reason enough."

A deep chuckle boomed up from Big Bull's chest. "What I think, you're an Injun-lovin' bast—"

Tenney's right hand held his filled glass; he flicked its contents into the giant puncher's face.

Big Bull took a stumbling step backward, pawing at his eyes. A bellow started from his throat, but it died in a wheezing grunt as Tenney's fist sank into his kettle gut. Tenney chopped a second punch to his neck and, as Big Bull sagged toward the floor, slugged him on the point of his jaw with all his weight behind the blow. It snapped Big Bull's head backward and dumped him with a crash on his back.

"I'll tell you what, gentlemen. . . ." Tenney took a bandanna from his pocket and wiped off the whiskey that had spilled on his hand. "You say anything you want to each other. You can even say it about me.

But not to me, all right?"

Big Bull groaned. Tenney stepped around him and walked out of the Lady Gay.

The spasm of violence had channeled off about half his temper. At least it was down enough that he judged he could return home now and not let Bettina's coldness get under his hide again. Besides, he was ravenously hungry, and if she hadn't thrown out that roast, he was prepared to do justice to his postponed supper.

Tenney was turning in to his front path when he heard Bettina scream.

He bounded onto the veranda and into the house, his Luger in hand. Bettina came stumbling down the hallway, hands pressed to her cheeks. Her face was nearly as white as her shirtwaist and full of a deathly shock. He seized her arm.

"What is it?"

"He was. . . ." Pointing down the hallway, she spoke in a husky whisper. "He was there. God! *He was there!*"

Tenney moved swiftly past her and into Joe-Jim Izancho's room. Its only occupant was the sleeping boy. But the window was wide open, the muslin curtains bellying on a night breeze. He went to the window and peered out. The spill of lamplight showed an empty yard. If Jim Izancho had been here, he had departed as speedily and silently as you'd expect him to.

Bettina's cry had also drawn Bob Threepenny, who was patrolling this street. Equipped with electric torches, he and Tenney made a search of the yard and outsheds in back of the house. Predictably they found nothing at all, not even a sign beneath the window of the Apache's coming and going.

After telling Bob Threepenny to station himself beside the woodshed and keep a watch on the place tonight, Tenney went back into the house. He found his wife sitting on the parlor sofa, her face composed. But her hands were clasped whitely in her lap; her expression was frozen.

He seated himself in an armchair facing her, then leaned forward with elbows on his knees. "Betts."

She did not reply.

"Betts . . . I want to know exactly what you saw."

"I . . . I went to look in on the boy. He was there, bending over him. His face was all painted. And . . . and then he went out the window so quickly I was hardly sure he'd been there. But he was."

Briefly Bettina's eyes closed; her teeth dented her underlip. Then she opened her eyes. "Frank . . ." A shrill note touched her voice. "I want that boy out of this house. Tonight."

"Betts, listen —"

"I want him out! Do you hear?"

"Betts, be reasonable. Where can I take him?"

"I don't know! I don't care!"

"Honey, listen," he said sharply. "He didn't come here to do mischief, only to see how his son was doing. No reason for a vendetta against us. *We* helped him, not the contrary."

"I don't care! Just get that boy out of here!"

Tenney sensed that her edge of hysteria was only partly rooted in the unexpected appearance of Jim Izancho. "Look," he said patiently, "keeping him here could be our way to nab Jim. I'll have a man watching the house every night from now on. If he comes again —"

"Frank . . . *I don't care*." Abruptly her voice turned matter-of-fact and brittle. "It is not my duty to play nurse to a killer's son."

"You blame a little boy for what his pa's done?"

"I . . . blame . . . *you* . . . for . . . everything." Bettina said the words through clenched teeth, spacing them. "You've defended that . . . that murdering siwash from the start! You've as good as accused my brother of cold-blooded murder!"

"Betts, we're been over all that. I know how —"

"Know *what*, for God's sake?" She came to her feet with an angry hiss of skirts, the inheld wrath pouring out of her. "You know *nothing!* All you've done is guess, Frank, and every guess you've made has ruled against my family and in favor of that killer! Yet you *know* that *he* has killed and that he's tried to kill again!"

"And you know your brother didn't, eh?"

"Yes! I know Roger. I know him as well as I know anybody alive. And I don't care what sort of hell he has raised at one time or another, *he is not a killer.*"

Tenney nodded wearily. "Fine. Maybe it'll prove out that way. I hope so. But meantime, Betts . . . just what the hell do you expect of me?"

"For a start, I want you to remove that boy from this house. I don't care where you take him or what you do with him. I want him out. Now."

It was a testing, Tenney knew. Quite often when something got Bettina's hackles up, she would try her imperious Warrender will against his. Not nearly as spoiled as her brother, she was just spoiled enough to find that particular tack irresistible at times. And Tenney cared for her enough to let her have her way now and then and not argue.

But this was a challenge more intense than any she'd offered. The tension in her voice held the twang of a tautened wire. It bordered on an unspoken threat. And he had no intention of yielding to an ultimatum of that sort.

"No," he said coldly.

"Very well. You'll have your way . . . and I will have mine. I am packing my things tonight, Frank. And tomorrow I am leaving you."

CHAPTER TWELVE

As soon as Tenney entered the office the next morning, O. D. Bangs could see his temper was up. For that matter it must have been pretty high last night, when he'd kayoed Big Bull Anders for wrongly shading a remark. O.D. had heard about it later on from one of the saloon loafers. Had something happened since to make him even more touchy? It was a curiosity for sure. Tough as he could sometimes be, Tenney had never angered easily.

O.D. said a mild good morning, then handed Tenney his written report on the night's watch. Noting the plain impatience with which Tenney scanned it, O.D. thought this, too, was unlike him. Something was really digging at him . . . maybe more things than one. Also his eyes were slightly bloodshot, like those of a man who'd put away several healthy belts of liquor and then slept it off. But Frank was no great drinker, either. It could explain, though, why he'd failed to show up to spell O.D. last night, as he'd promised. Goddam hypocrite, O.D. thought. He made enough fuss about another guy having a snort or two. . . .

Finished with the report, Tenney opened a filing cabinet drawer and stowed it in a folder and banged the drawer shut. "Go get some sleep," he said curtly. "Dil Mudd will be in to look after things when he's had breakfast. You and Bob Threepenny will relieve Dil at the usual time this evening."

O.D. made no effort to conceal his disappointment. "Ain't we going on the search today? For that 'Pache?"

"No."

Obviously Tenney was in no mood to offer an explanation, but O.D. pressed for one. "Jeez, Frank! How come?"

"I've something else on the fire. Anyway, I've caught some sleep; you and Bob have been up all night and yesterday, too. Tonight you'll hold the fort in town and spell each other."

"Hell —" O.D. clamped his jaws to fight back a yawn. "I'm fresh as a daisy. Whatever you're about, I'd admire to trail along."

Tenney said flatly, "Forget it," and walked to the gunrack on the north wall. He took down a Winchester rifle and checked the action while O.D. glared at his back and groped for terms in which to express his resentment without putting Frank too much more on the peck. Tenney wasn't ordinarily this closemouthed, which doubly convinced O.D. that he had something on his mind.

There was a sound of footsteps in the corridor; they paused by the open door of the sheriff's office. Still glaring, O.D. swiveled his glance that way. Two men were standing there. One was a tall, slender jasper, elegantly dressed, with a Malacca walking stick in his hand.

"Excuse me," he said with a ready smile. "Sheriff Frank Tenney?"

Tenney walked to the desk, broke out a box of cartridges from a drawer, and began filling the Winchester's magazine. He gave the newcomers the barest of glances as he said, "I'm Tenney."

"I'm Sidney Marston, Sheriff." The slender fellow nodded at his companion, a rumpled, chubby, balding fellow who had a camera and tripod slung over his shoulder. "This is my colleague, Mr. Fleming."

Tenney jerked a nod toward O.D. "Bangs, my deputy. What can I do for you?"

"Well, sir, maybe we can do something for each other." Marston cleared his throat. "I have a proposition which may interest you. Perhaps you're familiar with my name . . . or at least with a best-selling book that bears my by-line. The title of it is *With Passion Cold.*"

At once, O.D. was all ears. Wow . . . *With Passion Cold!* The book in question was a yellowback non-fiction thriller that he had avidly perused nearly a year before. It was a "true account" of a multiple murder committed in Iowa by a maniac, who had slain, violated, and hideously butchered three teen-aged girls.

"Hey, I read that!" he said excitedly. "It was a helluva good book!"

"Thank you." Martson inclined his head and smiled at Tenney. "And you, Sheriff. Have you, by chance —"

"No." Finished with loading the Winchester, Tenney raised his eyes. "But from what I've heard of your book, Mr. Marston, I wouldn't use the pages to wrap fish in."

Marston's smile twitched. "Ah? But, as you haven't read it, you've passed a prejudgment on the work. Admitted?"

"Man doesn't have to open a garbage can to know what's inside. Isn't it true, Mr. Marston, that every respectable publisher of trade books in the country declined to bring out your masterpiece?"

"Flagrant shortsightedness, Sheriff," Marston said blandly. "Nothing else. That book has made me, as its author and ultimate publisher, and the small firm which distributed it, a great deal of money."

Tenney nodded impatiently. "Especially after it was banned in Boston, eh? Get to the point."

"The point, sir, is this: Day before yesterday, I read in a Tucson paper of the very interesting business that's developed in your bailiwick. It has all the earmarks of being a suitable subject for my next book-length undertaking. I've pulled a set of clippings from a press morgue on this Jim Izancho. His is a most fascinating history. Reservation youth . . . first-rate scholar and star athlete at Carlisle . . . disqualified would-be Olympian . . . performer with Buffalo Bill's show. And now, of course . . . hunted killer. His apparent reversion to the ways of his savage forebears is particularly intriguing. And that very ingenious use of rattlesnakes. Now, there's a truly bizarre touch."

"I can see why it would appeal to you."

"Money always has an appeal, Sheriff. And that's my real point." Marston paused. "My proposal to you would be in the nature of a collaboration. I understand you were a boyhood chum of Izancho's. The account in that Tucson paper did no more than state the fact, but if it's true —" He raised a quizzical brow. When Tenney made no response, he shrugged and went on, "If it's true, I'm sure the circumstances could be elaborated on quite entertainingly. And therein lies a pivotal hook on which to swing the whole story: boyhood friend of Apache killer has duty of running him down."

Tenney said thinly, "I'm a little busy —"

Marston raised a quick hand. "All right. Here it is. I want to go along with you on your hunt for Izancho. As long as it lasts — and no matter how it turns out — I want to be in on every stage of it. Mr. Fleming will accompany us to take exclusive pictures. No other writers or reporters, no other photographers, must be permitted along. As the officer in charge, you can ensure us that exclusiveness. You will have to confide in me. Everything about your past relationship with Izancho and your present feeling toward him. All proceeds from my story, when it appears, will be split 60 per cent for me, 30 per cent for you, and 10 per cent for Mr. Fleming. Believe me, Mr. Tenney, this will be no piece of cheap sensation-mongering — not merely another *With Passion Cold*. The major publishers will be vying to take on this book. Then, there'll be the magazine and newspaper serialization rights. . . ."

Tenney was already shaking his head.

O.D. could scarcely believe it. Jesus Christ! the man was dangling a sure-fire shot at fame and fortune in front of him and Tenney wasn't a lick interested!

Marston gazed at him for a thoughtful moment, then said almost tenderly, "Sheriff, I trust you're aware how this business has made you look a bit of a fool — or even villain — in the public view. Several of your townspeople I've talked to have suggested that, to put it as gently as possible, your loyalty to an old friend has made you less than zealous in prosecuting a search for him. Nonsense, of course. But the kind of nonsense that could jeopardize your career, your entire future. You need a friend. A press agent, let us say. I can make you a national hero. Consider that — and consider the alternative. Come now, man. Won't you cooperate with me?"

"Mr. Marston. To put it as gently as possible, no."

"Very well, then. I've used up my arguments. I still intend to do the story, understand."

"Your privilege," Tenney said quietly. "Just stay out of my way."

"Gladly. I suppose you won't object to Mr. Fleming taking at least one picture of you, your deputy, and your office."

Mr. Fleming was already setting up his apparatus, and O.D. happily struck a pose. But Tenney spoiled his big moment, thrusting out his jaw and saying flatly, coldly, "No pictures. Out. Both of you."

Marston's brows tilted ironically. "My portrayal of you, friend, can go either way. So far, you've barely had a nodding acquaintance with trouble. Before I'm through, you'll be a regular pair of sweethearts — I promise you. All right, Andy. Pack it up and let's go."

The two men left. Tenney, occupied with scribbling some notes on a pad, seemed hardly to notice their going. O.D. gave a mental shake of his head at such stupid goddam intransigence. Then the glowing dawn of an idea began to warm his brain. By God, just maybe, now . . . !

Tenney departed the office with O.D. beside him. The two of them walked down the basement corridor, up the stairs, and out into the hot sun while Tenney, consulting his notes, gave his deputy curt instructions on handling the day's affairs. O.D. nodded or grunted mechanical replies, his own interest having gone off on a bemused tangent of its own.

At the front of the courthouse lawn, Mr. Fleming had set up his camera and was waiting. Sidney Marston stood beside him, calmly smoking. When Tenney and O.D. were halfway across the lawn, Marston took the cigarette from his mouth and said idly, "Okay, Andy. Take it."

Mr. Fleming tripped the shutter.

Instantly Tenney quickened his pace toward them. "I told you —" His voice was chill with wrath as O.D. couldn't remember hearing it "— no pictures!"

Marston laughed easily. "Come on, fellow. It's a free country. You can't —"

Tenney reached the camera and bent, gathering the legs of the tripod together. He picked up the whole apparatus and swung it, once and savagely, against the hard-packed surface of the street. The camera shattered internally and sagged in on itself; the lens rolled out and lay in the dust like an unwinking eye.

Mr. Fleming let out an inarticulate bleat of anguish. Suddenly he hit Tenney in the face, then stepped back, wearing an appalled look. Tenney rubbed his jaw and smiled. "I'm glad you did that," he said.

The photographer didn't even attempt to retreat gracefully. He simply turned and ran, his short, fat legs pumping. Tenney followed him at an easy lope. On every fourth step he gave Mr. Fleming a hard boot in the rump, keeping it up clear to the end of the block. . . .

That action, thought O.D., was *really* out of character for Tenney. Though he actually found the incident kind of amusing, O.D. pretended to commiserate soberly with the furious pair. After Tenney had headed downstreet, he helped the battered and badly shaken Mr. Fleming gather up his broken equipment. He offered a placating sympathy with Sidney Marston's angry denunciation of Tenney's "highhandedness," agreeing there was no damned excuse for it. Sheriff was pretty much used to doing as he pleased, O.D. explained; he was apt to get overly sore-assed when anyone crossed him.

"He made my ass sore, all right," Mr. Fleming groaned.

O.D. grinned and said affably, "Listen, I like to ask you guys something: Supposing a fellow was to bring this here Apache to taw. Catch him or kill him, I mean. You reckon that fellow could get hisself written up and his picture took for this book o' yours?"

Marston smiled humorlessly. "I imagine a bit of space would be devoted to him, yes."

"Okay." O.D. dropped his voice. "Supposing this fellow could get you boys what you wanted from Frank. I mean, get you right in on the kill — with exclusive pictures and story and all. What'd there be in it for him?"

Marston's brows crawled upward with a mild interest. "Part of what we offered Tenney, I suppose. Not all of it, because the hook with Tenney was his being chummy with this Apache . . ."

"Okay, I get it. But how much, say?"

"Well, obviously an expansive write-up. One that would heavily extol this wonder-worker's heroism. Plenty of pictures, including poses with the captive — or corpse, whichever is the case." Marston touched his dapper mustache. "And 10 per cent of all royalties from publication."

"How 'bout twenty?"

"I might go to fifteen."

"Done," O.D. said promptly.

Marston laughed. "What are we talking about? How can you *promise* to deliver Jim Izancho for an exclusive scoop . . . unless you know something we don't?"

O D. scratched his chin, grinning. "Can't guarantee a damn thing. Just pitching pennies, I guess you'd say. But if you men don't make yourselves too hard to find in the next few days, I might just be in touch."

Marston nodded slowly, his pale eyes sharpening on O.D.'s face. "You'll be able to locate us at the hotel, Mr. Bangs. . . ."

Tenney had headed toward the livery stable after his chastisement of Mr. Fleming. O.D. idled along the main street, watching the livery entrance. Presently he saw Tenney ride out on his horse and turn along the highway east from town. Afterward, O.D. hurried on to the house on a quiet side street where he lived with his widowed mother. While he packed a hasty lunch, he told her — over her mild remonstrations — that he was in no need of sleep, that he was leaving for the day on business and likely wouldn't be back till nightfall.

O.D. returned downtown without delay; he rented a horse at the livery. Old Emery, the hostler, was full of curiosity about what was developing with that there Apache case. O.D. evaded his questions and, after some hesitation, slipped him a five-spot with the understanding that Emery, a garrulous soul, wasn't to mention to anyone else, mainly Tenney himself, that O.D. had rented a horse today.

With that pecuniary encouragement, Emery came out with a sudden and unexpected piece of information. Seemed the sheriff's wife had upped and left him. Yessir. Early this morning, she'd hired a dray to take her and a big pile of her belongings out to her folks' place, Big W. This news surprised the hell out of O.D., who hadn't been aware of any trouble between Frank and his missus. But it would explain why he'd been acting as touchy as a grizzly that had accidentally squatted in a puddle of turpentine. . . .

O.D. set a brisk pace on the highway, for he wanted to pick Tenney up as quickly as possible. Presently, with the aid of his binoculars, he made out the sheriff and his mount on the road far ahead. O.D. now slacked his pace, wanting only to keep Tenney in sight.

The sun was already high and hot, and it worked pleasantly into O.D.'s body. But in his state of having gone without sleep for well over twenty-four hours, the heat rapidly turned him drowsy and made him aware of just how tired he was. He yawned repeatedly, pinching himself and fighting off waves of fatigue.

Blinking and nodding, O.D. went to sleep in the saddle a couple times. And after the second time, when he jerked awake once more, he realized he had lost sight of Tenney. This shocked him wholly alert, and in a wild panic he rapidly scanned the landscape with his glasses. In a moment he found Tenney again. The sheriff had left the road, and unless O.D. was mistaken, the point at which he had turned off it marked the rutted old trail that led to Jim Izancho's place.

What the hell did Tenney hope to find there?

His weariness banished by a rising excitement, O.D. moved on quickly. He swung onto the turnoff and followed it till it bent upward toward the forested hills just short of Izancho's layout. There O.D. cut away from the wagon trail and put his horse up the wooded slopes. At last he came out on the summit of the pine-clad escarpment that overlooked the burned remains of the Izancho place.

O.D. dismounted and, binoculars in hand, made his way a short distance downslope. He found concealment behind a screen of brush from where, through a break in the trees, he could con the scene below. Almost at once he located Tenney. The sheriff had dismounted close to the pine knoll where Izancho's squaw and granddaddy were buried.

But exactly what the hell was Tenney up to? He was walking around gathering up stones of a more or less uniform size, about as big as a man's fist, and dropping them in a pile near the graves. Then he hunkered down and began arranging the stones into odd patterns on a grassless stretch of ground.

Abruptly, O.D. snapped his fingers; he laughed quietly. Christalmighty, yes! A message, wasn't it? The lines and swirls of stone Tenney was laying out were intended to convey a meaning of some kind. And who would that message be for if not his pal, Izancho?

A flare of wild suspicions swept O.D. Were Tenney and Izancho somehow in cahoots? Or was this merely an attempt by Tenney to get in touch with his old buddy? After thinking it over, O.D. inclined toward the latter probability. Tenney had been acting sort of off his feed, but that could be put down to the trouble with his wife and feeling sore about having to hunt down a siwash buddy turned criminal. For O.D. hadn't a jot of doubt that Frank's dedication to his duty was unshakable, old friend or not. Others might doubt, but O.D. knew his boss too damned well to think otherwise.

That still left the question of just what Frank was up to.

O.D. watched him complete the tidy arrangement of rocks. Then Tenney walked back to his horse, mounted, and rode away from the place without a backward look. Now, as O.D. trained his glasses wholly on the pattern in stone, he swore in baffled disappointment. If the cryptic design was supposed to spell out anything, the sense of it was lost on O.D.

An Injun code of some kind? More'n likely. But a fat chance he had of doping it out. Hell!

Then O.D. chuckled. Hot damn! No need to cipher the sonuvabitch, maybe. If Izancho showed up here, and evidently Tenney believed he would, all O.D. had to do was wait right smack where he was. And pull a bead on the Apache as soon as he showed himself.

Still chuckling, O.D. walked back to his horse, collected his rifle and canteen and sack of grub, and returned to his vantage point. He seated himself on the ground with his back comfortably propped against the bole of a big pine. The brush screen would hide him from any but a close scrutiny by any observer from below.

It was nearly high noon. The midday warmth baked a resinous smell out of the pines; the heat and pine odor and a mild breeze soughing in the branches conspired to make O.D. feel as restful as he ever had. Soon he was struggling to keep awake. When he found himself actually dozing off, he dug out his sandwiches and ate them, hoping food would stir up his juices a mite. Instead, the meal sat heavily on his belly.

Finally he came to a drowsy decision that forty winks wouldn't do any harm. And dozed off in a sitting position against the tree. . . .

He woke abruptly enough. Yet it took several confused moments to shake away the fog of sleep and realize where he was. Then he realized with a sense of bewildered shock that it was nearly sundown. He had slept away the afternoon. Jesus! Quickly sighting downslope through the lengthening shadows, O.D. glassed the arrangement of stones. Had they been disturbed in any way?

Yes, by God! A number of the rocks had been rearranged. Somebody had come and gone down there while he'd slept.

A clot of bitter disappointment thickened O.D.'s throat. Goddammit to hell anyway — he'd muffed the chance of a lifetime!

He rose to his feet, grunting with a twinge of cramps. Then, as an afterthought, he once more steadied the glasses on the stones. He'd memorized the previous arrangements; maybe the changes would offer a clue to the sense of it.

No. No use. To him it was all Greek. Or Apache. Shit!

Around him, the stretch of shadows lent a somehow ominous touch to the waning light. A ripple of gooseflesh prickled O.D.'s hide. Suddenly he wanted very much to be away from there. Anyway, he was shortly due back in town to take over the evening watch. Best he get moving before Tenney's suspicions were aroused . . . man could always find an excuse for being just a mite late.

As he tramped back toward his horse, O.D.'s anger simmered quickly away. It was almost gone by the time he took up his reins and stepped into the saddle. A fresh anticipation honed his thoughts.

Izancho had left a message of his own. For Tenney. And Frank would be coming back to learn what it was . . . wouldn't he?

CHAPTER THIRTEEN

Tenney had never been anywhere near Rattlesnake Bluff. No business of his had ever brought him to its vicinity, but he would have steered clear of it in any event. The isolated, loaf-shaped rise and its surrounding area were said to be infested with rattlesnakes. Tenney wouldn't have described his loathing of the reptiles as a genuine dread, but he knew it amounted to that.

And now, against all misgivings, he was bound for Rattlesnake Bluff. It would take him half the day to reach it on horseback, and he didn't press a hurried pace. Either Jim Izancho would be there or he wouldn't. He hadn't set any particular time for the rendezvous, an omission that might be set down as a reversion to an uncivilized man's indifference to time.

What would happen when they met? It was a disquieting question. Jim his friend had become Jim the renegade killer. And

Tenney the sheriff was duty-bound to bring him to justice. Jim would have no illusions on that point, and would be inclined to take it damned seriously. Maybe killing serious. Was that why he'd consented to the meeting?

No use thinking on it, Tenney knew. He was the one who'd asked for it; Jim had accepted. He knew what he had to say to Jim. All he could do was tell it and hope Jim would listen. That was all he needed to think about.

At least Jim hadn't forgotten the code the two of them had devised when they were boys. Setting out messages in the form of stones or sticks was so common with Indians that they hardly even thought about it. But the custom had intrigued young Frank Tenney, and he and Jim Izancho had worked a few improvisations of their own on the old Apache method.

It had seemed possible and even likely that a grieving Jim Izancho would be drawn, and, Tenney had hoped, before long, to visit the place he and his family had called home, where the graves of his wife and grandsire were. So yesterday Tenney had left his message in stone close to the knoll where Sally and Cow Bird were buried. He'd simply asked Jim for a meeting. Returning to the place this morning, he'd found Jim's reply in a stone diagram that directed him to a large boulder a hundred feet east. Beneath it, Tenney had found the scrap of paper with two words etched by a charred stick: RATTLESNAKE BLUFF.

At Jim's motives for accepting the invitation, he could only guess. Maybe they were as mixed as his own. So far, Jim had directed a vendetta solely against those who'd wronged him. He'd robbed to obtain his needs, but had committed no wanton acts of carnage. If this was madness, there was a method to it. The big question was . . . how far did Jim intend to carry it?

On the answer to that would hinge the outcome of their meeting.

Tenney was unpleasantly aware that not only was he placing his neck under the ax, he was prepared to stretch to breaking the law he was pledged to uphold. Yet his friendship for Jim wasn't the main consideration. It might be next to impossible to run down a man of Jim Izancho's desertcraft unless you blanketed the whole county with posses of men. Even then the outcome would be doubtful. Adding to Jim's enemy list could prompt him to widen the range of his depredations; he might inflict a lot of damage before he was brought down.

To avoid that, Tenney thought, made any amount of law-bending and risk to his own hide worth the candle. . . .

It was past noon when Rattlesnake Bluff came into sight. The lofty and rambling formation reared out of a rugged desertscape; its sandstone cliffs and abutments were eroded and pitted and creviced. Not much vegetation grew on it except near the base. Tenney pulled up his horse and lifted his binoculars to study its facing flank, sweeping it from top to bottom. He found no sign of Jim Izancho, nor had he expected to.

The Apache had picked an ideal place, from his standpoint.

Tenney had almost wondered if a dormant streak of sadism had caused Jim, knowing his friend's aversion, to choose Rattlesnake Bluff as their meeting place. The more reasonable explanation, however, was that Jim wanted safeguards against being taken in a trap. Looking at it that way, he had chosen strategically and well. From any number of concealments on the bluff's ragged summit a man could see for miles on all sides and not be seen himself. He could watch all approaches to the bluff and, if he saw the makings of a trap being set for him, could fade quietly away down one of the shadowy draws that laced the slopes and be gone long before the jaws closed.

Tenney's mouth was dry as dust as he rode steadily nearer. Finally, as the first rock lift of ridge began to make the footing treacherous, he stepped from his saddle and ground-tied his horse. And he started to climb. Despite the general steepness of the formation, the going wasn't as rough as he'd anticipated. Those deep and shadowed draws that scored its sides provided places a man could ascend easily if slowly.

Jim, he knew, would show himself only when he was ready to. Very probably, he was watching Tenney at this moment, and he might be almost anywhere. But logically he would be near the summit, where he could command the best view. It would be easy, terrifyingly easy, for him to draw a bead on a lone climbing man with that Winchester he'd stolen from Hardy's Gun Shop.

Almost unconsciously, Tenney's right hand sought his left arm. His fingers traced the faint ridge where the ends of broken bone had knit together years ago. And this reminder gave him a sudden lift of confidence. He knew, without being able to spell out a cold reason for his certainty, that *Jim Izancho would not take the life he had once saved.*

The chatter of rattles crackled along his taut nerves like an electric shock.

The rattler was coiled on a sunny shelf of rock just feet ahead of him. For a moment Tenney was a man close to panic. He pulled his Luger and fired. The snake's ugly snout dissolved in a crimson smear; it flopped and rolled in its dying constrictions.

Tenney stood in the clammy wash of his sweat, listening to the shot echoes die into silence. Then he raised his voice in a shout: "Jim!"

Jim . . . Jim . . . Jim!

Only the stony throwback of his own voice answered him. Go on, he told himself, go on. His legs felt leaden as he plunged on and upward.

It came dimly back to him: Jim's long-ago telling that the Apaches regarded the rattlesnake as an evil to be avoided at all costs, but one to be propitiated, rather than combated. God, Tenney thought dumbly, it was as though Jim, in embracing the serpent as his instrument of terror, had aligned himself with . . . *with what?* Get off that goddam nonsense, he thought then. You're spooked already and you're spooking yourself worse. . . .

"Stop there, Frank. Throw your gun away before you come up here."

Jim Izancho's voice came from surprisingly close at hand. Tenney peered to his left and right and then upward. All he saw were folds of sun-baked rock.

But the steep cleft yawned ahead of him; there was nowhere else to go. Tenney laid his Luger on the ground. His driving legs carried him on and up for another six yards, and quite abruptly the cleft ended. He was inside a wide natural amphitheater formed by vaulting walls of rock and littered by crumbling slabs that had sloughed away from them.

Jim Izancho was nowhere in sight. But he made a sudden appearance, stepping out from behind a rock slab.

For a shocked moment Tenney simply stared at him. In this year of grace you didn't expect to see — outside of old photos or Wild West shows or cheap-thrill cinemas — an Apache decked out in full regalia for the war trail. Jim was wearing a calico shirt, a muslin breechcloth, and a headband of some dark material, all forming a blend of dull hues. Noting his tall moccasins with the stiff, upcurling toes, Tenney had the odd, inconsequential thought: There's the deer-hide he stole. A rifle fitted with a leather sling hung from Jim's shoulder; a bow and quiver of arrows were strapped to his back, and a kit bag was slung from his belt.

Jim was cradling a shotgun in the crook of his arm; his black eyes were watchful. Otherwise, his face, streaked with broad bars of blue and vermillion paint, was as impassive as stone. "That shot," he said. "One of my friends?"

Tenney's knees felt weak. He saw a low rock in a shady place and took his time about settling his butt on it. "That's right. So this is where you snare 'em?"

"This is where," Jim said matter-of-factly. He sank onto his haunches a few yards away, laying the shotgun across his knees. "The company could be worse."

Tenney took off his hat and sleeved sweat from his face. He pulled out a bandanna and ran it around the sweatband of his hat while his glance moved up and around the circling walls, and then came back to Jim Izancho. "Tired, Jim?" he asked tonelessly. "You must be getting tired."

"About half as tired as you look." The Apache's voice held a fleck of amusement. "How is my boy? He didn't look too bad the night before last."

"He's better and better."

Jim nodded impassively. "And Roger. How's Roger doing?"

"I've bad news for you. Your friends missed."

"Oh?" Again the hint of amusement. "de Groot, too?"

"Bad news again. Billy got bitten, but he'll live."

"I've made my point with Billy," Jim said almost indifferently. "As for Roger, there's plenty of time. I have all the time in the world, Frank."

"You think. Listen, Jim. . . ." Tenney hesitated, trying to phrase his feeling. "Maybe, just maybe, there's been a kind of justice in how it's gone till now. . . ."

"Not your kind," Jim Izancho said gently.

"All right. Listen to me. Those men were guilty as hell and no court would have brought in a verdict of guilty. So I can accept it as far as it's gone. But it's gone far enough."

"Uh-huh. What will you do about it, Frank?"

"Ask you to quit. That first of all. Damn it, Jim, you've had your pound of flesh! Stop now — before it's too late."

"That first of all," Jim echoed musingly. "What's next?"

"Clear out of the country. With my help, you can do it. I can arrange it on the quiet. But, once you're out, it's quits. You're never to come back here."

A slow smile broke Jim Izancho's face. "I

put myself in your hands. I take your word, is that it?"

"That's it. And I take yours, Jim."

"There's my boy. I won't leave without him."

"You won't have to. He'll be well enough soon."

The Apache nodded slowly, thoughtfully. "You're the law, Frank. White law, and you believe in it. So, why? Is it for friendship or what?"

"That," Tenney said grimly. "But I've other friends too. A lot of them live in this county. Whites, Mexicans, Indians. I'd put more than one twist in the law's tail to keep any of them from getting hurt. Or killed."

"Which could happen if I stay around, eh?" Jim rose to his feet in a catlike motion, stretching his long arms. The great muscles coiled and corded under his calico shirt. "You know what I did, Frank? I made that climb to the heights. I made my medicine and I'm a man. A warrior of the *Be-don-ko-he*."

"You're a criminal," Tenney said quietly. "There's no such thing as a one-man war, Jim."

"Frank, there's a war. I didn't start it. But I lost a wife in it."

So did I, Tenney almost said. But it wasn't close to being the same, he knew. "Your son's lost a mother," he said harshly. "You want to lose him a father, too, stay around. You want the only friend you have left to hunt you down like a rabid wolf, stay around too. Because that's what you'll make me do, *sheekasay*."

The Apache was silent for a moment, his face immobile again. Then he said, "I would trust you, Frank. That's not the question. I just don't agree there's enough justice done."

"You mean Roger —"

"And the Senator. Maybe the Senator most of all."

For a moment, Tenney stared at him uncomprehendingly. Then he understood. "You think the *Senator* gave the order to . . . ? Hell! You're wrong, Jim."

Jim Izancho's face smoothed to a metallic mask. "I think I'm right. *You're* the one was wrong about him before — remember? It's clear enough, Frank. Burn the Injun out. Get him off the land. Yount and de Groot and Roger were just the hands. Senator Warrender was the brain —"

Jim broke off suddenly. His gaze cut past Tenney and upward. And he moved in almost the same instant, swift as thought, throwing himself aside and groundward. As he did so, the gunshot sounded from above and back of Tenney.

Jim's body was twisted by the bullet's impact before he hit the ground. He landed on his side and shoulder and rolled over twice, coming to a motionless sprawl on his back.

Caught in the blurred shock of the moment, Tenney stood paralyzed. Then a yell of triumph caused him to swivel his head to the left, his eyes turning up, up toward the rim of a deep saddle that cut between two looming arches of rock. O. D. Bangs was lifting into sight, his rifle raised high in one hand as he let out another exultant yell —

A movement in the tail of Tenney's eye brought his glance sweeping back. He saw Jim Izancho roll off the ground and onto one knee in an unbroken motion, his shotgun coming up, a hammer earing back. A burst of gun roar crashed back and forth between the walls.

The full charge of Double-O Buck took O. D. Bangs in the center of his body. It seemed actually to lift him in a toe-arched pose — a fragmentary illusion that was ended by the graceless slam of his body against one of the flanking rocks. He crumpled like a puppet with all its strings cut at once. Then his body spilled headlong down the thirty-foot wall and crashed onto the rocks a dozen feet from Tenney.

Jim was already inching to his feet now, a side of his shirt plastered with blood and sand. He had one hand clamped over it; the other hand held the shotgun on Tenney, finger ready to the trigger. And Jim's face told Tenney he had never stood closer to death than at this moment.

"You needn't have coppered your bets this way, Frank," Jim Izancho whispered. *"Why?"*

"If that's what you think . . . you'd better pull that trigger."

Jim straightened slowly to his full height, still holding his side. Blood welled between his fingers. And slowly he let the shotgun slack down. "I don't know, any more." His voice seemed oddly remote. "I don't know, any more. . . ."

"I want you to listen," Tenney said carefully.

"Are there any more besides him?"

"I don't know. Will you listen?"

Jim Izancho's expression was not angry now, not even puzzled. Merely distant and watchful. He motioned gently with the shotgun. "Get down on your face. Stay that way for five minutes."

"Jim —"

"It's all said. Down."

Tenney dropped to his hands and knees

and then stretched out on his belly. Jim moved over to O.D.'s rifle, on the ground near his body, and picked it up. He hefted it thoughtfully, then gave it three hard swings against a boulder. Afterward, he tossed the barrel-bent weapon aside.

"Five minutes," he said. "Remember."

The pebbly ground rustled under the soles of his moccasins. And he was gone. . . .

Tenney lay unmoving. Five times over, he counted off to sixty, silently. There was a strange and somehow narcotic calming in that meaningless turnover of numbers. His brain felt closed around by a numb shell when, finally, he climbed to his feet and tramped over to O. D. Bangs.

The blast of buckshot had cut O.D. nearly in half. Tenney knelt by him but did not touch him for several moments. *You poor, glory-hunting son of a bitch,* he thought with a dismal and weary bafflement. *Was that all there was about it . . . glory? "O. D. Bangs" in large print on a news page? Or was it to steal my thunder? My job? What was it you were after so goddamned bad? . . .*

Not that it mattered any longer. Except that a chance of bringing Jim Izancho's spree of terror to a quiet end here and now had been wiped out. All that remained was to pack O.D.'s body back to Friendship and, by far the harder task, think of some way to break the news to his mother.

Tenney packed the body across his shoulders down to the base of the height. A logical guess and a few minutes of searching turned up O.D.'s horse in a clump of chapparal at the bottom of a gorge not far away.

Tenney had dully wondered just how O.D. had managed to follow him as far as the bluff without being seen by Jim Izancho from his position at the summit. This explained it. O.D. had trailed him from town and, once he'd fixed the direction in which Tenney was moving, had been able to keep fairly close behind him and remain unseen while catching only an occasional glimpse of Tenney. Riding along the bottom of this long gorge that meandered from the west, hidden by its high walls, O.D. had successfully evaded even the Apache's keen attention.

And Jim? Despite his precautions, he'd not really looked for such a ploy. Because, quite simply, he had trusted Frank Tenney.

After loading the body on O.D.'s pinto and tying it in place across the saddle, Tenney caught up the animal's reins and swung onto his own mount. He headed back toward town.

He'd covered perhaps a mile or so when two horsemen came into view from across a rise. It was with a start of surprise and suspicion that Tenney recognized Sidney Marston and his associate. Mr. Fleming was leading a pack horse with his photographic equipment (no doubt including a new camera) lashed to its back.

In a couple minutes, when they were near enough to identify the horse and tied body, both men pulled up.

"My good God. . . ." Marston's words held a hushed shock. "What happened?"

Tenney felt a cold rush of understanding and then a hot wave of anger. It was hard to keep his voice steady. "Pretty damned obvious, isn't it? I take it Bangs told you gentlemen what he had up his sleeve. And you were to record his great moment for posterity. Is that it?"

He laid the words down hard and flat, making no effort to conceal his contempt. Marston's pale face slowly colored. "If it is, what of it?"

Tenney wanted to say more but abruptly he checked himself. To give this pair even an inkling of what he had tried to do and how the effort had fared would be distorted by Marston to their advantage. He started to rein past them, and Marston lifted a hand sharply.

"Wait a minute, Tenney. Whatever's happened is news. All Bangs told us was he thought you'd left a message for Izancho. He was to follow you and we were to follow him by signs he left. That's all we know. Be reasonable, man. You can't suppress a story of this nature. It's too big. Why not come clean with us? You won't regret it. Otherwise. . . ." Marston's smile failed to temper the suggestion of a threat.

"I'll tell you just one thing." Tenney stabbed a finger at him. "If the pair of you damned jackals aren't out of this county by tomorrow, I'll have you both in the clink for a month. You won't have to do anything. You won't even have to sneeze hard. I'll throw you in and I'll throw the key away. Now get the hell out of my way."

CHAPTER FOURTEEN

Roger Warrender was as bored as he could ever remember feeling. Since the night of the rattlesnakes, he'd been confined to Big W headquarters by the Senator's orders. And he was going to stay right smack there, close to home, till that siwash killer was apprehended. After several days of it, he was willing to do almost anything to relieve his desperate boredom.

Each morning, a full two thirds of the Big W crew was split into search parties that combed the surrounding range for any trace of the Apache. Roger had pleaded with his father to let him join one of the groups, but the Senator was adamant. That siwash was tricky as hell. No telling what he might pull next, and a long shot from ambush could kill a man as quick as any other way. . . .

Izancho had already amused himself in another manner. Who else would have released a dozen or so de-rattled diamondbacks among the ranch buildings the night before last?

God knew how he had managed it, with guards nightly patrolling the place and a big searchlight, the kind that was installed by seaside harbors, set up to sweep the yard. Somehow, though, he had stolen deep into the headquarters area undetected. Their first inkling that a fresh rash of venomed death was at large came when a guard was struck by a snake in the dark. His boot had saved him from a flesh bite, but pandemonium had followed through half the night as the crew had fanned among the buildings, dispatching rattlers. One unnerved puncher had fired at a suspicious shadow, only to wound a fellow crewman.

There was a fine psychology behind the Apache's ploys of terror. Beyond the very real danger it created lay a constant and apprehensive fear. Everyone on the place was on his jittery guard against a menace that would strike without warning. It was a tense and temper-fraying way to live, and the potential threat was underscored by a deeper, chilling knowledge that they were dealing with an enemy who was playing a grim game for his own amusement, mocking their seeming helplessness.

For the posse of ranchhands had turned

up nothing. It was like skirmishing with a ghost. Some of the people from town and other ranches had joined the hunt, augmenting Big W's forces, but putting this increased pressure on the fugitive had yielded no better results.

Senator Warrender was taking fresh steps now. He'd telegraphed the governor's office, requesting that a detachment of state troops be sent to Buck County. He'd fired off a second telegram to the commandant of old Fort Apache, where the U.S. Army was still garrisoned, requesting similar aid. What Frank Tenney was doing, if anything, about the situation, nobody at Big W had more than a vague idea, for the Senator had refused to have any further contacts with the sheriff's office. Outsiders had conveyed a few morsels of information, including news of O. D. Bangs's death at the Apache's hand. But the circumstances surrounding it were anything but clear. . . .

This Sunday morning, Roger was trying to chase his ennui by showing a rather leery Tony Soto (who knew nothing of cars and wasn't particularly curious to learn) how to operate the Senator's battered old Ford, long since abandoned for his personal use in favor of the fancy Stafford. Roger was having only indifferent success with either project, but what the hell, it was one way to kill time. Sitting in the driver's seat while Soto stood warily by, Roger explained the proper method of getting the vehicle started.

"This is your ignition key," he told Soto. "Turn it and you're ready to go ahead. Then you push this dingus to the left to put it on battery. See, where it says *Bat?* No, wait. First you got to retract the spark and advance the gas or the sonuvabitch will bust your arm off. All right. Push the spark up, push the gas down. Now you switch to battery."

A coughing buzz sprang from the engine. Soto jumped backward a foot.

Roger laughed. "Don't be so goddam squirrely. That's just the contact in the coil box. Now, up here" — he got out of the car and walked around to its front — "is the crank. Watch what I do now. I push the crank in till she catches. See this wire sticking out of the radiator? That chokes it. You pull out the wire and bring her around careful to pull gas in. All right? Now you give the crank a spin, and soon as she catches. . . . Okay!" Roger ran back and leaped on the running board. "Now you advance the spark and retard the gas and switch over to magneto. Where it says *Mag,* see? And that's all. She's started up."

"Thass all?" Soto said incredulously. "You got to do all that jos' to *start* it? Chrissake, Rodge! Is faster you jos' saddle the horse."

"You'll pick up the knack soon enough," Roger assured him kindly. "I'll drum it into your head till it runs out your goddam ears. Now. Want you to say it over till you got it right. Okay. . . . Spark up."

"Spark op."

"Gas down."

"Gos down."

"Switch to battery. . . ."

By early afternoon Soto had loosely mastered enough of the machine's intricacies to drive it slowly around the place. The old contraption was noisy as hell, and Soto, with Roger in the seat beside him, added to the racket by beeping the bulb horn as he tooled happily between the ranch buildings, caracoling the vehicle first in one direction and then another.

"Wow, hey, Rodge. Is some fon!"

"I told you. Just watch you don't go running into something. . . ."

As they swung along the gravel drive where it curved past the main house, Bettina stepped out on the veranda. She called angrily at the top of her voice: "Will you little boys *please* go play somewhere else? Mother has a dreadful headache and she's *trying* to sleep!"

Roger, knowing exactly how to needle his sister, turned his head toward her and formed go-to-hell with his lips. Bettina whirled back into the house and violently shut the door behind her. Roger and Soto hooted their mirth as they rattled back toward the outfit's working area.

A reckless impatience had taken hold of Roger; he nervously snapped his fingers. "Damn, I wish that Malcolm of mine was fixed. We could go for a real buzz. . . ."

"Wha's the dif'rence?" Soto asked practically. "Your pa, he say you stay on the place."

Roger rolled his burly shoulders with irritation. "Piss on that," he growled. "I'm tired of cooling my heels around here. No danger in a car on the open road, even if that damn Apache was inside ten miles of here, which I doubt. Let's go for a spin. Take her out, Tony!"

"Bot the Senator —"

"He's out on posse with the rest. Won't be back till sundown. We won't be gone a half hour. Come on, roll her!"

Soto hesitated only a moment longer. Then he flashed a grin and brought the

Ford peeling around in a broad circle that ended at the front driveway. From there he headed out to the highway and turned west, toward town.

"Let her out!" Roger yelled.

Wind whipped their faces as the tall open car sluggishly picked up speed. You couldn't nurse much "go" out of this old crate, but even so it was great just to get out and away for a while. . . .

They had driven past the limits of the Big W range before Roger began to feel a sober trepidation. This was a desolate run of country, great masses of red boulders bulking on either side of the road. Not that there was anything to be worried about, Roger told himself. All the same, he abruptly told Soto to turn back.

Nothing loath, Tony halted the car on a broad gravel shoulder, swung it carefully around, and headed back toward the head-quarters. After a quarter mile Roger felt easier. Soon as they were out of these damned rocks. . . .

The rifle shot came like a whipcrack above the engine's clatter.

Were they being shot at? Frantically Roger twisted his head to the right, toward the shot's seeming direction, and saw nothing. He had no time to consider anything else, for the car made a sudden swerve to the right.

Roger swung his head back with a yell of "Tony!" And in the same shocked instant saw that Soto was slumped across the steering wheel.

The Ford was already veering out of control. Roger grabbed at the wheel, but the drag of Soto's limp weight on it prevented him from turning it in time. The right-hand wheels struck a steep embankment; the whole car slewed. It tilted wildly and for a moment hung suspended on two wheels as it skidded downward. Then it crashed on its side.

For a confused space of time, Roger lay dazed and helpless. Then he realized he was sprawled half in, half out of the car, his face partly shoved in the sand. Soto's body was jammed atop him. He felt a hot drench of wetness on the back of his neck and knew this was blood. Soto's blood dripping on his neck.

A horrified yell clotted in his throat. He fought free of Soto's pinioning weight. Scrambling out of the overturned car, he staggered to his feet. As he stood with his head down, swaying back and forth in a kind of trailing shock, a shadow fell across the embankment and touched his feet.

Roger looked up. *Holy Jesus!*

The Apache was standing on the road shoulder above. He seemed to loom gigantically against the sun.

Details of his costume and painted face stood out in Roger's dazed vision with a strange clarity that was sharp as ice. He was carrying a rifle in one hand. What appeared to be an ordinary length of iron pipe was secured to his back by a rawhide sling. And that seemed very peculiar to Roger. In the stunned idiocy of his surprise and terror, he thought that piece of pipe was a very peculiar thing.

Jim Izancho moved so swiftly that his hand was clamped around Roger's throat before he knew it. With a mighty wrench the Apache wheeled him and flung him stumbling away. Roger plunged to his hands and knees. The gritty pain of his fall spurred him back to sensibility.

He surged to his feet and spun around, his shoulders hunched with temper. He was met by a massive fist that landed a single crushing blow to his solar plexus. Roger sank down, gagging and doubled up with agony. Jim Izancho hauled him upright with an effortless yank and hurled him away in a wild stumble that ended in another bruising fall.

The Apache stood over him, grimly waiting, and Roger got the idea. He was being herded in a particular direction. Roger wanted desperately to fight. But he knew that pitting himself against the animal power of this man would be worse than futile.

"Go to hell, you son of a bitch." He hacked the words from his throat with a gummy spittle. "You can't make me go with you. Goddamned if I'll walk a step. . . ."

The Apache's hand went into the kit bag at his side and came out with a coil of braided rawhide cord. In a couple quick movements, as it seemed, he'd looped an end around Roger's neck and tied it fast. Then he turned and started up the embankment.

"Wait —" Roger croaked.

Jim Izancho gave a hard yank on the twelve-foot cord. Roger let out a choked cry and stumbled back to his feet. Izancho moved at an even, flowing stride. It took several more painful tugs of the cord to persuade Roger that the only way to avoid them was to fall into a jerky trot behind the Apache and keep it up. . . .

My God, he thought dumbly. He was waiting for us in the rocks. But how? Jesus, how?

There could be only one answer. And the implications of it were frightening. Somehow Izancho had managed to keep a close surveillance on the ranch and not be detected. While searchers were combing the country miles away, he was nearby, ever watchful for the main chance.

Jesus God, Roger thought. And you handed it right to him. . . .

He was numbly aware that Izancho was leading him north and west. The route he chose lay across almost barren valleys and ridges characterized by expanses of broken and sun-blasted rock. It was clear that the Apache was deliberately choosing as brutal a route as possible. To baffle trackers no doubt, but incidentally increasing the misery of his captive.

Roger had lost his hat when the car went over; the sun beat relentlessly on his bare head. His jacket felt like a hotbox and presently he shed and dropped it. Long before the pace began to really tire him, his throat was parched with thirst worsened by the constriction around his neck. Any effort to speak brought a vicious pull on the cord that was so painful he desisted after the third attempt.

What will he do? What will he do?

That refrain of fear kept pounding behind

every flicker of thought. Roger was no more cowardly than any normal man, but he had good reason to be sick with fright. Jim Izancho had killed Trooper Yount. God, the *way* he had killed him! And Roger Warrender had been with Trooper on the fateful night Izancho's family was wiped out.

He knows, Roger thought. *God, he knows. No use denying it. But O Jesus, I don't want to die. Please God, I don't want to die. Do something, God help me please. Just get me out of this and I'll never ask for anything again. I'll never more do a wrong thing in my life, I promise. Please, God!*

They were crossing an indented rise sparsely laced with galleta grass. Suddenly the Apache whirled back toward Roger, seized him by the shoulders, and flung him to the ground on his face. A moment later, Izancho flattened out beside him. The Apache's left hand held a keen hunting knife to Roger's throat. He was staring intently ahead of them . . . at something Roger couldn't make out.

But in a moment he did. Ahead of them a group of four horsemen emerged from a draw and picked their way in a loose file across the stone-strewn ground. One of the heavily armed posses of Big W men. Their way would take them athwart the direction Izancho had been moving, not three hundred feet from the fringe of galleta grass where the two men lay.

A cry formed in Roger's throat. But it did not well into sound. Let a hint of an outcry escape him and he'd be dead in an instant. He tasted a bitter despair as the riders vanished slowly behind a ridge.

The Apache dragged him to his feet and they resumed their trek.

Knowing he was being taken farther and farther from the few sanctuaries of civilization put an edge on Roger's dread. So did the absolute silence of his stone-faced captor. Not once in the passing hours did Jim Izancho utter a word. . . .

Roger was no weakling, but, within a couple hours of this hard pace over the roughest kind of terrain, fatigue was eating at his body. Whenever he faltered, his neck was seared by another savage tug. Striding on and on at the same springy tread, the Apache seemed indefatigable. Roger lost track of direction as well as time. He did have a vague awareness that the sun blazed somewhere at his back and to his left. So they were still making north and the hour was late.

Only once did the Apache halt. Again

something had taken his attention, and Roger saw it was a good-sized rattlesnake coiled on a rock. He slumped on the ground and dully watched as Jim Izancho unslung the pipe from his back. Now Roger saw that a wire with a loop at its end was threaded through the pipe. After making a few deft passes at the snake, Izancho snared the looped end of wire over its head. He drew the wire taut through the pipe and held the squirming rattler helpless as he took a bulky folded canvas bag from his belt and shook it out. He put the snake inside, disengaged the wire loop and quickly secured the bag's mouth with drawstrings. Then he caught up his prisoner's leash once more and they pushed on.

Roger was plodding and trotting and lurching in a nightmarish haze of exhaustion when he felt the ground start to slant sharply upward. Now they were climbing steadily. Roger had almost reached the outside edge of endurance. He was sobbing with exhaustion; his eyes swam in a red blur of pain. Repeatedly he stumbled and fell, bruising and cutting his hands and knees, and still he was yanked up and onward in that relentless ascent. . . .

And then the pressure was gone from his neck. He realized he was lying on his back in a shadowy place.

Groggily, as the red throbbing washed out of his eyes, he raised his head and looked around. He was on the sandy floor of a cave whose rock walls arched to a low roof. This must be the Apache's hideaway, such as it was. Odd pieces of gear and various supplies were stacked by one wall.

There was no sign of the Apache. Painfully Roger struggled onto his elbows. A tin can full of water was on the ground near him. He seized it and greedily drank it down. Water! It sent a flush of life through his parched and battered body.

Roger climbed to his knees now, looking wildly about for a weapon or anything that might serve as one. Then the Apache appeared in the low, narrow slot that served as the cave's entrance. He ducked inside and without preliminary caught Roger by the collar and hauled him up and out of the cave.

Roger was propelled roughly ahead of the Apache for twenty stumbling paces. He was jerked to a stop at the edge of a deep hole about six feet in diameter. Apparently it was a natural pit, even though its ten-foot-high walls had been additionally hollowed out around the bottom to make them steeper.

Roger peered down. He gave a hoarse cry and took a step back. The Apache's hands gripped his arms and forced him back almost to the brink of the hole. Roger's nerve broke completely. He gabbled with terror.

The bottom of the pit was squirming with rattlesnakes. There were at least a tangled dozen of them. Obviously they had been captured and placed in the pit. But God! Why would even a madman collect a slew of deadly diamondbacks for no other purpose than to dump them in a sheer-sided hole?

The answer came with a horrifying shock that chilled Roger to the bone. *What other reason could Izancho have?*

For a moment, his tongue was stilled by a freeze of terror. Then he began to struggle wildly. He might as well have fought the clasp of a steel vise. Jim Izancho did not budge an inch. But his remorseless grip forced Roger forward, forward, till soil at the pit's edge crumbled under his feet.

Roger let out shriek after shriek. The clods of falling earth irritated the rattlers; they hissed and thrashed. A piece of ground sloughed away under Roger's left boot; his foot dangled over space. His weight was tipping forward. A babbled paroxysm of pleading broke from his lips. . . .

Then the hands dragged him back to solid footing and let go of him. Roger fell to the ground, clawing at it with his hands, sobbing. Jim Izancho spoke for the first time. His words came slow and hard and clear, like measured strokes of a bell:

"It won't be that easy, Warrender!"

CHAPTER FIFTEEN

Bettina picked at her breakfast, giving slight replies to her father's strained attempts at conversation. It seemed to her that of late everything had gone wrong that could go wrong. The break with Frank. The kidnaping of Roger. And now her mother's nervous breakdown. Behind all this lay a kind of dismal conviction that had grown steadily since her return to her old home a few days before.

Home. Odd how she had continued to think of Big W as home during her two years of marriage to Frank Tenney. Or was that natural enough for a new wife? She'd had to return to the great ranch for this brief time to learn that home was a state of mind. Home belonged to a safe and untroubled time that was no more. Nothing any longer seemed as it had been. And the ranch itself resembled a fortress under siege, rather than anyone's idea of a home.

Finally the Senator said abruptly, "My dear, you've not heard a thing I'm saying."

"I have, Pa. Really. I'm blue, I guess." Bettina added belatedly, "About Roger," and felt a quick guilt because for the moment she'd forgotten about her brother.

"Ah. And the other thing?"

She nodded.

The Senator reached across the table and patted her hand. "You'll get over it. Anyone can make a mistake. Frank wasn't the man for you, that's all. As you know, I've never approved of divorce, in theory or in action. Now, by the Lord Harry — I've come to believe it's an institution that has its place!"

Bettina felt a stir of protest, but didn't voice it.

Divorce? Of course the *idea* of it had crossed her mind more than once. But she wasn't yet prepared to give it serious consideration. Not even with a father whom she had practically worshiped all her life. There was so much to consider. She felt confused and uncertain as to her true feelings about Frank. And there was the child she was carrying. . . .

Correctly interpreting her silence, the Senator cleared his throat and said brusquely, "Well, well. Time enough later to attend to that matter."

"Are you going out today?" Bettina asked.

"Later on, yes. Did you think I wouldn't?"

Looking at him, she felt a familiar welling of affection. There was a core of unshakable iron dignity in this man who had sired her, something that all his worry and near despair could not touch. True to form, he was immaculately dressed for breakfast, as he had dressed for every meal in her memory. But there was a gaunt and haggard strain in his face that no amount of affected poise could hide.

"You're not as young as you were, Pa," she said gently. "It won't do Roger any good if you drive yourself to death looking for him."

The Senator smoothed his mustaches. "Sitting around and merely waiting would do me even less good, I'm afraid. Anyway . . . we should have the answer soon. One way or another, we'll have it."

Bettina wondered how he could be so sure. Word from both the governor's office and Fort Apache had been disappointing. Neither state nor federal troops could be spared to fill Buck County's present need. All available forces were standing by pending further developments on the tense situation between the United States and Mexico's Huerta regime; in case of emergency they would quickly be deployed along the border. The citizens of sparsely populated Buck County would have to stomp their own snakes.

Yet, so far, nobody had caught even a glimpse of the marauding Apache. Except, presumably, Roger . . . and God only knew what had become of him by now. A few hundred feet beyond the overturned Ford, all track left by Jim Izancho and his captive had petered out.

For three days, scores of men drawn from every corner of the county and from across the county line had been scouring the mountains and desert for any clue to Roger Warrender's fate. Thus far they had turned up nothing.

Reading her thought, the Senator smiled faintly. "We'll have the dogs out today, Betts. Harley Moss has brought a pack of hounds over from Price Wells. And a telegram from Finn Lafferty was brought out from town this morning. He will be arriving from Phoenix early today."

"Finn Lafferty . . . is he that pilot?"

"Right. He will land his aeroplane here, on the flats yonder. After he's been acquainted with all facets of our situation, he'll begin a search by air. Lafferty has done this sort of work before. A balloonist or an aviator can spot things from aloft that a whole army of men on the ground would miss — What is it, Celestina?"

One of the Mexican maids had appeared in the doorway of the dining room. "It's a man to see you, sir. He is from Señor Haskell's ranch. He says it is urgent."

"Very well. Send him in."

The maid went out. In a few moments, a middle-aged cowhand entered the room, hat in hand. "Howdy, Senator."

"Hello, Bill. What brings you over?"

"Old Milo allowed you'd want to know right away. This 'Pache fellow showed up at our place last night."

"Thunderation! What happened? Out with it, man!"

"Well, wasn't nobody seen him. But the dogs set up a ruckus. Time anyone got on the scene, he was gone."

"Then, how the devil can you be sure it was him?"

"Coming to that. We looked around and found they was a case of dynamite missing from the tack shed. Some tools, too. Sledge hammer and a single-jack. Young Tom and young Ed was set on going right after the man who took it. Old Milo wanted the boys to wait till morning. But you know Tom and Ed; they wanted to get right on the trail. So they went out with dogs 'n' torches."

The Senator nodded impatiently. "Well?"

"Milo didn't get no sleep after'ards, waiting on his boys to get back. 'Bout dawn he hears a shot outside — we all heard it — and finds Tom layin' on the front porch. Just Tom, and he's been shot. Still alive but in bad shape. Milo sent Hank Sims to Friendship to fetch Doc Courtland and the sheriff, and me to fetch you."

The Senator had surged to his feet, gripping the edge of the table. "Is he fit to talk? Tom?"

"Milo hopes he'll be fitten right soon. The old man has the whole crew out looking for Ed. Case they can't find him, only Tom can say what happened."

"Yes. How do you know it was Izancho?"

"Figures, that's all. 'Pache's been lifting things in town. And he visited our outfit quite a few times 'fore he went hostile. He *knowed* we had dynamite in that shed. I come in our outfit's truck, Senator. Want to ride back with me?"

"I do," Stuart Warrender said crisply. "If there's room in the back for my horse."

"Sure is."

The Senator's tinge of weary discouragement had vanished. While he readied himself for the day's outing, he had Celestina summon his foreman, Tim Lester. He told

278

Lester to have a dozen crewmen saddle up and head for the Haskell place, where he'd be awaiting them. When Finn Lafferty arrived, Tim was to give the pilot all the information he'd need. The Senator had orders for Bettina, too. She was to escort her mother to Friendship, as the Senator himself had planned to this morning. Diego Baca would take them to town in the Stafford.

Bettina stood on the porch and watched the Senator depart with the Haskell crewman, the truck sending up billows of dust as it swung onto the highway. Already the sun was high and vicious; the day would be another scorcher.

She glanced toward the four armed men steadily pacing the yard between the house and the headquarters working area, tramping endlessly back and forth. There was a mild activity around the corral, where the crewmen were readying their horses. Otherwise the place had a drowsy and deserted feel that seemed peculiar, probably because things had been so frenetic during the preceding few days as the ranch had been besieged by reporters from near and far, many of them representing big-city dailies. Finally the Senator had stationed a guard at the gate with orders to turn back anyone who even smelled like a journalist.

But of course the whole world hadn't gone mad, Bettina thought: only the Warrender part of it. All because of one man. And to think he was Frank's friend!

Yet, again and again, almost guiltily, she'd found herself thinking of the sensitive, concerned man who had brought his ailing son to their home because there was nowhere else to take him. Always she forced that image away and let her mind's eye picture only the painted savage she had seen bent like a bird of prey over his son's bed.

Impatiently Bettina thrust both memories out of mind and turned back into the house. She gave the housemaids their orders for the day, then summoned Diego Baca, the ranch's handyman-chauffeur, and told him to bring the Stafford around to the front porch and load it with Mrs. Warrender's bags, which were packed and ready in the front hall. Afterward she went to her mother's room.

Eleanor was sitting on the bed in her traveling suit, looking sweetly drowsy. Obviously she had taken another strong dose of sedative for her nerves, and Bettina thought it was just as well. The quiet and modest daughter of a genteel New England family, Eleanor Warrender had never truly adapted herself to this land or to her husband's high ambitions. Roger's disappearance had been the final straw that had tipped her into a nervous collapse.

Bettina sat beside her mother and pressed her hand. "Diego is fetching the car now, dear. We'll have you in Friendship in no time. The Willses are expecting you. Everything's going to be fine."

Mrs. Warrender gave a faint, sleepy nod and smile.

Bettina could only hope they'd decided on the proper course for her. Dr. Courtland had suggested that the best thing for Eleanor would be to get away from the ranch and its tensions for a good while. Mayor Wills and his wife were old and understanding friends, and a phone call by Bettina had quickly confirmed that they would be happy to have her mother as a house guest.

"I'm sure you'll be comfortable," Bettina went on. "A nice long visit is just what you need, dear. You'll see."

Mrs. Warrender blinked at her daughter. She smiled and nodded.

Bettina quietly left the room and went down the hall to look in on Billy de Groot. He was still asleep or pretending to be.

Bettina believed that by now her cousin had quite recovered from the snake bite and was feigning a residual illness in order to avoid being up and around. Billy had become extremely withdrawn. His fear of the Apache persisted so strongly that only here, safely in his room at the tightly guarded house, did he feel secure. Poor Billy! The son of one of her mother's first cousins, he possessed in full the highly neurotic temperament of family on her mother's side. . . .

Bettina wanted to check on Tony Soto, too, before they departed. The Mexican youth had lain unconscious in the overturned car for at least an hour, bleeding steadily from a serious wound. He'd been in critical condition when, after being found by a neighbor who was returning from town, he was brought to Big W.

Soto had been installed in a room at the end of the hall. Bettina softly opened the door and, seeing Tony was awake, crossed to his bedside with a smile. "How are you this morning, Antonio?"

Soto's dark eyes were listless and sunken. "Not good, Señora," he husked faintly.

Certainly she could discern no improvement in him. Dr. Courtland had confided that he had little hope for Soto's complete recovery. If he lived, the internal damage he'd suffered would almost assure him a life of semi-invalidism. Either prospect was one so bleak for this active, high-spirited young man that Bettina hadn't found the heart to tell him.

"I think maybe I don' feel bad so long," he whispered. "Don' you say so, Señora?"

"No," said Bettina. "Good heavens, no."

"The doctor, I think he say so."

"Hush, Tony. Here. . . ." Seeing that sweat beaded his forehead, she wrung out a cloth in a basin of water on the bedside stand and gently wiped his face. "You have a chance to recover. But you must be still and you must *want* to live."

"Oh, *sí*. I care to live." His fingers plucked restlessly at the coverlet. "Bot there's a thing I mus' tell, Señora. If I do not live, it mus' be known. *Dios!* I wish there was a priest. . . ."

"I am going to Friendship, Antonio. If you wish, I'll ask Father Schoenbraun of your local parish to come out. I'll bring him back with me. But I don't want you to think about dying."

Soto shook his head weakly. "Is hard not to think of. But I guess I don't want no priest yet. Only, if I go sudden, Señora . . . there's a thing the priest must know for my absolution. I tell you so you will tell him and he will know."

"What is it, Tony?"

283

He talked faintly and haltingly, keeping his eyes averted.

Bettina's blood went hot and then cold. *Dear God . . . dear God!*

She didn't know what she'd expected to hear. Perhaps a recitation of some minor and purely venial transgressions. Anything other than a declaration that her brother and Yount and Billy had been truly responsible for the killings of Jim Izancho's wife and grandfather.

Soto's words came more strongly as he warmed to the story. He seemed determined to leave out no excruciating detail. After her first unspoken flare of disbelief had subsided, Bettina knew with a sick conviction that she was hearing the unvarnished truth. Soto was ridding his soul of a knowledge that had festered in it.

Afterward, a long silence followed his words. Then Bettina said slowly, almost inaudibly, "I see. I want to know one thing. And I want the truth from you, Antonio."

"*Sí.*" His eyes stayed averted.

"Did my father give the order to burn those Indians out?"

"No. This was Rodge's idea."

"Thank God for that much," Bettina murmured.

"Bot — uh . . ."

"What?"

"The Senator, he knows of it. Later, he found out from Rodge what they did — him an' Billy an' Trooper. Rodge, he tell me that, too. The Senator was mad on 'em, but he say no one else mus' know."

A kind of blankness slid over Bettina's mind.

Honesty was a watchword with any Warrender. It was the foremost key to holding one's honor forever unblemished. So she'd been raised to believe. How glibly the Senator would quote Polonius: *This above all: to thine own self be true. And it must follow, as the night the day, Thou canst not then be false to any man.* Of all the lessons she had taken from the father she revered, this had been the one most religiously cherished.

But we're to cover up when it touches us. Is that it, Father?

Yes, that was it. Undeniably, one reason she hadn't seen it was because she hadn't wanted to. And it meant Frank had been right, after all. God help me, Bettina thought in the dull glaze of her pain; Frank was right. . . .

Tenney left his horse at the livery barn, where he parted with the men of his posse who had returned to town with him. Most of them said they were prepared to take up the weary search again tomorrow; they would rendezvous at the livery in the morning. These six men, along with a dozen others who had split off during the homeward journey and headed back for the ranches or farms where they lived, were a good, steady crew of fellows, Tenney had found. There wasn't a slacker among them.

Yet a tired discouragement threaded the men's talk as they broke up now and headed for their homes. Tenney hunched his slicker-covered shoulders against the steady rain as he tramped across town through the darkness, heading for his own home. He was drag-footed with fatigue. His thoughts budged like chilled molasses.

The way he had driven himself on this man hunt had gradually dispelled the rash of doubts his fellow citizens had entertained about him. For a while it had been damned rough. Sidney Marston had promised him trouble. He'd fulfilled that promise by writing an inflammatory article that was picked up by a major wire service. Careful not to state flatly anything he couldn't prove, but skillfully stressing Tenney's old friendship with that murdering siwash Indian, Marston had increased public distrust and hostility to where nearly all able-bodied local men had refused to serve on any posse headed by him. Scattered groups of men had gone out on their own, but their searches had been disorganized and chaotic.

Tenney had found it necessary to trim a couple more loudmouths to size in order to squelch the talk. In this country even a sheriff was still expected to take on such challenges man to man. After the results were in, a few local fellows had consented to go on posse with him, and every day since, more of them had joined up.

But the seeming hopelessness of the hunt was starting to grind them down. Tenney with the rest, though he'd been pessimistic about their chances from the first.

Early today, when a rider had summoned Dr. Courtland and him out to the Haskell ranch, there had been the tingling hope that at last they were downwind of something positive. But it hadn't worked out that way. While Dr. Courtland had patched up Tom Haskell, the latter had regained a tatter of consciousness. Enough to tell briefly and weakly what had happened to him.

Tom's story had added little to what they'd already known or guessed. On horseback he and his brother Ed had quickly overtaken the dynamite thief, who was afoot and burdened by the heavy tools and a weighty box of explosives. However, all it had gotten them was a serious wound apiece, for the robber had laid up ahead and opened fire on the glares of their electric torches. Tom had a hazy memory of being picked up and carried a ways before all consciousness had left him. But the facts that his attacker had tied off his wound and carried him home and fired a shot to alert Tom's pa all pointed to Jim Izancho — whom Tom Haskell had befriended — as both the dynamite thief and Tom's savior. And a little later, when Haskell riders sent out to look for Ed Haskell found him at the place where he and Tom had been shot, his wound had also been tended.

The smell of the Apache was strong on the strips of calico he'd used to bind the brothers' wounds. Harley Moss's hounds had picked up the scent at once, and swiftly they were on Jim Izancho's trail, the large combined posse of Tenney's and Senator Warrender's men following them closely. It had seemed the best chance yet to bring down the Apache. The possemen were mounted on still-fresh horses; Izancho was on foot and burdened with the heavy box and tools he'd refused to abandon.

Then, a little before noon, the cloudburst had struck. In minutes the trail had been wiped out and the hounds left milling in a hopeless, baying confusion. . . .

Losing the trail had ended the brief alliance between Tenney's and Warrender's forces. The Senator's icy disavowal of his son-in-law hadn't relaxed by a jot. The only thing they'd agreed on was that every effort must be made to take Jim Izancho alive: only he knew the truth of Roger Warrender's fate. Now, with the trail erased, the Senator had declared his intention of continuing the hunt separately as before, and he'd dispatched four of his men back to Big W headquarters to augment the guard he'd placed on it. His fear was obvious: that Izancho's theft of dynamite meant he intended to pursue his vendetta by blowing up ranch property. Tenney had to concede grimly that this was a damned likely development, if Jim's pattern of vengeance remained confined to the Warrenders.

But God knew where or how he would strike.

Three days before, Tenney had solicited both the governor and the Army for help, only to find that Senator Warrender had beaten him to it. But the answer to both men's requests had been the same; no aid could be expected from those quarters. And unless the hunt was pressed by a veritable army of men, it was probably doomed to failure. By now the members of his posse were starting to share this conviction. The rain had slacked off, but a monotonous drizzle had kept up all day, dampening their chances and the men's general mood.

Tenney slogged onto the muddy street where he lived. Seeing the rain-misted squares of lamplight that marked the windows of his home did nothing to lift his clammy spirits. Today's fiasco had been like a rank climax to the bitter chain of events that had lately dogged him.

Above all, there was Bettina.

A pain stirred in him. God, the things people said or did in anger. And had to follow through on because pride wouldn't let them do otherwise. Other differences had come between Bettina and him. Never anything so sharp that a little talk or letting off of steam wouldn't reduce it to laughable proportions. But this damned business! What would happen with them now? He had no idea. He knew only that he'd never felt so utterly empty and alone.

But how was it with her?

Along with everything else had come the reporters. Following Marston's dramatic exposé, they'd descended on Buck County like a horde of locusts. Some of them, whetting knives for Tenney in particular, had trailed along with his posses. "For God's sake, Frank," Major Wills had implored him prayerfully, "be tactful with them, won't you? No ass-kicking. No busting up cameras, all right? Just try." Tenney had tried. But the questions the journalists had put to him, and the way they'd phrased them, had been damned near enough to drive a man to the conclusion that under some conditions homicide might be justifiable. . . .

Tenney swung up the path to his house and let himself into the closed veranda. Dilworth Mudd was slacked there in a wicker chair, rifle across his knees. Dil had been assigned to watch the Tenney home on the off chance that Jim Izancho might come again to check on his son. A thin hope, for of course Jim would anticipate such a move. As much as he'd anticipate that Tenney had posted a similar guard at Jim's own, burned-out place.

Dil gave him a big horsey grin. "Evening, Frank."

"Dil. Anything to report?"

"Huh-uh. You?"

"Not much." Tenney eyed him irritably. "What the hell are you smirking about?"

"Nothin'."

Dil went on grinning. *Jesus,* Tenney

291

thought wearily. "Go on home," he said. "I'm back for the night."

"Sure, Frank."

Tenney opened the front door and stepped into the lamplit hallway. As he hung up his hat and shed his dripping slicker, he was surprised to catch the warm odors of cookery. Mary Bettinger, who had served the Tenneys as hired girl, had taken over the job of caring for Joe-Jim Izancho during his absences. But Mary's job didn't include preparing his supper. That was nice of her, he thought as he headed for the kitchen.

Before he reached it, he heard a splashing and a childish squeal of laughter. Seemed the little fellow was out of bed at last . . . and Mary was giving him a bath.

Tenney came to a stop in the kitchen doorway.

There was a wooden washtub in the middle of the kitchen floor, and Joe-Jim was splashing in it like a small brown seal. And a woman was kneeling by the tub, her sleeves rolled high and her back to the doorway, scrubbing him. No, Tenney thought . . . it couldn't be. Yet it was not Mary!

Bettina laughed. "Hold still there, you —"

At that moment she turned her head and saw him. And came to her feet and slowly turned to face him. Her arms were soapy and her pug of hair was mussed and damp; the front of her middy blouse was wet.

"I . . . I had to bring Mother into town." Her face was flushed and almost smiling. "So I. . . ."

One of them moved first, but he never knew which one. Only that his arms were full of her, the damp clinging ripeness and warmth of her. And everything was right again.

CHAPTER SIXTEEN

When the rain started, the first, fat drops spattering on his face, Roger stirred and groaned. Then he roused himself from a near coma, licking his cracked lips and blinking his crusted eyes. The pelting drops had an irritating effect on the rattlers. Once more, they began to stir and hiss.

But Roger hardly cared. Water . . . rain! Suddenly the sky split open and drenched him, cooling his parched and broiled flesh. The rattlers were furious now, thrashing against their tethers and striking this way and that. Roger opened his mouth to the rain and drank deeply. He summoned enough strength to give another fierce wrench at his bonds.

They held fast. But hope surged in his wakening brain. Wetted uncured rawhide was supposed to stretch after a bit. If that goddam Indin didn't come back too soon, he had a chance! Even if he couldn't break the rawhide ropes, he might finally slip free of them. . . .

It had been a long three days and nights of spine-crawling terror for Roger Warrender.

Through the first two days of his captivity, Jim Izancho had kept Roger in a simple agony of anticipation. Would he or would he not throw him into the pit of rattlesnakes? Izancho had been satisfied to drop an occasional hint that he would . . . after letting Roger have all the time in the world to think on it. Waiting could be an exquisite form of torture in itself.

During all that time, Izancho had spoken little, giving no responses to Roger's threats and pleas, his taunts and his curses. In fact he had paid his prisoner almost no attention. He'd left him tied in a corner of the cave and once a day freed him long enough to take nourishment and to relieve his bowels and bladder. Roger had soiled himself several times during the interims, and the Apache had been indifferent to that, too.

When Izancho did say anything, it took the form of a low, idle, musing soliloquy on the subject of venomous snakes, spoken precisely as if Roger weren't present at all. For instance (had run one of his suggestions) if a man were dropped in a pit with a dozen or so rattlers in it, in a little while he would be so impregnated with poison that his body would bloat and split open. At least there was a notion abroad to that effect, and it should be interesting as hell to test it. . . .

Most of the time, Izancho was gone from the place, ranging afar to hunt for food or perhaps more snakes. During his absences Roger would savagely fight the ropes, only to tighten them more and finally to desist against the pain of his torn wrists.

Early yesterday, quite suddenly, something in Izancho's demeanor had changed. Not his granite-faced taciturnity. Just a conveyed hint of excitement, as if he had reached a decision of some kind.

Before Roger could even think to query him, Izancho had seized him and dragged him out of the cave. Close to the pit of snakes, the Apache had sunk four cedar posts into the ground at a distance of five and more feet apart, forming the corners of a square. Several feet beyond each side of the square, he had driven in other stakes. Throwing Roger on his back inside the square, Izancho had lashed his wrists and ankles to the four corner stakes. Then he'd tied four big rattlesnakes to either side of him and by his head and feet, their tails secured to the outside stakes. Afterward, leaving Roger hedged around by writhing, angry serpents, he had departed.

The torment was ingeniously devised. The diamondbacks were tied just near enough to attempt venting their fear and rage on Roger, not near enough to harm him . . . quite. They would strike and draw back and strike again, only to be pulled up a few inches short of his arms and legs and head.

Roger had gone frantic with terror. He had strained at his bonds. Shrieked till his voice had dropped to a raw husking. None of it had availed him anything. Finally he had slipped into the quiescence of helplessness, and so, as the hours crawled by, had the rattlers.

A leaden numbness compounded of dread and resignation sat in his belly. Now and then, the tethered snakes stirred back to torpid arousal. *Suppose one of them was to pull free!* But as the hours had worn on and the sun arced higher, even that fear had come to be of less moment. Spread-eagled, with arms and legs stretched so tight by the biting thongs he could hardly move a muscle, flinty pebbles gouging his back, sun flaming on his eyelids, he had begun to know considerably worse than discomfort.

Night had brought little relief. Roger had been tortured by cold and thirst and vermin, made putrid with his own foulings.

Sometimes he heard the snakes rustle. His brain wandered in and out of its own twilight. A new day of blazing sun and further dehydration came almost welcomely. But the freshened agony of it seared his flesh past bearing. He had been clinging to a bare thread of awareness when the sky had begun to darken. It took the flick of falling moisture to reach his waning sensibilities.

Fully drenched now, he came back to life and struggled once more. He could feel the rawhide turning slick and greasy and the hope that flushed through his veins gave him new strength. He would slip the ropes! He would be free!

The rattlers were whipped to a wet fury that, for the moment, Roger ignored. Their rawhide fetters were being wetted down too, but they couldn't exert the pull he was putting out. Once freed, he could step out between any two of them. Then, by Christ, he would see about that sonofabitching Apache. His swollen throat growled with an exultant mirth. Let Izancho try to pick up his trail in the rain! The Senator would have men out looking for his son; he would have the country full of search parties, and in a little while Roger was bound to raise one of them —

With a lurch of gray horror in his guts, giving out a groan of despair that was almost a sob, Roger sank back on the soaked earth.

Jim Izancho was tramping into sight through the rain, a bulky box held on one shoulder. He walked slowly but unbowed under its weight. Yet, for the first time, the Apache showed fine traces of wearing down.

Not even glancing at Roger, he set the box carefully on the ground. A sledge hammer and a single-jack were lashed to his back by a rope, and he let them fall, along with his rifle and shotgun. Then he peeled off his calico shirt. A dirty bandage circled his torso. The muscles stirred like thick snakes under the smoky shine of his wet skin as he slowly tore away the bandages.

Izancho examined the wound in his side and then changed the bindings, taking a fresh wrap of calico around his ribs. Roger dully noticed that the injury was surrounded by a livid spreading discoloration which showed it wasn't a recent one. Izancho must have had it for days, yet in all this time he'd shown Roger no indication of a serious hurt. God . . . the man must be made of iron!

Afterward Izancho stepped into the cordon of rattlers, pulled out his knife, and severed Roger's bonds. By now Roger's misery was too great for him to care that he was incapable of movement. The Apache picked him up and dragged him away from the snakes and dumped him on the ground.

For the first time since he'd brought Roger to this place, Jim Izancho addressed him directly: "I was looking to take you alive, Warrender. I waited a long time for the chance."

Roger managed to sit up. By nature fastidiously clean and natty in his person, he felt a sudden and violent revulsion at his condition. A funny time for it. He peered out of his utter misery at his captor and managed to make husking speech: "I know that."

Izancho squatted down, facing him. "I was going to put you in the pit." His tone was matter-of-fact, even conversational. "Not right away. You had to think about it a good while. I suppose you know that, too."

"Uh."

"Well," Izancho went on gently, speculatively, "I changed my mind, Warrender." His gaze moved to the wooden crate he had brought. "I have a better use for you. After that . . . who knows?"

Roger looked at the box a few feet away. He saw the black stenciling across its top:

DANGER —
HIGH EXPLOSIVES.
THIS SIDE UP.
NO. 1 DYNAMITE — 1½ X 8 IN. 50 LB.

300

"What're you going to do?"

Izancho smiled. "You wonder about that. It won't bore you, I promise."

Again the rawhide leash was fastened to Roger's neck. Izancho secured the tools on his own back, together with his weapons. He hoisted the case of dynamite to his shoulder and then yanked his prisoner to his feet. Roger gave a howl of anguish as the band of half-raw flesh around his throat was savaged by a wrenching agony. Other miseries flailed him at every lurching step he took, his body weakened by inactivity and hours of being stretched immobile. He fell several times, and then the Apache slacked his pace a little and Roger was able to stumble awkwardly in his wake.

Gradually his muscles loosened and he could manage an easier walk, but it brought no relief. Izancho simply picked up his own stride and Roger could barely match it. He felt an edge of urgency in the driving pace Izancho set. Whatever goal he had fixed on, he was going straight for it.

After a while, the rain lessened to a gray misting. As he had before, the Apache chose a rugged and pathless route. Roger hadn't even a vague idea where they were heading. There was no sun, and none of the landmarks he could make out seemed familiar.

He was almost numb to pain, but nearly dead on his feet with fatigue, when Izancho finally halted, toward nightfall. Obviously the stop was compelled not by consideration for his captive but by his own perceptible sluggishness. His infected wound was bothering him. Izancho found some prickly pear and mashed its paddles between two rocks to make a poultice for the wound. This he bound in place with a hint of rough impatience that seemed to be daring his body to fail him.

Roger, drenched and shivering on the ground, watched in a haze of stupefaction. He was almost beyond caring, and he numbly reflected, with a kind of doomed and feverish satisfaction, that presently he would be too far gone to be of any further use to the Apache. But Izancho had thought of that. He built a fire in a sheltered pocket of rocks, then made Roger strip and warm himself by the blaze. He propped Roger's clothes on sticks to dry out and gave him a couple of cold meat sandwiches, which, as strength and awareness picked up once more, Roger found himself too famished not to wolf down. Except for his moccasins, Izancho didn't remove his own clothes, merely squatting by the fire till they dried on his body.

When Roger was dry and dressed again, the Apache tied him hand and foot and then stretched out by the fire himself. Drugged with warmth and weariness and a full belly, Roger dropped off to sleep at once.

Before true dawn came, they were on the move again. Roger felt stronger for a time, trotting along fast enough to keep slack in his rawhide collar. But the Apache seemed to press harder and faster now, calling on some fierce reserve of energy. Roger had to put all his concentration on merely keeping his feet under him. The landscape was rougher than ever, covered with a rubble of splintered red rock, showing little vegetation outside of the tough, twisted manzanita and more kinds of cacti than he could remember seeing.

The dawnlight was increasing. And quite abruptly Roger knew where they were. They were climbing into the *mal país* above Big W's northwest range. God, yes! He knew this country well. It also lay close to Izancho's burned-out place.

Vaulting like a goat across the desolate scape, balancing his burden and tugging his captive along, Izancho seemed imbued with the untiring fury of a man nearing his objective. Again and again Roger fell and was dragged back to his feet. His palms and knees were raked bloody by cactus spines and jagged rocks; the legs of his breeches were bloody tatters.

Suddenly Izancho stopped. Roger's quivering legs gave way and he sank to the ground, looking dumbly around him. They were atop a ridge of volcanic rock which at this point formed the west bank of the Santa Agrita River. Its yellow torrent surged below, swollen by yesterday's rain.

Izancho set the case of dynamite on the ground. He forced his powerful fingers under the end of a topboard and pried up, wrenching it away. One by one, he tore away the topboards. And then understanding hit Roger like a cold wind. . . .

"No," he said hoarsely.

"Yes," said Jim Izancho. "You watch."

Not only did Roger watch, he was forced to assist the Apache's activities. Holes to set the dynamite charges had to be drilled by hand, and that meant plenty of muscle work with the sledge hammer and single-jack. The work would take many hours, and in the broiling heat of a new day, it was savagely brutal work for anyone unaccustomed to it.

Izancho was showing more and more signs of depletion. Having driven himself close to his limit, he was satisfied to take long breaks, during which he kept an eye on Roger's labors and also watched the range of hills to the south. The risk of discovery was high now, for to complete this job he must remain in the open and in one place for as long as it took. If search parties were out and any of them chanced this way. . . .

Roger was nudged by fresh hope, but not very strongly. He was veering close to utter exhaustion once more, his legs so wobbly they threatened to collapse. He thought of feigning complete fatigue and decided against it. Once Izancho was assured he couldn't get more work out of him, he was likely to consider Roger's usefulness at an end. And then. . . .

But would he? No, by God! He wouldn't kill his prisoner, for an obvious reason. No doubt it was his main reason for keeping Roger alive. And that was that he might have need of a hostage.

Roger gripped the handle of the sledge. If the son of a bitch would relax his vigilance for a moment or so! One good lick with this baby would do it. But Izancho was sitting on a rock some fifty feet away, and even if he were to drop his guard, Roger knew that he himself was too drained to move anywhere near fast enough. . . .

A humming noise grew out of the hot silence.

Roger paused in his labored sledge blows, listening. The Apache had already come to his feet, his face turned southward. Roger looked that way but could see nothing. The sound resembled nothing so much as a gargantuan insect, its buzz muted by distance but coming rapidly nearer. What the hell?

Then it came to him. An aeroplane, sure!

A moment later, the plane came skimming into view, zooming low across the south hills. It dipped lower yet as it neared the two men, and Roger clearly saw the pilot's goggled face and his flapping yellow scarf. The craft was a Curtiss biplane, an entirely open affair, and damned if it didn't look like the one he'd seen race against an automobile over at Salt Flats not six months ago.

Hell, yes! It was none other than that daredevil nut Finn Lafferty. The yellow scarf was his trademark.

The plane swooped above them, only yards away, it seemed, and then tipped up and winged northward above the river, describing a broad circle.

Roger glanced quickly at Izancho. His attention was on the circling plane and his face was tense as iron. This was one development he couldn't have anticipated. For Roger guessed that his father must have hired Lafferty to take up the search where ground posses had failed.

Maybe . . . ! Roger measured the distance from himself to Izancho. The latter's attention was wholly on the plane and he was turned somewhat away. Desperate enough to take the chance, Roger tightened his grip on the sledge. But Izancho glanced his way now.

"Throw that hammer away from you," he said quietly. "Then go down on the ground. On your face."

Roger groaned a low curse and did as he was told.

The plane wheeled out of its arc and came roaring back, dipping low once more. Deliberately the Apache raised his .45/70 Winchester and began shooting. He got off shots as fast as he could, and the pilot pulled the stick hard for altitude. As the plane cut upward above them, Izancho was still pumping off a shot a second; he didn't stop firing till the fifteen-load magazine was empty.

On the twelfth shot a plume of dark smoke leaped from the engine. The machine began to cough and miss as the plane sailed higher and higher. It streaked against the sun and was invisible for a moment. Then it plummeted back to sight and continued to lose altitude as it vanished over the far rim of hills. . . .

At first Tenney was puzzled by the sound. It seemed to come from a height of land to the east. He pulled up his horse, raising a hand to halt his possemen. They all sat listening, quietly commenting.

"One o' them aeroplanes. Sounds like she's in trouble."

"Must be that aviator fella Warrender brought in, huh?"

"Must be."

As they watched, the plane appeared from across the chain of hills. Smoke was trailing from it, and its engine was sputtering. It passed from sight behind another rise of ground. Tenney swung his mount that way, and his men followed.

In ten minutes they crossed the last ridge and came into a shallow and level valley. The plane had pancaked to a stop toward the valley's end. It didn't appear badly damaged, except for a broken strut. The pilot seemed to be unhurt. He was beside the craft, scooping up double handfuls of sand and heaving them on the smoking engine. Apparently he'd successfully doused the fire, but he was cussing a blue streak as the posse came up.

"Ah, the damn scut has grounded me and for a long time, I'm thinking." Disgustedly the pilot spat the remnant of a wet cigar from his mouth. "What a vile place to set her down! Christ, it's the whole damn engine I'll have to dismantle now. And be cleaning the grit from every piece by hand."

Tenney stepped to the ground and walked over to him. "I'm Frank Tenney."

"Ah, the sheriff you'd be. Finn Lafferty."

They shook hands. Lafferty was a short, wiry man in a leather jacket and khaki breeches and high-laced boots. When he yanked off his helmet and goggles, he revealed a face that was big-nosed and blue-eyed and feisty with temper.

"Too bad about your ship," Tenney said. "Anything we can do?"

"Ha! Point me toward town. Better yet, loan me one of your hayburners and a spare equalizer if ye have one. I'd not mind a crack at the red bastard who shot up me darlin'."

"What?"

"Aye, it was that Apache o' yours. Emptied a rifle at me, cool as you please."

"Where did you see him? Can you show us?"

"That I can. It's no great distance. But I think you'll not be taking him any easy way...."

Lafferty mounted up behind Tenney and directed the posse eastward. As they rode, he told with many epithets what he had seen on the bank of the Santa Agrita.

"If I take the scut correctly, he is setting charges to blast a ditch through this great ridge of rock. To divert that river, perhaps? Though why he'd be doing it is more than I can rightly tell."

Tenney understood only too well. This was Jim's *coup de grâce*. He meant to carry through exactly the threat Senator Warrender had once feared.

Then the fear had been groundless. Now it was all too certain. Jim Izancho intended to cut off a great ranch's source of water. He meant to strike at the heart of Big W's existence by turning its range bone dry.

CHAPTER SEVENTEEN

Tenney had known that if they did catch up to Jim Izancho, taking him either dead or alive would be a bitter task. When Lafferty told him where Jim was positioned, he judged it was going to be far tougher than he'd ever guessed. He was right.

On its eastern flank, except where a loop of the Santa Agrita River touched it, the hogback ridge was bounded by other, less lofty heights of land. The rest of the hogback was skirted by a small, deep, almost flat valley that opened onto Izancho's basin flats to the southwest. Only that ridge stood between the river's present course and this valley, whose floor was lower than the river bed.

The valley's only vegetation was low scrub that gave no cover at all. There were a scattering of large boulders here and there, but they'd serve only for taking shelter behind. From his vantage above, the Apache could cut down anybody that attempted to cross the valley. You couldn't get anywhere above him, because that hogback spine of rock was the highest point for a good distance around.

And Jim was ready. As the posse fanned out in their slow approach of the hogback, he opened fire from the rim. Bullets kicked up dust close to their horses' feet. Close enough to alarm the animals and to give a clear warning that he wouldn't hesitate to draw blood if necessary. Tenney knew that leading a charge on the ridge would be suicidal. One man with a repeating rifle laid up at its summit could drop every one of them.

Since they were as close as Jim would permit them to get, Tenney signaled a turn. He led his posse onto the gentle swell of a flanking rise. It was several hundred feet from the hogback ridge and too low to offer any sort of vantage in their favor, but it was high enough to spare them from getting caught by the head of water if the charges went off and the Santa Agrita came pouring into the valley.

From what Lafferty had told him, it seemed a good bet that's what would happen. "The scut knows his dynamite," the pilot had said, and had described how, as nearly as he could tell from a couple of quick passes overhead, Jim apparently intended to set the charges. He was setting the drill holes one above the other in an ascending line across the narrowest section of the ridge. The first shot would take out an immense chunk of rock at the western end of that section where the ridge tapered off. A second charge, laid above it, would gouge another vast gap behind the first. The third explosion would complete the channel. On each detonation, the rock should spill in the direction of least resistance so that the final one would hurl fragments of rock toward the valley and not into the river. . . .

Tenney deployed his men across the shallow rise, telling them to cling to rock cover wherever they could. Some of his posse were scouring the *mal país* to the west, and he sent a rider to fetch them. He dispatched Bob Threepenny and two others to find Senator Warrender and as many of the Big W search parties as they could. Maybe their combined forces couldn't make an outright charge on the Apache's position, but they could surround him in a vast cordon of men that a lizard couldn't slip through. And if they undertook to charge his position, even Jim Izancho couldn't defend all sides of it at once.

Of course there was Roger. Lafferty had

said Roger was with the Apache and apparently unharmed . . . so far. And his continued safety might depend on their acceding to Jim Izancho's demands. A crooked smile touched Tenney's lips. Yes. Jim would have thought of that.

Tenney trained his binoculars on the hogback's crown. No sign of life on the side of the ridge he could see. But work would be going on atop it. Jim needed time. Even if he also put Roger's muscles to the job, they'd be a long time setting those holes by hand. No telling how long they'd been at it already, but Lafferty had reckoned a good part of the work was done.

Weeks ago, Jim Izancho had studied this deeply fissured ridge with a painstaking eye to blasting out an irrigation trench. He would rethink his calculations with the same care. If successful, he could deal a crippling blow to Big W. And perhaps ruination to the Warrenders.

Yes, in time the new channel might be dammed off. But this was Jim's own land. He had the right to dynamite it as he chose. The Warrenders had no rights on it at all. Even if Senator Warrender could swing enough influence to void Jim's ownership, it would mean a period of dragged-out litigation. Then title would revert back to Milo

Haskell, whose old feud with Stuart Warrender might be enough to stiffen him against any plea or threat offered by Warrender. Even if Milo considered that this way of striking at an old enemy was beneath him, and gave his consent to a dam, repairing the damage done to nature's work would be difficult and costly. Moving the necessary equipment back into these rugged hills would be a mighty chore in itself. Assuming that all problems could be overcome, it might be a year or more before a dam was installed. . . .

Meantime the hottest stretch of an Arizona summer lay just ahead. Long before it was over, the Santa Agrita's ponds and flowages that had always supplied the Big W's inner range would be dry. Cattle would die of thirst. They would die by the hundreds. And very possibly Stuart Warrender's longtime fear would be realized: the heart of his little empire would be wiped out. . . .

The sun beat fiercely against the rock-studded rise. Crouched against a giant boulder, Tenney felt sweat pour down his ribs and puddle in boots. His eyes ached from a steady watch on the hogback. A sparkle of flinty light danced off mica-shot boulders; heat hung like a shimmering veil above the valley floor.

Wait. What else was there to do? Some part of the decision belonged to the Senator, after all. Warrender's son. Warrender's ranch. What happened in the next few hours could decide the fate of both. Yes, the Senator deserved a vote in this. . . .

Tenney reached in his pocket and pulled out a folded paper already worn at the creases from much handling. The note had come in yesterday's mail. It was from Jim. Short and to the point, it had asked Tenney and his wife to do their best for Joe-Jim. The only life he could have given the boy was that of a father on the run. He had nothing else to give. And it was signed simply: *Sheekasay.*

Despite the terseness of the message, Tenney knew by this parting token that Jim had concluded that Tenney hadn't betrayed him at their ill-fated meeting. And somehow, even now and after all that had happened, it was a good thing to know. As he read the note over, Tenney felt a hard tightness in his throat. *Jim,* he thought. *Oh, hell, Jim. Sheekasay.*

Not wanting to think about it any more, he blindly thrust the paper back in his pocket.

Jim needn't have asked. One of the things

Tenney and Bettina had talked about last night was the care of Joe-Jim. No matter what happened with his father, they would raise him as one of their own. Both of them wanted as much; there was hardly a need to discuss it.

Other matters between them hadn't disentangled so readily. Talking for hours, both had warmed the edges of their tempers. They had a long way to go in finding a real understanding, Tenney wryly knew. But, for the first time, he could believe they would. Bettina had shed a lifelong belief in the Senator's godlike attributes . . . and that was something. It left her free to love a father shorn of a righteous façade. Realizing that the cost of ambition could be too high seemed to promise another change: in Bettina's regard of the man she had married. . . .

The ground trembled to the explosion. A dark eruption spewed from the hogback's summit. A massive slough-off of rock and rubble crashed into the valley. As the noise of falling rock died away and the dust settled, Tenney saw that a deep notch had been pared out of the ridge's west flank.

A perfect shot. Two more like it and Jim Izancho would taste the wholeness of his revenge. He should be sated with it.

A ripple of grim murmurs ran through the watching men.

In this country, water was a commodity more precious than gold. It gave the white Westerners their tenuous hold on a land whose other natives, such as the rattlesnake and the Apache, had fitted themselves to its fierce demands. Jim Izancho had exploited the fears and weaknesses of his enemies with an unerring shrewdness. The physical harm he'd wreaked amounted to very little. It had been within his power to do much worse. He had chosen the far deadlier tool of psychological destruction and attrition. Nobody whose life had been touched by it would forget it. . . .

Tenney remembered his own reply to a youthful and unusually persistent reporter, who'd said earnestly, "Say, listen, Sheriff. I understand your reluctance to discuss all this. Hits pretty close to home, don't it? But they say you know this Indin better'n anyone. What I want to ask is, what's this guy's *real* angle? What do you think?"

Tenney had stared at him for a long moment, finally saying, "You've read the facts, haven't you? By now it's all in print for anyone to see. I don't think they've overlooked a damned thing. Facts of his life. All that's happened to him."

318

"Oh, sure. Read every scrap I could dig up. But I want to hear what you think. I really do."

"Well," Tenney had said, "I'll tell you. I don't know the answer. I really don't. But it's possible, just possible, that he got to feeling awfully sick, way down deep inside."

The rest of Tenney's posse arrived. He sent this group of men to circle the valley to its far side and there take up positions watching that flank of the ridge.

Shortly afterward, a second detonation sent another rumbling slide of dust-shrouded rock into the valley. The results of this shot were largely hidden from sight, but Tenney didn't doubt it had significantly extended the channel.

The men muttered and swore and fingered their rifles.

Some of them were all for making a charge on the ridge without delay, but Tenney quelled that notion. Roger Warrender's life was at stake, he reminded them.

So they continued to wait. The sun crept higher. So did men's tensions.

Warrender and his men arrived about noon. Tenney picked them out across the valley, a close-riding group of fewer than a dozen men. Bob Threepenny was with them.

Tenney felt a thin disappointment. It would have been better for his plan of surrounding the ridge if his messengers had been able to round up all the Big W crewmen and their cohorts. But, of course, the crew was split into a number of search parties and Bob had chanced to find the Senator's own group first. The two other men Tenney had sent out might still locate more Big W parties and fetch them here.

Anyway, Stuart Warrender himself was with this bunch of men, and for once he couldn't fail to heed what Tenney had to say. Not with his son's life in the balance.

The Big W men put their horses up the long rise, and Tenney came out to greet them.

"Senator. . . ."

Warrender pulled up his big iron-gray. Even with a harried impatience plain on his face, he bore himself with that impenetrable dignity that made you forget his "Senator" was a courtesy title.

"We heard the explosion," he said coldly. "There is no time to lose. Why are you holding your men here?"

Tenney glanced at Bob Threepenny. "Did you tell him?"

Bob nodded. "All that you said to."

Looking back at Stuart Warrender then,

Tenney said slowly, "Maybe you misunderstood. He's got Roger up there. He's unhurt, Lafferty says. But if we rush that ridge —"

"My son is a Warrender," the Senator said harshly. "He will not buy his life at such a price."

For a moment Tenney wasn't sure he'd heard right. "Senator, you —"

"There's been one explosion," Warrender cut in. "How many will it take to breach that ridge? Lafferty . . . you saw the situation from above. Have you an idea?"

Finn Lafferty had moved up beside Tenney. Standing carelessly hipshot, he puffed on a cigar and nodded judiciously. "Well, sir, a fair one. I'd say three in all. But I'd reckon ye didn't hear that first one —"

"First what?" The Senator rose in his stirrups, blue eyes hot and tense. "Do you mean . . . there was. . . ."

"Aye, one shot previous to that you heard. So I would guess one more to go, d'ye see. And that will do it."

"Damnation!"

The Senator started to swing his horse around. Tenney moved forward and caught his rein. "Wait a minute. Wait, damn it!"

"What?"

"You run into his gun from one side,

you'll be cut to pieces. *Wait.* Let's get our men strung out around the valley. Then — once they're in place — we can all of us converge on the ridge at once. But gradually. Every man on foot, moving from rock to rock. There's no way he can cover every side. . . ."

"And give him time to finish the job?" the Senator shouted. "Christ, man! Let him see what we're up to and he wouldn't wait! He'd set that last charge in place right away. God — maybe he is now. . . ." His words trailed; a berserk look twisted his face. "Let go, damn you!"

He wrenched his rein from Tenney's grasp and wheeled his horse, all in one motion. Then he spurred downslope, waving and shouting, and his men pushed their horses after him. Some of Tenney's men caught the fever; they ran to fetch their own mounts.

Tenney started yelling orders to the contrary. But hardly a man of them was listening. It was as if a tight-wound spring had been suddenly released. For days these men had been prey to a common tension that had swelled to explosive proportions: now they were eager to be in on the kill.

Up on the ridge, Jim Izancho opened fire. Only the fraying blooms of powder smoke marked his position. He had stationed himself between two slim pinnacles of rock at the south rim of the ridge. He fired coolly, methodically, deliberately, making every shot count.

Two Big W horses went down. When that failed to slow the Senator's men, he picked off two of them, one after another, tumbling them clean out of their saddles.

Halfway to the ridge, the charge faltered.

Some of the Big W men pulled up their horses and began firing at the pale plumes of gunsmoke that were the only giveaway to the rifleman's position. Senator Warrender spurred on, followed by the rest of his men. The Apache's cold accuracy sent two more riders, the ones closest behind him, spilling from their saddles.

That broke up the charge. Any man who reached the bare ridgeside would be an open target along the whole rugged climb to its summit. They didn't stand a chance and they knew it. Already a good half of them were abandoning their horses to seek shelter behind whatever sizable boulders were handy. The rest merely pulled up their mounts and lent the Senator a covering fire as he raced heedlessly for the base of the ridge.

Warrender reined his horse to a halt and

half fell out of his saddle. He began a scrambling ascent of the rough escarpment. He was wide open to a shot from above, but Jim Izancho had ceased shooting now. Several of the riders spurred forward once more, only to be driven back by the Apache's instant resumption of fire.

But he hadn't once drawn a bead on Stuart Warrender, whom he easily could have picked off at the start. And he did not fire now, as Warrender toiled slowly up the sun-scorched face of the ridge.

The Big W men continued to direct a desperate fire at the Apache's position. Uselessly, Tenney knew. And quite unnecessarily. Jim had no intention of shooting Senator Warrender. At least not right away.

Jim Izancho was letting the Senator come straight into his hands.

CHAPTER EIGHTEEN

Both physically and mentally, Roger had reached a state of numb misery that put him almost beyond fear. But not quite. When the first explosion came, the earth quaked and shuddered so violently he thought the whole ridge was breaking up under him. He shrank against the ground, his terror unabated as the shower of dirt and rock rattled down on all sides of him. Yet when the tremors and the rain of debris were done, he was unhurt.

After he'd seen the posse coming across the valley, Izancho had bound Roger hand and foot and carried him to a deep pocket under an arching slab of rock not far off the rim. That arch had protected him from the deadly downpour just now. But, Jesus, the Apache was taking the worst kind of chance, firing off dynamite this near them. Of course he couldn't leave the ridge without drawing the posse's fire.

Roger lifted his head, straining his ears.

Silence now. He didn't know where Izancho had taken shelter from the explosion, but he wondered with a wild flare of hope if it wasn't barely possible the son of a bitch had been killed. However, he doubted that he'd be that lucky, and he was right.

In a moment Izancho came clambering across the rocks to see how his prisoner was faring. Roger pressed his back to the ground, praying with a sick fervor that the Apache wouldn't inspect his bonds. Izancho's eyes had a weary glaze and he was moving slowly. An infected wound and the relentless pace he had set himself were telling on him more and more.

After a cursory look at Roger, Izancho left him again, stumbling a little as he moved off. Directly he was out of sight, Roger hitched himself onto his rear and again set his wrists against the jagged sliver of volcanic rock on which he'd been awkwardly sawing the thongs that secured his hands at his back. By craning his head backward, he could tell that the flinty strands were hardly frayed at all by his savage persistence. But the flesh of his wrists was worn raw, streaming blood from a dozen wicked gashes.

Still he worked on, doggedly and numbly, raking back and forth, back and forth, against the saw-edged projection. His muscles were nearly spent from weakness and strain and cut-off circulation. By now Roger was almost numb to hope. Yet a man had to keep trying, if only to the urge of blind, involuntary reflex.

Just after Izancho had tied him up and dumped him here, Roger had heard the fusillade of gunfire as the Apache shot it out with the posse. After that had come a long stillness broken only by occasional scraping noises as, he assumed, the Apache capped and fused his dynamite cartridges. He could do that while he was laid up on the rim and watching the posse's activities. Once prepared, the charges could quickly be wedged in place. The laboriously chipped-out holes were ready to receive them, and if the Apache hadn't somehow miscalculated — on the placement of his charges or the strength of them — his scheme should come off without a hitch.

Unless the son of a bitch dropped from weakness before then. Or unless he overestimated the size of a shot and blew them both to hell.

The rolling earth shock of the second blast, when it came, momentarily persuaded Roger that he'd bought it there and then. He felt the volcanic folds of the ridge literally heave beneath him. The leaning slab that sheltered him actually groaned and tilted a few inches. He thought it would come down on him. But when the hail of debris had died away, he was still alive and even miraculously untouched.

God! And his wrist bonds were worn nearly through at last. He could no longer feel his hands except for a slickness of blood . . . but as he resumed the sawing of rope on rock he felt the jerky stretch and fray of the thongs.

Somehow, though he was now so light-headed he feared he might pass out, Roger doubled the fury of his effort. Izancho had not come to check on him again. The sounds of soft scraping told him the Apache was occupied with readying the third and last charge.

Unexpectedly there was another outbreak of shooting. Men below the ridge (they sounded nearer than before) were concentrating a fierce fire on the rimrock. Roger heard the scream of lead ricocheting, and the steady, unhurried roar of Izancho's Winchester as he replied to their fire.

Silence then. Another spasm of gunfire. And more silence.

God! What was happening out there?

Unheeding of pain and blood in his violence to free himself, Roger wrenched savagely at his bonds. Suddenly a strand parted. In a frenzy he fought free of the remaining turns of rawhide. With a scrambling haste he swung his legs around to rip his ankle thongs back and forth over the sharp fragment. He had a much greater mobility now — and the tough Cordovan leather of his boots protected his ankles. Just a dozen furious slashes severed the rawhide.

Roger staggered to his feet and almost fell down again. All the punishment he had absorbed seemed to savage his body at once as he lurched forward, swaying for balance.

Those minute scraping noises had ceased again. Cautiously Roger edged toward where he had heard them. The surface of the ridge top was irregular with spires of volcanic rock. Roger stumbled across the sharp-edged terrain, twice falling to his hands and knees. He was no longer aware of pain. One thought filled all his mind: to get his hands on a weapon.

The Apache would be setting the third charge in place. It wouldn't take him two minutes. This could be Roger's chance. His only one.

Ahead of him on the rimrock rose a pair of pinnacled rocks. Roger saw the open box of dynamite, an open carton of copper detonators and a coil of fuse, a knife lying on the ground, and a litter of fuse scrapings around it. An exultant croak squeezed from his throat.

Limping over by the rock pinnacles, he braced a hand on one and looked wildly around. Where the hell was the Apache's rifle? His goddam shotgun? He wouldn't take both weapons with him, would he?

Roger was about to settle for the knife, bending to pick it up, when he saw the shotgun stowed under a flat shelf of rock just two yards away. Eagerly he pulled it out and straightened up with it in his hands, and then moved quickly out on the rimrock.

In the valley below him were horses, their reins thrown, and men crouching behind rocks. A couple of dead horses, too. And some dead or wounded men, it looked like. Roger waved the shotgun above his head and instinctively opened his mouth to hail the men in the rocks — then thought better of it. They could see him all right. Why alert the Apache? Be easy to slip down the ridge to safety while that siwash was occupied.

On the other hand . . . why? Roger was in a sorry condition, but the Apache was fast weakening too. Why not take him by surprise? Hell, yes, Roger thought with a mounting excitement. You got enough left to point a shotgun. You can still pull a trigger.

There was a shallow crevice in the lava close by, and it would just about hide a man lying prone. Roger lowered himself into the crevice and shrank down inside it. He laid the shotgun barrel on its edge and nestled the stock against his shoulder. Anticipation flushed along his veins like hot nettles. From here he could watch the Indian coming. Blast the son of a bitch before he knew what hit him. . . .

In almost that moment, Jim Izancho swung into sight from around a mass of rock, coming back at a laborious lope. Roger eared back the shotgun hammers. Izancho saw him and came to a stop, and did not reach for the Winchester slung to his back.

"Hold still," Roger whispered. "Watch the birdie —"

And pulled both triggers.

A futile click. And another.

No loads in the shotgun.

Izancho's giant chest stirred with silent laughter.

Roger rose shakily to his feet. A dizzy vagueness filled his brain. A brassy taste of fear and rage that was painfully familiar filled his mouth. Izancho was starting toward him now, but then pulled up sharply.

He was listening. And Roger heard it too: a faint scrape of something sliding along rock, and it was coming from somewhere below the rim. These were the sounds of a man climbing the steep ridgeside, Roger abruptly realized . . . and a fold in the rimrock had hidden him from Roger's view.

Quite suddenly the man lifted into sight, scrambling up the last few yards over a dip in the rim. For a thunderstruck moment Roger hardly knew his own father. The Senator's hands were raw and bleeding, his shirt torn, his clothes covered with dust. His white hair fell over his reddened face; through it his eyes glittered like a crazy man's.

At sight of Izancho he stopped. His hand dived for the revolver holstered at his hip.

Roger was momentarily frozen by the spectacle of this austere and dominating man as he'd never seen him. And in that instant Jim Izancho moved with that incredible quickness of his. He seized the Senator's arm, took the pistol from him, and threw it over the rim. Stuart Warrender struggled against his hold, but the Apache held him as easily as a child.

"Right here, Senator —" Izancho's laugh

boomed from his chest. "You came up to watch it, eh? It is set now: a full charge on a three-minute fuse. We'll watch it from right here, Senator. Both of us. . . ."

Roger came to his senses. He clubbed the shotgun in both hands and rushed at them, aiming a blow at Izancho's head. Holding the Senator one-handed, the Apache caught the swing on his lifted palm. With a powerful wrench that drove Roger to his knees, he ripped the weapon from his grasp and tossed it after the pistol.

Roger's ears sang dizzily. He shook his head, trying to clear it. The Apache's laughter boomed with a terrible, rollicking mirth that rolled like thunder in Roger's ears. *Christ!* He lurched to his feet and doubled his fists. Laugh, you son of a —

"The fuse!" the Senator screamed at him. *"You fool! Get the fuse!"*

Roger blinked. The dynamite. God!

He wheeled and started away, swinging his fists for balance, hardly able to manage a limping trot. Then the need for haste fed a stark frenzy into his muscles. It galvanized his legs to a furious, pumping run.

Roger plunged down a declivity into a rough-bottomed fissure. He raced toward its end and the socket in stone that he had spent hours helping drill out. He saw the protruding ends of the paraffin-coated packets, capped and fused.

Jesus — the fuse! Only a trailing sputter of it was left.

Roger dived for it.

When the man stepped out on the rimrock, Tenney quickly trained his binoculars on him. Then he swore in disbelief. It was Roger Warrender, waving a shotgun above his head. Quite abruptly he turned and faded back off the rim. The Senator was still dragging himself upward, and apparently his son hadn't seen him.

What did it mean? That Roger had subdued Jim Izancho? No. They would have heard a shot. That was the only way Roger could take the Apache.

The men around him were still muttering their surprise when Tenney said sharply: "All right, let's close in now. We'll fan out and go on foot. Go slow and use the rocks for cover all you can. We don't know what's happening up there. . . ."

Before a man of them could move, things began to happen on the ridge almost faster than anyone below could follow. The Senator had achieved the rim, only to be seized and disarmed by Jim Izancho. Roger charged into sight now, swinging the shotgun at Izancho, and he was knocked down and disarmed too. His father seemed to be yelling something at him . . . now Roger was on his feet and retreating. Or was he? Anyway he was out of sight again.

Tenney thought then: Christ! The dynamite!

He lowered his binoculars. "Hold your fire!" he yelled at his restless men. "You might hit Senator Warrender! Hold your fire!"

The Apache was making no effort to pursue Roger. He still had an iron hold on the Senator and his head was thrown back. He was laughing. . . .

Tenney came off the rise at a run, and his possemen followed him. The Big W men in the valley were on the move too, all of them heading for the ridge.

It was then that a third blast filled the rocky scape with thunder. The earth throbbed like a live thing. The barrier ridge shook with a force that sent cataracts of rubble cascading down its sides. Some of the possemen flattened themselves to the ground as a spray of dirt and pebbles fell around them.

The explosion had twice the power of any previous one. And it did the work.

A foaming, dirty torrent roared through

the manmade chasm and boiled onto the valley floor. Close to the hogback now, the men raced for its lower slope to get above the flood. Though they were nearest to it, the Big W men reached high ground no sooner than the rest, for they were carrying three wounded comrades and one dead one. But though the water was surging in the men's direction, it wouldn't rise very deeply toward this end of the valley. Seeking a new channel, the river would snake onto the basin flats southwest of here and eventually find a confluence with Saba Creek, over-flowing that smaller stream's banks. . . .

Tenney pulled up on the beginning slant of the hogback, raising a hand to halt the others. Rivulets of rubble were still sifting down; high on the ridge top a pall of dust was settling.

The ground shock must have knocked both Izancho and the Senator off their feet. Now the Apache was rising up and stag-gering to the edge of the rim. He stood with his feet apart, swaying like a tree in a wind.

"Frank," he called in a voice that held the clear calm of a summer day. "I'm giving my-self up. I'm coming down."

Men were bringing up their guns, and Tenney said sharply, "Hold your fire!"

Jim Izancho unslung the Winchester from

336

his shoulder. He moved forward, coming down the ridge at a painful half trot. Blood streaked his face; his teeth had a bone-white shine.

"Jim!" Tenney shouted. "Throw down that rifle! Throw it down!"

Izancho kept coming. And he brought the rifle to his shoulder as he came.

One of the possemen fired. The bullet's force threw Jim to his back in a skidding fall. He staggered up and plunged on and downward toward them, trying to aim the rifle.

This time a flurry of shots from the posse slammed him backward. He fell as heavily as a sack of rocks. Then his body rolled downward till it lodged against an outcrop.

"Roger!" The Senator's voice came as a high, thin shriek. "Rodge boy. . . ."

Like a summons out of Roger's childhood.

On his feet now, the Senator was looking wildly about him. Then he stumbled back off the rim and out of sight.

Roger would be hard to find, Tenney thought dully as he and the other men tramped slowly up the ridge to where Jim Izancho lay. Almost certainly Roger Warrender had been caught in the explosion he had tried to stop. On his father's order.

The men stood looking down at the

Apache's body. It lay on its back, mouth open, and already flies were settling on the face. Mute ingloriousness of death. All the pride and temper and splendid manhood that had been Jim Izancho, flung away to this.

Madness! Tenney thought. This was the finality of madness.

Senator Warrender appeared on the rim again. He stood there looking down at them, his mouth working with a horror of realization. No sound came from it. Some of his men were climbing up toward him. Before any of them reached him, his legs gave way and he slumped to the ground and sat there. His mouth kept soundlessly working.

A son and a ranch. He had lost both. But he could have saved one, Tenney thought. My God . . . what kind of a choice was that?

Jim Izancho had taken a fullness of revenge. Had used up his last reason for being. With life effectively done for him, he had forced them to shoot him down. Unreasonable? Senator Warrender still lived . . . would live with today and its moment of a mad choice until his dying day. *Then, who was the crazier one?* Jim Izancho or Stuart Warrender?

The fierce blaze of sun made an oven of

the bare rock slope. The men began to mutter and stir, lifting their voices then. They had lives of their own to pick up. It was time to be going home.

The employees of Thorndike Press hope you have enjoyed this Large Print book. All our Large Print titles are designed for easy reading, and all our books are made to last. Other Thorndike Press Large Print books are available at your library, through selected bookstores, or directly from us.

For information about titles, please call:

(800) 223-1244

To share your comments, please write:

Publisher
Thorndike Press
295 Kennedy Memorial Drive
Waterville, ME 04901